Baked Inn Love

ERIN BRANSCOM

For Dusty. For loving that single mom with two boys and building a life bigger than either of us could have ever imagined and adding two more hearts to the mix. I love you so much. You're my forever.

Baked Inn Love

~

Allie

You're fired.

"You're fired."

I'm quiet of the other end, sure I didn't hear correctly.

"I wanted to do this in person, but since you're working from home right now, it has to be done like this."

"What has to be done like this?" I ask my boss Albert as I slide a pan of cookies into the oven.

"We have to let you go. We just can't have people in your... position on the team anymore."

"My position? Meaning what, exactly?" I stand up and walk toward my rickety kitchen table, scored for free from a trash pile on the side of the street, which together with my laptop has been my makeshift office the past several months.

"The position of not being able to give what everyone else on the team is able to give," he says condescendingly.

"And what exactly is everyone else giving right now that I'm not? I work sixty to seventy hours a week and I'm only paid for forty. The only thing I'm not doing is traveling, and almost everyone is working remotely right now. So, what am I not doing?"

I freeze in front of my table, the full reality of what's happening hitting me. I mean, I've always known Albert is a slimeball, but I didn't expect to get fired. I basically lose a piece of my soul every week that I work for him, but I do what I have to do to pay our bills. Caleb is counting on me and only me to provide for him.

"You aren't pulling your weight."

"I see. You know my son just had a major kidney transplant surgery... Firing me means *we* will have no health insurance and no income to pay for medical bills. You're going to cut us off right before the holidays? Do I get a severance package or anything?" I begin to pace my kitchen, my toe rubbing on some of the worn linoleum that is peeling in our trailer that's seen better days.

"Human resources will be getting in touch."

I sit in one of my mismatched chairs and stare at my

computer but can't see a thing through my tears, anger, and fear. I realize I'm checking my work email out of habit while Albert still drones on about how I chose my family over the job he'd graciously handed to me. I realize work emails no longer matter and close the laptop.

I have always tried to keep my personal life separate from work, but I had no choice these past six months with my son being sick. He has a rare childhood kidney disorder and needed a transplant, which he had several weeks ago, and I've been at home with him while he heals since his immune system is still fragile. I've worked day and night at this kitchen table for 393 Creative. Far harder than I should've, apparently.

I never set a timer for my cookies, but I can always smell them right when they're done and know just before they burn. My mom calls it my 'baker's nose.' I've always been a great baker, and that's what I do when I'm stressed. These are pfeffernusse cookies, one of my specialties. The aroma of holiday baking in my kitchen right now is flooded with cinnamon, molasses, cloves, and nutmeg. I wanted to take them back to the hospital for all the nurses we made friends with on the transplant floor where Caleb and Evan had their surgeries. Now, after that phone call, I have bigger things to deal with.

My mom and brother will probably be relieved to hear that I can finally move back home to Freedom Valley. I've stayed in California because, despite how crappy the job was, the insurance was good and covered Caleb's transplant. But now that the transplant is done and there's no job holding me here, I can go back to New Hampshire and help out at the family inn. Evan keeps telling me they will have a job waiting for me whenever I'm ready.

I look over the trailer and mentally try to figure out how to make this work. My thirteen-year-old Toyota Camry has 290k miles on it—I'm not even sure it can make it from our small town of Poway out of California, let alone across the country. I glance over at Caleb, napping on the couch. Even if the car could make it, could his little body handle a cross-country road trip?

I pinch the bridge of my nose and lean back, taking a deep breath. I know what I need to do, but I don't want to do it. I hate asking for help from anyone. Knowing I don't have a choice, I call my brother at the inn. His girlfriend Beth answers. I haven't met her in person yet, but we text and talk on the phone regularly.

"How are you guys doing? Evan stepped out for a minute, but he'll be back soon."

I break down in tears just hearing a friendly voice. It hits me then that I really need to be with my family.

"Allie, are you okay? Is Caleb okay?" Beth's voice is now full of worry.

"We're both okay, but I just lost my job."

"Oh, no. I'm sorry," she says. "What are you going to do?"

"I don't even know. I want to come home."

"Okay, let's make a plan. I'm sure Evan and your mom can help, too," Beth reassures me.

"Right now, I'd love a plan. I need that, badly."

"I think I have an idea. Want to hear it?" she asks.

"Sure, I'll welcome any and all help at the moment," I admit. I'm so tired and overwhelmed from the events of the past few months, I can't even figure out what to make for dinner most nights.

"Okay... I've heard stories about your car, and no offense, but that thing can't make it across the country. What if one of us flies out to get Caleb and brings him here. My friend Logan is leaving LA next week and coming to New Hampshire to spend the holidays with us. He can give you a ride and help you get you and your things back home to the inn."

"What kind of person would volunteer to help a stranger drive across the country?" I have to ask.

"He loves road trips, and besides, he likes to help."

It seems awkward, spending all that time on the road with a person I've never personally met. "I don't know, I don't want to trouble him..."

"He's like family to me, which means he's like family to you now, too. It never hurts to ask."

My parents have always been big on family, and they

raised us in the same way. Even beyond that, we all have a habit of turning friends into family, too. I know how they feel about Beth, and now that I think about it, I'm sure my mom has mentioned Beth's friend Logan to me before. Can I take that chance, though? I realize I've got nothing to lose, and before I can change my mind, I blurt out, "Okay, I guess. I need to start making lists so we can make this happen." I start to cry with relief. "I've wanted to move home for years, Beth. *Years*. I've missed everyone so much."

"Everyone here has missed you, too. We talk about you moving back all the time; everyone is going to be so excited to hear the news. Plus, I can't wait to finally squeeze you both in person! We'll help you and Caleb both get back here quickly and safely."

"Okay, I have to start figuring this out while Caleb is still napping. Thank you, Beth. I appreciate Logan's help. You know, if he's up for it."

"I'm sure he'll do it. Logan loves to drive. And I think we'd all feel better for you to have someone to travel with. I think everyone will worry about you making that trip alone. It will be safer."

I hang up, feeling relieved. When my brother was stationed out here for the Marines, I followed him to go to college here and fell in love with the whole Cali vibe. Surfing, the weather, the food, the fun. But as a single mom, trying to keep us afloat with a job I worked far too many hours at, none of that really applies anymore because I don't get to enjoy the parts of California that I used to enjoy.

For a brief time, there was the hope that Caleb's dad Chris would come around and help us out, but that's never been the case. He refuses to accept Caleb; neither in his life nor as his son. Even Chris's parents want nothing to do with Caleb. You'd think that they'd want to meet their only grandchild, but they have ignored all communication I've tried to have with them. It makes me more sad than angry, because Caleb deserves better.

My family is always there for him, cheering him on, calling him every chance they can, donating their kidneys to literally save his life… The usual. It's been a long time coming for us to finally reunite with them for good; we just have to get home to New Hampshire.

I make a fresh pot of coffee, then put a few warm cookies on a napkin and carry them to my makeshift desk. I open my laptop and check my bank balance. There's a whopping $678 in my checking account. I have one more final paycheck coming, but even factoring that in, my savings won't get us too far.

I need cash, and I need it now. Ever the independent, I refuse to ask Evan or my mom for help. I can do things on my own; I *prefer* to do things on my own.

Looking around at our trailer, I decide that I will sell whatever anyone will buy, assuming anyone wants to buy any of our second- and third-hand furniture and DIY décor. Hopefully that will give me some extra money, and then maybe I will just donate the rest. I don't need to bring too much with me since we have everything at the inn.

Thinking about the drive, I look up how far it is from Poway, California to Freedom Valley, New Hampshire. It's... not close. I calculate gas and food and feel instantly overwhelmed thinking about how I am going to afford this, even if I split everything with Logan.

My eyes drift to my baker's rack and my oven, still warm from the cookies.

I get on the computer and make a post in our neighborhood group offering a pan of homemade organic cinnamon rolls for $40 each. I mention in the post that I'm moving and will be selling everything in the trailer, so I will be happy to make cash deals on anything they can see when people come to pick up their rolls.

Just as I hit the button to post, Caleb stirs on the couch and says, "Mommy."

I head over and snuggle him, telling him the news. "Baby, how would you like to go live with Grandma and Uncle Evan at the inn?"

He smiles big and wraps his little arms around me. "Yes! Do I get to play with his puppies?"

"Yes, buddy, you can play with his puppies. And Kase." Mellie, the housekeeper at The Golden Gable, has a son Kase who is around Caleb's age. "You guys will have so much fun together."

Talking about it out loud and making plans for the move has me starting to feel really excited and less overwhelmed by this new endeavor. Our current neighborhood is a mobile home park, and mostly a retirement community, so there aren't a lot of kids for Caleb to play with. The bonus is that he's had plenty of older, retired grandma and grandpas to spoil him, but I know he'd love to have kids his age to play with now that he's feeling better.

Not to mention, I'm thrilled that Caleb will get to be raised at the inn where my brother and I grew up. That he will get to experience the magic of fall, the smell of Sasha's cooking, and the place my dad loved so much.

Caleb starts playing with his cars while I check my post about the cinnamon rolls. It's only been an hour, but I gasp and put my hand over my mouth when I see I already have forty-three orders. Our community of grandparent-like figures have been so kind to Caleb and me; they've really spoiled us. I'm not surprised they want to support us.

For this number of cinnamon rolls, I'm going to be baking nonstop for the next several days, so I cut it off there. I go through my baking supplies and estimate that I have enough for only a few pans, so I put in a bulk order for more baking supplies to be delivered to me. I hesitate at the cost, but at least this way I can stay home and keep baking.

I realize it's going to be a long night and I pour another cup of coffee. My kitchen becomes a full-on baking zone, stopping only once to make Caleb and me bowls of tomato soup and grilled cheese, which we eat together at the coffee table watching *PJ Masks*.

After a while, Caleb starts yawning so I get him ready for bed, knowing I need to get back to baking anyway.

My phone rings and even though it's late, I know it's Evan.

"Hey, you," I answer on the second ring.

"So, what's going on?" he says, concerned.

"I'm sure Beth filled you in, but it's finally happening, Evan."

"I'm sorry about the job. But, on the bright side, you get to come home now."

"Do you know if she talked to Logan?" I ask hesitantly.

"Yes, that's the other reason I'm calling. He's agreed to help."

"What do you think about that?"

He's quiet for a beat, then finally says, "I'm not against it. Logan's a good guy."

"Why would he say yes to this?" I ask.

"Beth mentioned he usually spends the holidays with her instead of going home to his family, so he was planning on coming here anyway."

"He's really going to drive with me all the way to New Hampshire?"

"That's the plan. Mom's coming to get Caleb. I booked their flights."

"Okay," I say as my oven timer goes off.

"Are you stress-baking again?" he asks.

"Actually, I decided to use up my baking stash to make cinnamon rolls for some of the people in my neighborhood before I go." I don't want to tell him that I need the money, because knowing him, he would just send it to me, and I really don't want him to do that.

"I can't wait to have your cinnamon rolls again. Sasha is tired of baking and could definitely use your help when you get here."

I smile because I know he sees right through my bullshit and still decides not to call me on it.

"Love you, Evan. I gotta get to bed. You probably do, too."

"Love you, too. Can't wait to have you guys home."

We hang up and I look at the clock. Of course there's no bedtime in sight for me right now. I hate lying to Evan, but I need to get to baking if we're going to get out of here.

I catch up on our laundry and make bags for donation in between cinnamon roll orders. I haul the donation piles out to my trunk and wrap the cinnamon rolls once they're cooled and frosted. I add my signature ribbons to each package, including a handwritten thank you card expressing my gratitude for everything our community has done for us.

I finally turn off the oven and fall into bed around four. I know Caleb will probably have me up around seven and I'll need to get started baking again. *I can do this*, I lie to myself as I drift off to sleep.

~

You need me to
do what?

"You need me to do *what*?" I say as I stop the treadmill and step off, wiping sweat off my face with the bottom of my t-shirt.

"I need you to drive Evan's sister from California to New Hampshire. She's moving here and it's too far for her to drive on her own."

"Beth, I don't even know her. She doesn't know me. That trip will take almost a week," I say, trying to catch my breath.

"You said you'd agree to *anything* if I agreed to do the

magazine article," she says quietly.

"You're sneaky," I say as I nab my water and walk out to my rental car, adjusting my AirPods in my ears.

"How many miles did you just run? You sound out of breath."

"Seven. It would've been eight, but you told me I'm driving a stranger across the country. This sounds like that movie, *Trains, Planes, and Automobiles*."

"Allie isn't a stranger, she's almost my sister-in-law, and you're like my family, so she's basically your family now, too."

"Oh, is that how that works?" I ask. I slide into the driver's seat and lean back, taking a big drink of water. I sigh in defeat. "When do you need me to do this?"

"Evan's mom is flying out tomorrow to get Caleb and bring him back, then you guys can leave whenever. Evan already rented a U-Haul."

"Okay, I have a few meetings in LA today and then I was heading back. So I guess I'm driving to Poway now." I sag deeper into the driver's seat, closing my eyes.

"I guess you are. And the *good* news for you is that you get your magazine article." She laughs.

Beth is a talented author, but she has a painful life story and she doesn't want to expose herself to having to tell it. As her literary agent, I've been pushing her to put herself out there more. Despite a public presence being good media exposure—which means better book sales—until just recently, she had been adamantly refusing. Now that she agreed, she just spoke at a conference and has been more active on social media, so I've been fielding nonstop requests for her to do more events since the conference. I've been pushing her to let me get her publicist to schedule interviews and magazine coverage about her story and upcoming books, but she hasn't wanted to do any.

I realize this favor must mean a lot to her if she's willing to do a magazine interview for it. And of course, she's also my best friend, so I'd do just about anything for her anyway.

"Send me the details," I tell her.

"Love youuuuuuuuuu," she says. "Talk later, bye."

"Bye." I lean my head back against my seat. I recently moved from New York City to Boston to hopefully land a huge promotion. I've been working constantly, trying to prove myself for the new opportunity; I have a lot riding on this. When I planned my trip to New Hampshire for the holidays, I was really looking forward to just relaxing with everyone, not driving across the country with a girl I've never met.

Trying to shift my attitude, I focus on the fact that I do love a road trip. Who doesn't? New food to try, new things to see, and music to listen to. As long as this chick Allie is cool, I'm hoping we'll have fun.

~

CHAPTER 3

Allie

So, you'll let me help you?

Please don't break down, please don't break down, I silently pray as I circle the airport, waiting for my mom to come out of the arrival terminal. I don't have money for parking, and I don't want to take a sleeping Caleb out of his booster seat. I can't help but feel anxious and stressed when I hear and feel the sputters my old Toyota is making, but I try to ignore the glares from people who don't want me to pull in to idle and wait. I notice they don't do that for the newer SUV up ahead, just my old rusty Toyota.

I finally see my mom and quickly pull over to the curb, jumping out and hugging her. "I missed you!"

I grab her overnight bag and put it in the trunk then jump back in the car before I get more glares from the parking police. My mom climbs in and glances back at Caleb, smiling when she sees he is still holding one of his trucks in his hands. "He's out like a light."

"He's been so excited to see you and ride in an airplane. That's all he's been talking about."

"I packed very light to make room for some of the things he needs until you make it to New Hampshire. I know you're short on room."

I blink back tears as I flip my turn signal and cruise out of the airport. "I'm so glad you're here. I just want to get back home with you guys."

"I know, honey. It's time for you to get home and settled in. I know you've been having a hard time lately; you deserve a break. I set up your old room for you so you're comfortable, and there's plenty of room for Caleb, too."

"I can't wait for that, Mom. I feel like I have so much to do." I catch Caleb stirring in my rearview mirror. "Hey, buddy. Look who's here."

"Grandma, we're going on an airplane!" he says sleepily.

"Yes, we are. It's going to be so much fun."

Curiosity gets the best of me, and I can't help but ask my mom, "So, what's Logan like? I'll admit, I'm a little nervous about traveling across the country with a stranger."

"Oh, Logan isn't a stranger. He's Beth's best friend. Whenever he comes to visit, he fits right in at the inn, and even helps out sometimes. We've pretty much adopted him into the family—even Pete's on board. I think you'll have fun with him."

Like my brother, Pete's a former Marine and a pretty good judge of character. He wouldn't like Logan if he wasn't a good guy.

"Okay," I say, raising my eyebrows.

"What do you want to do for lunch?" she asks. "My treat."

"We have a lot to use up at home and I have to keep baking," I say sheepishly.

"Baking? What are you baking?"

"You can't tell Evan. Promise?"

She raises her eyebrows and purses her lips, but she nods.

"I needed cash for the move and I had a lot of baking supplies to use up, so I took cinnamon roll orders from the neighborhood for some extra money. I still have several more orders to fulfill, so I have to keep baking and packing until Logan gets here."

"Oh, honey, I wish you'd just let me give you some cash. You didn't need to do all that baking."

"Mom, thank you, I love you for that, but don't start. You know I like to pay my own way."

"Okay, but at least let me help how I can. I'll find

something at the house to make for us so you don't have to worry about meals, and I'll watch Caleb so you can focus on baking."

"Good, because I'm starving, and I can't stop baking until these are done."

"Logan's going to bring the U-Haul over tonight. He's staying nearby. That way I can help you guys load up before Caleb and I leave tomorrow."

We park and head inside. She pauses in the entryway to my kitchen and covers her mouth. "Allison Harper, what have you done?"

"Okay, don't freak out. I promise I have a system." I laugh at what my kitchen must look like to her, seeing more than thirty packages of cinnamon rolls spread out everywhere and not understanding how I work. Thankfully, they're all getting picked up by tomorrow morning. I'm sure I'll be up all night to finish the orders, but I can't complain. The extra cash will go a long way for the trip.

I'm so stressed when I think about how much the move is going to cost me. I still have Caleb's medical bills to catch up on, and I didn't plan for a sudden cross-country move.

My mom looks overwhelmed, but she takes a deep breath and says, "Okay, let's do this."

"I'm so glad you're here, Mom." I give her a big hug. We weren't always close growing up, but now that I'm a mom, I see parent-child relationships differently. It makes me even more grateful for her. I'm never taking living near my family for granted again.

Mom gets busy putting together a lunch for the three of us. I apologize for my lack of groceries, and she just waves me off. "It's no worries, honey. We are good with easy sandwiches."

I roll out more dough and get it rising before continuing to mix more. I quickly eat in between batches. As the dough rises, my mom and I pack more boxes and stack them in the living room. I wash all of Caleb's laundry and pack a suitcase for him to take with my mom, feeling a rush of sadness when I pack his little backpack with a few of his favorite toys.

"I'm going to take Caleb with me to the pharmacy to pick up his prescriptions," she says.

"Oh, sure. Thank you," I say as they walk out and I pull another batch of dough out of the mixer and begin to roll it out on the floured counter in front of me.

A little while later, there's a knock at the door and I open it to see a tall, dark blond Adonis with a chiseled jaw and neatly trimmed goatee. He wears a pair of blue jeans and a tight-fitting white t-shirt that stretches tight across his athletic body. My jaw drops and suddenly I feel very gross and in need of a shower. *A cold shower.*

My little trailer is so hot and muggy with the constant baking and I know I must look a mess. My dark, stringy brown hair clings to my neck. My face is flushed. I want a do-over. Just, no. I want to shut this door and go shower and look presentable and then open this door again.

Oh. My. God. Why?

"Uh, hi," I stammer, thinking there is no way this is Logan. This is not who I pictured. He has the most piercing blue eyes that make my heart race when he looks at me. He can't be more than thirty; I thought he'd be much older. Like an old-grandpa-like literary agent. In a cardigan. Like Mister Rogers. *Not a hot, young one!*

"Hi, you must be Allie?" he says in a deep, rich voice. "I'm Logan."

"It's so nice to meet you. Please come in. I'm so sorry about the mess. I've been... busy."

He nods and steps into the kitchen, doing a double take as he looks around the tiny kitchen covered in cinnamon rolls. "Wow. Any chance I can get one of those?" he says as he grins.

"Yes, of course," I say, scooping one out onto a plate and handing it to him. I can't make eye contact with him, I'm so nervous. This guy is who I have to ride to New Hampshire with? *This freaking guy?* He's so hot and I'm so distracted. *Holy shit.*

He moans as he bites into his cinnamon roll. "This is amazing."

My mom comes in with the prescriptions and gives him a big hug. "It's good to see you," she tells him. "I see you found the place okay. Thank you for helping. I don't know what we'd do without you."

"I know there's a lot going on back East. I'm happy to help. Where's—" Just then, Caleb comes barreling in and shoots Logan with a Nerf gun as a welcome. Logan just laughs, picks up the bullet, and follows him into the living room, where he finds a second Nerf gun and begins playing with Caleb, both laughing as they shoot at each other.

I shoot my mom a murderous glare. "Mom!" I hiss. "You did not tell me he looks like *that*." I pace the kitchen, smoothing my greasy hair back and fidgeting with my messy clothes.

She tries to hide her smile but can't. She laughs. "Like what?" she asks.

I shake my head and switch out the cinnamon rolls. I so badly want them all done so I can take a shower and crawl into bed, but I also want to spend the evening with my mom and Caleb before I don't see my son for a week. My heart hurts as I think of not being with him. We've never been away from each other.

"So, are these boxes all set for the U-Haul?" Logan asks, pointing at the tall pile I've stacked.

"Oh, yes, but I can do it," I stammer. I already feel like I'm asking too much of him, I don't want to burden him with more. Not to mention I am still shook at how freaking gorgeous he is.

He tilts his head at me as if to say *we both know that isn't happening* and he smiles kindly at me. "I'll just make a few trips out." He props the door open and starts carrying boxes. This is when I notice his massive biceps. My face is on *fire*, and it has nothing to do with the oven being on nonstop for two days straight.

I need that cold shower, *now*.

Mom orders a few pizzas and salads to be delivered for dinner. When I reach for my purse to hand her cash, she gives me "the mom look" and I just go back to baking and packing. Normally, I'd get my way, but right now, I'm just way too tired to argue with anyone.

The pizza arrives and it smells so good my mouth waters. I stack most of the cinnamon rolls on the now empty side table in the living room so we can eat.

I'm so nervous. I look like a hot mess, and I'm so hungry I'm afraid I'm going to shovel food in my face like a wild beast. Luckily, my mom breaks the ice so I can focus on eating and getting Caleb situated with his food.

"So, Logan, how's work?" my mom asks.

"It's been pretty busy. I just wrapped up a project out here in LA. I'm off for a week and then I start my new position in Boston. Thanks for asking, Margie," he says.

"How are things back home in Montreal?" Mom asks, then takes a bite of her salad.

Still nervous around him because I wasn't expecting him

to be handsome, I take a bite of pizza and scoot Caleb's cup closer to him.

"Okay, I guess. I'm in Boston now, and that's where I consider home."

"I'm going to make sure you have a room anytime you want to come visit the inn, okay?" She looks over at him and smiles.

"Thanks, Margie. How're Sasha and Pete doing?"

Mom smiles at me. "I told you Logan has helped out around the inn? One of his favorite things was baking with Sasha."

Ah, I think. Not only is this man fine, but he knows how to bake, too?

"Sasha's good," Mom says. "Just very busy with all the new guests we've had, thanks to all the work Beth did on our marketing. I'm hoping Allie will take over the baking for her."

"That would be perfect for me. I don't want to put Caleb in daycare, but I'll need to get started working again, right away," I say.

"Great. That's settled, then. You're our new official inn baker now. Sasha will be happy to hand it over."

"How's Evan been?" I ask.

"He's head over heels in love with Beth, so watching those two has been fun."

"I am so happy for them. He's healing okay?" I ask.

"Oh, you know your brother. He's already running again and trying to push it, but Beth keeps him in check."

I look at Logan. "So, you're a baker?"

Logan nods. "We had a lot of fun baking treats for the fall festival. I never realized I liked baking until then. I loved it, actually."

"Wow, what do you love to bake?" I sit up straighter and think maybe this road trip will be fun after all. We do seem to have some things in common.

"Anything really. My job is stressful sometimes. A lot of travel, constant meetings, and I'm always on the phone. Baking is relaxing."

Interesting. Smart, extremely hot, and helping me move across the country—and he loves to bake? Where did he come from? I shake my head in disbelief and take a bite of salad.

"This is good, Mom, thanks."

"I'm glad you're finally sitting down to eat something, honey. How many more batches do you have to make?"

"Six. Going to start back on them right after dinner."

"Oh, honey, you must be so exhausted. She's been baking nonstop for days now," she tells Logan.

"It's no big deal. I'll get them knocked out. The money will really help with the trip."

Logan looks up from his pizza and scans the kitchen, like he's just finally realizing what I'm doing with the cinnamon rolls and his eyes soften. "I can help you with them for a while before I go to my hotel, and you can get Caleb ready for bed."

My ovaries are throbbing. This man is liquid hotness.

"You don't have to do that, but I'd really appreciate it. I do need to give him a bath and finish packing him up."

"It's not a problem," he says. "This is great pizza. Thanks, Margie."

"Absolutely," she says. "How's Beth's book coming along?"

"Good, I think," he says, taking another bite. He chews and swallows before adding, "She's been busy with Evan and the inn, but she's really excited about what we have coming up. It's good to see her happy again."

"I can't wait to read it," she says.

I glance over at Caleb and the sadness from earlier returns. I would give anything to fast forward a week so we could just be settled in Freedom Valley.

"I'm going to miss you, buddy, but you'll have so much fun with everyone."

Caleb grins. "I'm going on an airplane! In the sky!" He spreads his hands wide and points up.

"Yes you are, honey. We're going to love living in New Hampshire with Grandma, Uncle Evan, and Beth."

"I heard about her family." Beth's husband and baby were killed by a drunk driver a few years back. It took Evan and Beth a while to get together because she was still dealing with grief. "So tragic."

"Yeah, that was hard," Logan says. "She's just now finally able to talk about it. She's come a long way, and your brother had a lot to do with bringing her back to the land of the living."

"She's been really good for him, too," my mom adds.

"They really are meant for each other," Logan agrees. "I'm really happy for them."

We finish dinner and clear the table. I wipe it down and begin to lay out more of the baking ingredients.

Logan leans in and says, "So you'll let me help you?"

I'm not usually one to accept help, but his tone is sincere and I'm bone tired.

"Do you want me to write the recipe down?"

"I watched you measure and put it in the notes of my phone earlier. Here, you can double-check," he says as he hands over his phone.

I take a glance and wow, that's my recipe. "Okay," I nod at him. "Thank you. I really appreciate this."

"It's no problem." He ties my bright red apron over his godlike form and I literally freeze.

My eyes can't stop looking at his arms as he begins to methodically measure out ingredients like he has been making these his whole life.

I head to Caleb's room and try to get my head on straight. I'm so exhausted I can barely function. "Hey, buddy, let's get you in the bath and get your jammies on. You have a big day tomorrow."

I pick him up, kiss his cheek, hug him tight, then carry him down the hall to the bathroom. His little arms hug me back and I set him down to start the water in the tub. I think about what our new life will be like in New Hampshire, about the new routines and traditions we'll make.

While Caleb plays in the tub, I pack a special bag for him that my mom can take, making sure I'm not missing any of his medications. I double check the bag again just in case, going over the list one more time, nervous I'll forget something for her to give him.

Anxious feelings run through me as I look over and see him playing. He has been doing well since his surgery, and I know he's in good hands with my mom, but not being with him even just for an hour makes me worried.

When he's all nice and dry and dressed, I snuggle him in his little bed and read him one of our favorite stories, *Love You Forever.* I look around the room that I made as homey as possible for him and know that I did my best, but now it's time to go home. We had a pretty good life here in this little home, reading so many books and stories, becoming friends with our neighbors, and making the most of what we had.

Caleb drifts off to sleep and I take a moment to wonder what our routine will be like in our new home. Confident that Caleb and I will both be happier there, I close the door and head into the kitchen. Logan already has one batch done and one in the oven, and he's rolling out more dough.

"This is a lot of work. You did all of these in just the past few days? You must have worked around the clock," he says. "When did you sleep?"

"I didn't," I say as I yawn and walk over to mix up the icing for the next few batches.

"You look exhausted. Why don't you go ahead and go to bed? You can take back over in the morning."

My mom sides with Logan and pushes me down the hall toward my room.

I realize I'm in no place to argue, so I trudge to my bathroom, take a hot shower, and fall into my bed.

The next thing I know, my mom gently gives my shoulder a shake. "Honey? It's time to get ready. We need to leave in about forty-five minutes for the airport."

"Oh my God, what time is it? I overslept! I don't even remember going to bed! I didn't even set my alarm! Oh no! My cinnamon rolls. I need to finish!" I scramble out of bed, pulling on pajama pants.

"They're all done, honey. Logan finished them last night. He said he couldn't figure out the bows you tied on them. He cut the ribbon and left those for you to do."

"What time did he finish? Oh my God, I feel so bad."

"I heard him leave around four a.m. I think he'll probably sleep for a while. Let's get going in case there's traffic."

I quickly pull on jeans and a t-shirt before brushing my teeth and heading to the kitchen. I pour myself a cup of coffee and splash some cream in it. I take in all of the completed cinnamon rolls, in awe because I can't believe he did all of this.

Caleb comes into the kitchen carrying his blanket, still in his jammies. "Hey, honey bunny. Are you excited to go with Grandma today?"

"Yes, but I'm going to miss you, Mommy," he says with sad eyes.

"I know, buddy. I'm going to hurry out to New Hampshire with all of your toys and we'll settle in at Grandma's. Remember that you have two new puppies to play with, and a new friend, Kase."

That seems to cheer him up and he eats some scrambled eggs at the table. He plays with his cars while I help my mom load their bags into the car. Too quickly, we are saying goodbye and promising to see each other soon.

~

I don't like surprises.

When I wake up the next morning, it's already nine. I have time for a quick run before I head over to Allie's and finish helping her load up her trailer with the last of her stuff. We still have to figure out what route we're taking, where we're stopping, and what our hotel situation will be.

I felt terrible yesterday when I realized how tight money must be for her to need to bake all those pans of cinnamon rolls for days straight. Although, I have to hand it to her. She's a fantastic baker, and that was a genius idea to quickly make cash for her move.

I get a text from Margie during my run.

Margie: Thank you for everything you're doing for Allie. She just dropped us at the airport and we're off to New Hampshire now. See you soon!

I send her a quick text back and I head back to my hotel, shower, and get ready. I take a few calls from clients and go through my emails. Before I know it, it's after eleven and I'm hungry.

I head down to my rental car and pick up Chipotle with extra chips and guacamole on the way to Allie's, hoping she likes it as much as I do.

I pull up to her trailer and park across the street. The sky is clear and the air has a musky, tropical scent. Poway seems like a nice little town, and I wish I had more time to explore.

As I approach the front door, I hear music playing. I knock, but she doesn't answer, so I open the door a crack. "Hello…?"

I ease in and look around. The giant piles of cinnamon rolls I'd finished baking this morning are mostly gone, and I spot her bent over, her butt in the air, packing books into a box. I have to admit, she has a gorgeous body and great curves.

And she's singing, hitting every note of Adele's "Easy on Me" with perfect pitch.

I set the food down on the table and lean back and listen. Damn. This girl can really sing. I could listen to her all day. Not only is she stunning, with her dark, wavy hair and mossy green eyes, but her voice is soulful, rich, and powerful.

She turns to tape up the box and gasps when she sees me, covering her mouth with her hand.

"Oh, wow, you scared me." She steps back and almost falls before steadying herself on the counter.

"Great pipes."

"Thanks," she says hesitantly.

"Where did you learn to sing like that?"

"My brother and I used to do some gigs in high school with a local band. We even wrote some songs together. He still plays sometimes, but I don't. Not anymore."

"Why not?"

She starts to speak then stops. She gestures to the chaos in the room. "Well, I've been kind of busy." She laughs. "Motherhood, work, and then Caleb got sick. It was always just a hobby, anyway."

"It sounded like more than a hobby."

I watch her face flush as she tosses her long dark hair over her shoulder. She stands up with the box, which I lean in and snag from her. "Let me get this."

She hesitates as our fingers brush when I take the box and set it by the front door. She seems shy and nervous around me, and I'm hoping she gets over that as we spend the next week traveling together. If she doesn't, it's going to be an awkward trip.

I decide I'm going to do what I can to try and make her

feel at ease. "Anyway, I brought lunch. Hungry?"

"You didn't have to do that. I'm not really hungry," she says, just as her stomach grumbles loudly in protest.

"Are you sure about that?" I ask then munch on a chip.

She smiles and shrugs her shoulders. "Okay, maybe I'm a little hungry."

I take the food out of the bag and set it out. "I see you've managed to get rid of most of the cinnamon rolls," I tell her as I open the containers.

"Yeah, people have been in and out of here all morning picking up their orders. So, what did you get for us?"

"My favorite bowls. I didn't know what you liked so I got everything I liked, one with chicken, one with beef. You can pick which one you want."

"Thank you. I do love Chipotle," she says as she points at the chicken.

"Me, too."

"Hey, thank you so much for all your help. I wouldn't have finished all those orders without you. You're a fantastic baker, by the way."

"It's no problem," I say. "I figure if the agent gig doesn't pan out, I can always open my own bakery."

"That's my dream," she muses, her tone faraway and almost dreamy.

"What?" I glance at her and her eyes captivate me. She and Evan both have the most striking green eyes.

"To have my own bakery back home in Freedom Valley. Someday." She shrugs.

"I think that's a great idea. Can you use the kitchen at the inn to get it going?"

She thinks about it for a minute and says, "Yeah, probably. I've already committed to baking for the inn so that has to come first, but I could probably bake on the side and build my own business, as well."

"Definitely needed in Freedom Valley. Everything Sasha and I baked sold fast, and it felt like we couldn't keep up with the demand."

She stands and opens the fridge as she asks, "Would you like a drink? I have water, and... water," she says meekly as she grabs two glasses, fills them with ice and water, and sets them on the table in front of us.

She's funny, too. I'm happy that she seems to be relaxing a bit around me. I smile. "Water is great, thanks."

We eat quietly. I sneak a look at her a few times. She's a woman full of surprises, that's for sure. I never expected her to be able to sing like that, for one. She's driven, ambitious. No one who bakes this many pans of cinnamon rolls isn't passionate about baking.

Pretty much out of nowhere, she breaks the silence. "What do you do for fun?"

I sip my water then reply, "I like to read, work out, listen to music, travel, and I guess now bake. What about you?"

She seems to be studying me but avoids my question. "Well, you're a very good baker. I heard from Beth that you're great to work with. Did you always want to be a literary agent?"

I think about this for a minute and finally say, "Yes and no. My family owns an investment company. Some of my siblings work in the family business. My family was disappointed that I didn't go into the finance industry, but I guess I've always loved books. I always wanted to go into publishing, and I've always been good at making deals."

"I can imagine it's a lot of fun working with authors and books."

"It can be. I love helping authors make their dreams come true."

"Maybe my future bakery can have a book shop in it."

"Now there's an idea." I grin. "So what about you?" I ask again.

This time she acknowledges my question. "What about me?"

"What do you do for fun?" I take another bite and wait for her response.

She leans back and says, "I don't really know."

How does she not know what she likes to do for fun? I press, "You don't know what you like to do for fun?"

She hesitates, as if conflicted. "I haven't had fun in so long, I don't even know what I like anymore." She takes another bite and looks away. When she sees I'm staring at her, she says, "What?"

There's no room in her life for fun? This woman has lost herself. I sit back in my chair and think about this.

"Well, you know what? That's changing now. We're going to have fun on this road trip and you're going to remember what fun means for Allie."

She peers at me. "What do you mean?"

"We're embarking on an epic cross-country road trip. Let's make the best of it. What do you say?"

"What do you have in mind?"

"See some fun things along the way, listen to good music, eat lots of greasy road food."

She hesitates, then says, "That sounds... actually amazing. I haven't had a break to just be myself in so long."

We both startle when a knock sounds at the door. Allie jumps up, wiping her hands on her napkin. "The last pick-up. Be right back," she says quickly as she walks to the living room and picks up the remaining pans and carries them to the door.

I hold the door for her as she carries them out and hands them to an older lady with white hair. The woman hands her an envelope and hugs her with tears in her eyes. I can tell Allie has been important to the people in her community and they're going to miss her.

I finish eating and pull out my phone to look up routes to

New Hampshire while she chats.

Allie comes back in to finish her lunch. "I have been looking up the best routes and thinking of lodging. We can also research cool restaurants and landmarks to see along the way."

She suddenly looks panicked. "Oh my God, hotels. I didn't factor in the cost of that." She suddenly sits upright and stares off in the distance, mentally calculating how much more it's going to be.

"Allie, it's totally fine. I worked it out with your mom," I fib, hoping she doesn't call me on it.

Her mouth goes into a straight line, confirming my suspicions that she's independent and probably wouldn't want me paying for things, so I don't push.

"Thank you for lunch and… everything," she says quietly.

"My pleasure. Let's get your stuff loaded up. I have a fun idea for tonight after we get all of this done."

"What is it?"

"A surprise."

She looks at me and bites her lip. "I don't like surprises."

"You'll like this one," I say.

~

CHAPTER 5

Allie

Don't knock it.

We load up the stuff I've decided to keep. I am planning on staying at the inn with my mom just until I can afford a place for Caleb and me. Not forever.

Logan figures out how to hitch my car to the back of the U-Haul, but he's holding on to his rental car for the night, saying we'll need it for his surprise later. I'm not thrilled about it since I hate surprises. Probably because I'm used to planning everything and making sure I don't miss something critical for Caleb. Being a single mom to a child who's been sick means I've always had to think ahead. I don't want to admit that it feels nice to have someone else do the planning for once.

When we finish loading everything and I close and lock the door for the last time, I am full of emotions. Most of all, I suddenly realize I'm filthy and need a shower. Logan said it was okay for me to get cleaned up at his hotel, so we head that way.

He pulls up to the front door, dropping me off, and tells me, "I'll be back in about an hour."

I nod and head up to his room. His bag sits on the chair in the corner. I set my stuff down on one of the beds and quickly get my clothes ready. I am nervous he'll make it back before I'm ready, and I want to be dressed when he gets here. He's given me no reason to believe he's not the perfect gentleman, but still, I just met him. Although, I have a feeling by the end of this road trip, we'll be close friends or archenemies as that's how road trips typically go.

What if he gets sick of me, though? I can't let that happen. I'll be quiet in the car, no snoring, no annoying him. I'll keep my head down and be grateful for the help.

I quickly shower and it feels so good to rinse off my moving grossness. I blow dry my hair, do my quick makeup routine, and put on a sundress and cardigan. I let my hair go curly and wild down my back and pull back the front into a knot on top. I try a little harder with my appearance than I normally would because I am not sure where we're going, and because he looks so good.

My phone buzzes and I flip it over to see a text from Logan.

Logan: Hey, I'm back. Wondering if you could run an errand for us while I get ready?

Me: Heading down now.

I put my stuff back in my bag and set it by the door. I swing my purse over my shoulder. I pause, then pull out a lip gloss and swipe it over my lips and tuck it back in my purse.

When I get to the lobby, I find Logan leaning against the wall. I appreciate how he gave me space by waiting down here for me. He looks amazing in his tight black t-shirt, blue jeans, and black boots.

His mouth falls open when he sees me. He quickly straightens and says, "You look nice."

I smile and thank him. "So, what's the surprise?"

"You'll find out." He hands me some cash and keys. "Can you pick up some snacks for the trip tomorrow?"

I nod but make no move to take his money. "Okay, but I've got this."

He reaches down, grabs my hand, and folds the bills and car keys into it. He locks eyes with me. "See you in thirty?" He saunters off as the elevator doors open.

I decide to keep track of what he spends and figure out how to make sure we settle up at the end of the trip.

I get to the store, not really knowing what to buy. He's a fit guy and looks like he eats healthy, but maybe he bends the rules for road trips?

I choose some things I hope he'll like—beef jerky, peanut butter cups, popcorn—and I pick up a case of water and apples to last us a while. I get back to the hotel and wait in the parking lot, texting my mom and Evan while I wait for Logan to come down.

Distracted by my phone, I don't realize the time has passed when there's a tapping at my window. Logan now has on black pants and a gray button-down shirt, with the sleeves rolled up over his massive forearms. *Damn.*

"Got the snacks," I say, motioning to the back seat as I open the door and step out.

"Perfect. Okay, first things first. Before we leave Southern California, is there any place you've wanted to go and haven't been?"

I think about this for a minute and finally say, "I always wanted to go to the beach more. I never made it down there much after I had Caleb."

Come to think of it, I realize I haven't been to the beach since the night I got pregnant with Caleb at a party at the beach. Not memories I'm fond of reliving.

He nods. "Okay, then tonight we're going for a drive to the beach and eating at a beachfront restaurant. And we're going to plan the next leg of our trip. Sound good?"

"This is your surprise?"

"And we're going to find out what you like to do for fun. By the time you get to Freedom Valley, you'll remember who Allie is." He takes his hand and lays it on my back as he guides me to my side of the car and opens the door for me.

Heat radiates through my chest. "Sure. Why not." My back still tingles from where he touched me as I slide into my seat. Gah. I feel like a high schooler again. *Why am I like this?*

We drive the coast for a while until we get to Cardiff, and he pulls into a beautiful restaurant called the Charter House. "Do you like seafood?"

"I don't really eat it that often, unless you consider fish sticks for Caleb as seafood," I say and laugh. "My cuisine is usually four year old friendly."

"Let's try some new things. It'll be fun." He walks around and opens my door for me.

"Thank you. What a gentleman," I quip.

We enter and are led to what seem like the best seats in the restaurant, looking out over the ocean. The view is breathtaking. The server hands us menus and Logan asks, "How does the three-course dinner sound?"

"Amazing. I'm so hungry. It all sounds so delicious."

"Okay, why don't we order different things and we can both try them all?"

"Let's do it," I say, feeling excited.

"I am thinking about getting clam chowder, prime rib, and

key lime pie. What are you thinking?" he asks.

"How about lobster bisque, the Baja salmon, and carrot cake. Sound good?"

"Perfect," he says.

The server comes and Logan tells her what we want. I glance out at the waves, admiring how the sea foams against the sand and boats dot the horizon.

"I bet you'll miss this view and the weather," he says.

I really won't. California was never meant to be my forever. I can't wait to go back to New England and enjoy all the seasons. California has had some fun times, but it's time to go home.

I think about the holidays coming up and all the memories we'll make.

"I bet it was hard to be away from your family all those years."

"It was," I answer. "But I learned a lot being on my own out here."

"I could see that—both learning how to be independent and still wanting to return home. I really love being at the inn. That's why I'm heading there for the holidays."

"Do you miss your family in Montreal?"

"I miss Montreal. But… I'm not very close to my family, aside from one of my sisters and her partner."

"How many sisters do you have?"

"Two. Kathryn, the one I talk to, is a teacher, and also a

black sheep like me."

"I can't imagine you being a black sheep," I say, meaning it. He seems to have it together. A great job he's good at, friends, and he seems happy.

"My father is disappointed in who I've become. He assumed I'd carry on the family business, but his dream wasn't my dream."

"What about your mom?" I ask, searching his eyes for an answer.

He gazes out to the beach, as if the answer he wants to give will be rolling in with the waves. "She's different, lost. She does whatever my dad wants."

I don't even know what to make of this. What a strange family dynamic.

"What do you mean?"

"She lives to please him. Does a lot of society type things. Sometimes she's like a robot. I didn't grow up in a very warm and cozy house like the inn. I think that's why I love spending time there. The people are so real and normal; it's easy to feel like I belong when I'm there."

"I get it. It's a special place."

I think about all the things I've missed over the years. Just little things like family dinners or having coffee with my mom in the morning will be nice. Spending time with my brother and Sasha and Pete.

God, I miss home. It makes me sad Logan didn't have that.

I guess I didn't realize how special the inn really was as a kid. As an adult, I see it differently.

Our food arrives and we split everything, which was a good call because each dish is delicious.

"I think I'm going to like finding myself again. This trip will be amazing if it's anything like this food."

Logan laughs as he eats a spoonful of lobster bisque. "Thanks for coming here with me. I rarely get to just let go and explore and have fun. Work tends to keep me on the go."

"So, Las Vegas is our first stop tomorrow?"

"I figure we can get there early so we can go explore a little. I was thinking we shouldn't plan each leg until the day before so we have some spontaneity."

"Sounds good." I sit back, so full. "I think we're going to have to take these desserts to go."

"I agree. Let's drop them in the car and walk this off on the beach." Logan hands the server his credit card before I can say anything.

"I can get half," I say as I reach for my purse.

"It's my pleasure," he says. "I'm actually really glad we're getting to take this trip. I'll admit, when Beth asked me, I was nervous to meet you. But now that I have, I think we're going to have a lot of fun."

"Me, too. Thank you for being willing to do this."

Logan signs the check and we head toward the beach. I take off my sandals as we reach the sand. It feels soft and cool under my bare feet, making me wish I had been able to enjoy simple things like walking on the beach all this time I've been in California. As we walk down the shore, I stare out at the tide for a while. It'll probably be a long time before I see the Pacific Ocean again.

"What are you thinking about?" he asks as the waves crash below us.

I sigh and my shoulders relax. "I'm nervous to start a new life back there."

"That's understandable. You left after high school, and now you're coming back as a parent with your own child. Your identity is completely different."

"That's part of the problem," I sigh. "I don't even know who I am anymore."

"Can I ask you something?"

"Sure."

"Why'd you stay here after Evan moved back?"

I think about this for a while and how to answer it. Why did I stay? I guess because I think I held out for a dream that I thought I wanted but didn't ever happen.

"I know it sounds stupid, but I kind of thought Caleb's dad would eventually come around. We'd only been dating for a few months when I got pregnant, but I thought we were serious. It turns out he was just a rich, frat boy who came slumming for me and now won't acknowledge Caleb."

I feel him tense up next to me. He reaches over and puts

his hand on my arm. "That's messed up, Allie, I'm sorry. Although, it sounds like you might have dodged a bullet there."

I close my eyes for a minute. I know we did, but it still hurts the same. Being rejected never feels good.

"Doesn't sound like he deserves you guys."

"He missed out on a great kid," I say. My stomach clenches when I think about the rejection I've felt for Caleb. It's not fair. Chris didn't have to be with me, but why reject his son?

"Anyway, I also stayed because I had a job with good insurance. I'd already been saving to move back when Caleb got sick. By the time we finally figured out what was wrong, we were on the transplant list for a kidney, and I was afraid to leave his surgical team here. Now that we've got him transferred to a new medical team in New Hampshire and a specialist in Boston for follow-up care, I finally feel okay about moving home."

"What was your job?"

"I worked for a marketing company."

"That's so different from baking. Do you really want to bake at the inn?" he asks.

I kick a few pebbles and pause to think about my answer. "I think I'd like to open up my own bakery eventually. I love Freedom Valley, and I always dreamed of having a little house on main street with a white fence and my own bakery shop. A place for people to come in for coffee and a pastry and work on their laptops, engage with the locals, and enjoy treats. I'd also like to offer specialty cakes for parties and celebrations. A place for Caleb to pop in after school and grow up with a family business like Evan and I did with The Golden Gable Inn."

Logan looks over at me and says, "That's definitely doable. You have a lot of exciting things in front of you."

"I do. Exciting, but overwhelming at the same time."

"Anyone who makes forty-three dozen cinnamon rolls in four days is a determined person. I have no doubt you'll achieve anything you set your mind to."

I laugh. "I guess I did a little overachieving there."

"And you seem like a great mom. Caleb is lucky to have you."

I anchor my attention on him. I feel like he's someone I've known for a long time even though we've only just met. It's like he really sees me, understands me.

"Thanks for that. There are days I question whether I'm doing enough or if my best is good enough. It's nice to be told those things." Not paying attention to where we are walking, I start to lose my balance and trip, and Logan reaches out and catches my arm, steadying me.

We both laugh and he looks at me, "You alright?" Before I can answer, his phone rings with a FaceTime call. "It's Beth. Let's take it."

He holds his phone up and we stand with our backs to the

ocean as Beth appears on the screen.

"Hey, how's it going? Oh my, that view! Look at you two! Where are you?"

I smile and wave, feeling nervous because Logan is so close and he smells so good.

"We just had dinner and we're doing some exploring before we head out in the morning," Logan replies.

"I knew you two would hit it off." Beth grins. She turns and picks up Caleb and holds him up. "Look who I have."

"Mommy!" Caleb squeals, "Hi!"

"Hi, honey. How was your airplane ride?" My heart swells as I see him safe and happy with Beth.

"Good. I liked it."

"Evan just got back with them. We're making cookies, aren't we, buddy?" Beth says.

"Where are you?" Caleb whispers.

"Let me show you, buddy," Logan says, flipping the phone around and showing him the beach and ocean. It makes me aware of just how close we've been standing and I step away a little.

"I also wanted to do something special for you guys," Beth tells us.

"What's that?" Logan asks.

"A client I freelanced for has an amazing Airbnb right outside of Las Vegas, and they had an opening. I guess he liked my work, because I was able to get the property tomorrow night for you guys for free."

"You didn't have to do that," I hedge.

"It's my pleasure," she says. "Take lots of pictures, okay? I'll email you the information when I hang up."

"Thank you," I say.

"Evan and I are happy to do anything to help you guys. Can't wait to see you both. Anyway, we have to go check on the cookies now. I am not the baker of the family... I heard that's you, Allie. I better not let them burn." She winks. "Drive safe!"

"Bye, thanks again." Logan ends the call, then slides the phone back in his pocket.

"That was really nice of her," I say as we make our way back down the beach. It's

starting to get chilly and I pull my cardigan tighter around my shoulders. "By the way, I can help you drive," I say.

"It's okay, I enjoy driving and road trips," he says.

"I'm good with playlists." I shrug with a smile. "That's what I can offer."

"It's a deal. So, what did you end up getting for snacks?"

"A little bit of everything, I guess."

"Good. I'm serious about my road trip eats," he teases as we approach the car. Once again, he opens the door for me.

"Thank you, sir." I smile and tuck my dress around my legs as I slide in, except the hem still manages to slide up mid-thigh. I quickly fix it and shuffle awkwardly, setting my purse down at my feet. As he walks around the car, I take a deep breath. I'm a little more relaxed around him now that we've spend some time together. It's hard not to be when he's so down to earth and kind. I can't imagine anyone not liking this man.

Logan gets in the driver's side. "Okay. Last chance. What else do you want to see before we leave California tomorrow? Speak now or forever hold your peace," he says, his eyebrows arching mischievously.

I wonder if this would be too much. "Well, I've always wanted to see..." I stop myself and shake my head. "Never mind, it's too far."

Logan put his hand on my arm. "No, that's not how this works. Tell me what you were going to say. We're on a quest to find Allie this trip," he says, his jaw twitches as he tries to keep a serious face. "What'll it be?"

"Okay. I've always wanted to see the Santa Monica pier, especially at night. Is it too far?" I feel guilty, not wanting him to be too tired for our drive tomorrow, but it's still kind of early.

He looks at his watch. "Nope, it's about thirty minutes up the coast. Alright, here's my phone, I have some playlists you can choose from. Are you feeling eighties? Nineties?"

"How about I surprise you and we do a mix?"

"Oh, how about that, says the woman who doesn't like surprises. Now she wants to do surprises."

"Oh, whatever," I say, playfully.

Logan nods, tapping his fingers on the steering wheel as he eases out into traffic and we head up the coast.

ZZ Top's "La Grange" fills the car and we both ease into our ride. "You're going to be a kickass road trip partner, you know that?" Logan tells me and smiles approvingly. "You pick both excellent snacks and music. So far, you're two for two."

"You haven't even seen the snacks yet."

"I'm sure you are a great snack picker."

"I'll try not to let you down," I say as I scroll through his playlists. "Your playlists are amazing. I'm a big music fan."

"I travel a lot and I like to rotate through them. I also listen when I run."

"Wait, like, you run on purpose? Like, for fitness? Is someone chasing you? Why would you do that?" I look at him, pretending to be shocked.

Logan laughs. "I like to stay in shape. It helps me keep up with my busy workload."

"I'm sorry I added more travel to your schedule. I feel bad. Thank you for helping me make this trip."

"It's okay. I haven't taken time off in a while, and to be honest, I probably really needed the break."

"Well, if you're sure..."

"I'm sure. Now, let's talk about stopping points. We're headed to Las Vegas already. But after that I think we should stop in Moab, Denver, and Chicago. What are your thoughts?"

"That all sounds really great."

"You can call the shots, Ace."

Ace.

Time seems to slow as memories take over. Ace. He called me Ace. Could he know that's a special nickname for me?

I lean back into my seat, watching out the window as we drive north. We get to the pier and it surprisingly isn't too crowded. We walk and take pictures before finding a place to sit, looking out at the ocean and listening to the waves crashing. We eat our desserts, trying each other's and soaking in how peaceful it is.

I wish I had had the time and money to take Caleb more places in California. Maybe someday we'll come back.

"What's on your mind? You look lost in thought over there."

"This has been fun. Thank you for tonight."

"It's no problem. It's funny how Beth has had to remind me to slow down and enjoy life. I had to remind her to do the same a few months ago, and that's how she ended up in Freedom Valley with your brother. I need this break, too," he admits.

"You're right. It's time for new adventures."

"Let's head back to the hotel. I'll get you your own room and we'll rest up for tomorrow. I want to head out early.

The faster we get to Vegas, the faster we can explore. Sound good?"

Oh my God. We were so busy getting packed up and ready for his surprise dinner, I didn't even consider where I was staying. I forgot to get a room.

Frustrated that I didn't plan for this, I say, "Yes, but I can get my own room." I pull out my phone to search up the hotel's website.

Logan looks at me and says, "If you're not feeling like spending the money, you can stay in my room. It's pretty late, and we're just going to crash and get up in a few hours anyway."

My eyes dart to his.

"I promise to be a perfect gentleman," he adds, his tone serious.

I think about it for a minute and decide it's probably a smart move. I'll be spending a lot of money on the trip for lodging, not to mention food and fuel. I need to stretch every dollar of my cinnamon roll earnings as far as I can. Plus, I'm exhausted and just want to fall into a bed and crash. And he has two beds in his room. It'll be fine, I reassure myself.

"Okay, if you're sure you're cool with it. I appreciate the offer."

Logan nods. "Sure thing. Okay, DJ Master Allie, put on some tunes. I'm feeling nineties. What about you?"

"You got it." I pull up the playlist on his phone. "Hold

up, you have Jamie Walters' 'Hold On'?" I cover my mouth, trying not to laugh. "Such a cheesy song. I'm getting nineties *90210* vibes."

"Don't knock it," he says as he sings along. We both laugh at how incredibly off-pitch he is.

"Logan, you and I are going to have a blast, and I appreciate you SO much, but you can't carry a tune…" I laugh and playfully push his shoulder. And it's a hard shoulder. Full of muscles. *Get your mind out of the gutter, Allie.*

He interrupts my dirty thoughts. "I know. And I still sing anyway. But now that I know that you *can* sing, I'll make *you* sing all the way to New Hampshire."

"I've been known to sing in the car," I say. "I know all of Jewel's songs by heart. She's one of my favorites."

"I met her once. Through her agent."

I gawk at him. "You, uh, know, Jewel? Like as in Jewel Kilcher, the singer?"

"Yep. She was really nice and down to earth."

"I've always wanted to go to one of her concerts. In fact, I thought it would be fun to busk her songs somewhere for fun. Did you know she wrote her first song busking across the country?"

"Busk as in sing on a street corner for money?" he asks.

"Yeah, I always thought it might be fun."

"Do you know any of her songs well enough to do that?" he asks, looking over at me.

"I know all of her songs well enough to do that. Too bad we packed my guitar in the U-Haul. I could have sung our way to New Hampshire for gas money," I joke.

"Wait, that's not a terrible idea," he muses.

"I was just kidding. I can't do that."

"Why not?"

"Because that's probably how you get kidnapped and murdered?" I deadpan.

"I would never let that happen to you," he says.

I don't doubt that he wouldn't keep me safe. He's built like a professional athlete and he looks very alpha male protective. Hmm. Maybe?

Logan stops at the red light behind a big SUV. "I know where your guitar is in the back of the truck. Let's get it and see what happens. What if we do it on the strip in Las Vegas? We'll cross that off your bucket list."

"Oh my God." I laugh. "This *is* wild. Let's do it. Okay, let me make a list of songs I can do and practice them. I'm rusty on my guitar, but we'll see what I can come up with!"

"This will be so much fun."

"And, at least if I suck, no one will know me."

He looks over at me and his gaze lingers a little longer than normal. "You won't suck."

"Okay, we can try."

We sing along to the music the whole way back to our hotel. We make it back to the room way after midnight.

"We'll probably regret this in a few hours." I sigh.

"Nothing coffee and a good donut can't fix."

"I can get up early if there's coffee and a donut involved."

Logan's mouth twitches in a smile as he unlocks the door and opens it, holding it for me. He sets his stuff down on the dresser and empties his pockets.

"Why don't you get ready first and I'll go after you?" he says then yawns.

"Okay, I'll hurry," I say. I step into the bathroom. I wash my face and brush my teeth, trying to rush so we can get to sleep. I open the door and tiptoe out in an old t-shirt and shorts, self-conscious about my lame pajamas. Logan doesn't even seem to notice as he passes me and heads in with his clothes and travel bag.

I lay out my clothes for tomorrow and crawl under the covers, relieved to finally be able to rest after our long day. The shower starts and I fall asleep thinking of Logan showering. Let me tell you, it was the start of some good dreams. *Damn.* This is going to be a hard road trip if he keeps being so freaking nice and hot.

I faintly hear him come out, get into his bed, and whisper, "Night, Allie."

I say goodnight while fighting a yawn and we sleep until the alarm goes off a few short hours later.

CHAPTER 6

~

Logan

And that's when I start
falling for her.

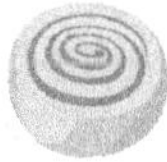

Standing outside in my black track pants, a navy t-shirt, and my Nikes, I remember how good it feels to wear comfortable clothes and to take time off. I click the pump to automatic then head to the back of the truck to fuel it up while Allie's inside getting us coffee and donuts. I pull her guitar from the pile of her belongings and tuck it behind the seats in the cab, where she can have quick access to it if she wants.

As I watch Allie come out wearing her jeans, faded Def Leppard t-shirt, and Converse, I can't help but think that this chick is cool. I'm looking forward to getting to know her better. In some ways, she reminds me of Beth. I have no doubt those two will get along great.

"You got my guitar!" she says, delight evident in her tone when she spots it. She looks at me skeptically. "But... I'm not really sure this is such a good idea after all," she says.

"Come on, it'll be fun. You can tell Caleb stories of the time you sang for our dinner," I say. "It's time to do something out of your comfort zone. Be brave. Have some fun."

"Speaking of Caleb, I think it's a good time to check in with him," she says. "You mind?"

"No, not at all." The truck bounces over the rutted road as we pull out of the parking lot and onto the interstate.

I really like her kid. I haven't been around too many kids in my life, but yesterday I found myself really having fun with him. That Nerf gun fight we had was epic. I wanted to be around him more; I was kind of disappointed when he had to leave and fly out with Margie.

Who am I?

"Hi, Evan, just checking in. How's everyone doing?" She listens, then I hear her say, "Hi, baby, I miss you! How did you sleep? Aww, I'll be there soon! Pet the puppies for me. Okay, bye, honey. Love you."

She's such a good mom. The kind of mom I wish I had growing up.

I grip the steering wheel tightly as I drive. She chats with the others a while longer then finally hangs up and looks over at me. "Why so serious?"

I glance in her direction then turn my focus back to the road. "I'm thinking my blood sugar is depleting," I lie. "Hand me another donut?"

"Sure, chocolate or glazed?"

"Chocolate," I say, glad I was able to deflect the conversation from what's really bothering me. My family isn't a topic I like to discuss. They're one major reason I haven't gotten married or had a family of my own—because I didn't have the best role models. My family is manipulative, greedy, and money-driven, and they measure value based on the money or power others have. It's just not a life I want any part of.

I think that's why I've always connected with Beth so well. She's down to earth. Non-materialistic. Real. Just like Evan and his mother, and the staff at The Golden Gable. No pretention, no agenda. It's the first time and the first place I've ever truly felt at home.

"Why don't you play something to make sure your guitar's ready to go? I'm guessing it's been a while since you played it."

"Sadly, you're right. I used to play Caleb songs at bedtime, but we stopped when he got sick. And it wasn't like I could play in the hospital."

I can't imagine what that must have been like for her.

I've only ever been responsible for myself. I can't imagine having a child, let alone one that went through major health challenges.

She leans over her seat to grab the case. She clicks open the locks and pulls out the guitar, then rests it on her lap.

"Let's give it a shot," she says as she sticks a guitar pick between her teeth and adjusts some of the strings.

She plays some chords to warm up.

"That doesn't sound too bad," I say. I do my best to keep my eyes on the road, but they want to be on her. Her hair is pulled up in a messy bun and her legs are tucked under her. *Damn, she is beautiful.*

I honestly should not be having these thoughts. Her brother could and probably would kill me if I ever crossed the line. I'm sure he'd pick me apart, limb by limb, if I ever did anything to Allie. I don't blame him. I'm the same way with Kathryn.

When Kat and I chose jobs our family didn't approve of, we ended up becoming a two-person support system. My sister and I had each other's backs when our family turned theirs on us.

"Let's see if I can still remember this," she says, and begins to strum a tune I clearly recognize as a Jewel song. I don't know that much about music, but it sounds pretty spot on to me.

When we're about an hour outside of Las Vegas, she clears

her throat and begins to play "When You Say Nothing at All" by Allison Krauss. To be honest, her performance gives me chills. It soothes me and excites me all at once; her voice is so calming.

She's doesn't seem nervous at all. In fact, she exudes confidence as she plays, getting lost in the music, closing her eyes. I'm starting to see that one of the most beautiful things about her is her confidence.

When she finishes, I try to catch my breath. "Damn, Allie. You're really good. I have goosebumps," I tell her and show her my arms.

She smiles and leans back, her guitar resting on her lap. "I have really missed this."

"I know that all too well. It's easy to get caught up in the daily grind and not make time for fun. I've been doing that myself with work lately. I haven't made time for myself, relationships, or friends."

"Do you have a girlfriend?" she asks, looking at me curiously.

"No. I was seeing someone for a while, but we weren't serious. I was so busy with work and didn't make time for her, so she moved on."

"Maybe it wasn't meant to be. If it was, I bet you would have made time."

Ohhhh. Burn. But she's right. If I had been into Jessica as much as she was into me, I would have been around more and focused on her. For the past few years, the only thing I've really made time for is work. Maybe this trip isn't just about Allie finding herself, but me doing the same.

I shake myself out of my thoughts and tell her, "We're going to be eating *good* tonight."

She laughs and tucks the guitar back into the case. "Yeah. Watch, we'll make five bucks."

"Even if you make nothing, it'll still be fun. I mean... We're in Vegas," I say. "Have you ever been before?"

"Nope. How about you?"

"Not unless you count a few meetings here and there. This will be my first time driving across the U.S. like this. But I have heard only good things about Vegas!"

We pull up to our Airbnb. I get our bags and take them inside and Allie follows, taking pictures for Beth.

We pause when we enter. We look around and then at each other.

"Oh my God!" Allie says.

"This place is amazing!" I say at the same time.

This is a huge house for two people, with floor-to-ceiling windows that overlook Red Rock Canyon. The house has the most incredibly gorgeous landscaping of green, tropical trees and plants. Pops of pink, purple, and yellow flowers flow through the property in terra cotta pots. Plants and beautiful rugs make the inside space cozy, yet modern and contemporary.

"Do we have the right house?" she asks.

"Yes. Are you sure you want to head into the strip now?" I ask, looking at her. "Because this place is amazing."

"You know… Maybe you're right. We should just hang out here."

"Nice try. You're not getting out of singing."

She returns my smug smile. "Fine, but we should go when it gets dark. This is too beautiful not to enjoy," she says as she gazes out the window at our backyard. "Oh, Logan," she says, pretending to faint as she stares to the side.

"What?" I say, curious to see what she's found. A huge infinity pool hidden away from the view looks like it's calling our names. "What are you waiting for, Allie?" I say, kicking off my shoes and emptying my pockets.

"Wait, what are you doing?" She looks at me like I'm crazy.

"Last one to the pool is a rotten egg!"

"What are you, five?" She laughs.

I run down the deck and jump into the pool, diving in. I come to the surface and yell, "It's heated!" I look up at her as she leans on the railing of the deck with one eyebrow raised, looking at me like I've lost my mind.

"You're missing out!"

"I don't have my swimsuit," she says, waving her hand at the pool.

"It's a private pool. No one can see us. Just swim in your underwear like me."

She glances around and looks hesitant as she says, "Okay, you said I have to live big on this trip... Here goes nothing. Turn around and don't look, okay?"

As hard as it is not to look at her, I face the other end of the pool. I'm trying my best here to be a gentleman, but Allie is really growing on me. I came on this trip with reservations, but she's pretty great. She's got that whole girl next door thing going on. I really only said yes to this as a favor to Beth and Evan, but here am I catching feelings.

I rest my forearms on the edge and look out over the canyon. It's so beautiful here, definitely not a part of Las Vegas I've ever been to before. Usually when I travel for work, I see the airport, hotel, gym, and our meeting locations, then I fly back home. I need to make more time to explore, to fully live my life and not just live for work.

I hear a splash and turn around to see Allie swimming toward me. "Isn't it great?"

She nods. "You were right."

"I'm sorry, what was that?" I joke. "Please repeat that so I can get it on a recording to remember for later."

She swats my arm playfully as she swims up next to me and puts her arms up to look at the view too. She glances back at the house. "So, just how successful of an author is Beth?" she teases.

"She's always been great, but she's finally getting recognized for it. In fact, we just landed a new book deal."

"That's really exciting for her."

"Are you a big reader?" I ask.

"I wish. I haven't had time for that in years. I'd love to get back into reading more for fun, just for me."

"You should read some of Beth's books. She's great, and one of them was just optioned for film."

"What does that mean?"

"Someone wants to make a movie out of it."

"No way! That is really cool."

"Yeah, things are finally going her way. I'm so glad she has your brother and Golden Gable."

"Thanks. Can I ask you something?" she asks as she floats next to me, still in her t-shirt but I notice her jeans are in a pile on the deck. I nod and she says, "Why didn't you and Beth ever date?"

I chuckle as I flip onto my back and float next to her. "We just don't click like that. And besides, I'm not really the relationship type."

"What do you mean?"

"I'm just not a family man type of guy," I say. "I am committed to my work, and that's about it."

I regret these words as they spill out of my mouth, and that surprises me. I have never had regrets on not wanting my own family... Until now. Being around Allie and her son are making me rethink that, causing a pit in my stomach.

"That's okay, it's not a requirement for life," she says

reassuringly.

"Do you think you'll ever get married?" I ask, trying to change the subject. I'm honestly surprised someone ever let her get away. Caleb's dad must be an idiot.

"I haven't really thought about it. It's just been Caleb and me, and we're happy. But maybe someday, if I met the right person, it might be nice."

The way she says this gets me thinking. What do I want? Am I truly happy with the way my life has been? I'm thirty-two and I'm starting to think it might be nice to have someone to share life with. I've honestly been working so hard to be successful on my own that I haven't even stopped to really have a life of my own.

We swim for a while and take in the view. Allie gets up to explore and finds some floats in the shed while I grab a few bottles of water and towels.

"This is the most relaxing road trip I have ever taken," Allie says, grinning at me as we float around without a care in the world.

"And it's just getting started," I tell her.

She closes her eyes and leans back.

"I'm starting to get hungry."

"Me, too."

"Want to grab a quick lunch then take a hike or something?"

"Let's do it," she says. She rolls off her float and makes her way to the stairs. I jump out of the pool and follow her to the patio. She grabs two towels and hands me one. Once dry, we head to our rooms.

"Let's just hit a drive-thru before we hike?" I say as I shut the door.

"Sounds good," she calls back.

We unhitch her car from the back of the truck. We find an In-N-Out Burger then head to the canyon for a picnic.

We pull into the parking lot and Allie pulls a blanket out of the trunk. I grab our bag and drinks and we walk over to a covered picnic area. Allie lays down the blanket as a tablecloth and I set our food down.

"Fancy," she says as she slides onto the bench across from me. My eyes catch hers and I still for a minute. Her bright green eyes lock on mine and make me forget about where we are.

She breaks my trance with a smile and says, "What?"

"You have really pretty eyes."

"Thanks," she says, her cheeks turning pink.

We start eating and the awkward moment passes. If we're not even one full day in and it's already getting hard not to stare at her, I wonder what the rest of the trip is going to be like. *Pull it together, Logan.*

When we finish, we collect our trash and dump it in the bin.

"Let's take lots of selfies on this trip and we can make a

fun collage of them at the end," she suggests. "It'll be fun. Pictures are kind of my thing."

"Okay," I said. We take a few pictures of the cliffs behind us, and Allie somehow captures me in a funny one that looks like I'm holding up the cliff with one of my hands.

"Okay, that's enough for now. Let's go explore," she says.

Being with her, spending time away from work like this, I realize I need to make time to take more breaks—that I need to make more friends and have more fun. The problem is, I don't think I want to be just friends with Allie. I want to kiss her. I want to hold her. I want to know her more. I want to hear her dreams, figure out what she likes to eat, and get to know her. And I haven't felt this way about a woman, *ever*. Sure, I've dated and had fun, but this is different. It *feels* different.

"What are you thinking about?" she asks, locking those emerald green eyes on mine again.

"Ready to head to your busking?" I ask her. "Maybe you'll get discovered," I tease.

Allie laughs, "Yeah, this just might be a disaster, but we'll fulfill my teenage dream of playing Jewel songs and maybe I'll make some loose change. Bucket list moment right here."

"No one even knows you here, so if you mess up, just keep going."

"Who says I'm going to mess up? Now you just jinxed me." She laughs.

"Sorry," I say with a laugh. "I'll be there for moral support."

She looks at me suddenly and says, "What if someone tries to kidnap me?"

I look over and reassure her, "Like I'd let that happen. We'll be in a busy, well-lit area."

"Okay," she says, looking a little relieved.

"Alright, m'lady. Get your guitar," I tell her. We climb into her Toyota and head to the Strip.

During the twenty-five-minute drive, Allie applies some dark lipstick and adjusts her outfit. "How do I look?"

"Perfect," I tell her, and it's not a lie. She's ridiculously hot, and it's taking everything in me to not flirt with her—and to remind myself that this is Evan's sister, which makes her off-limits.

We pass by a t-shirt stand and just from the look she gives me, I can tell she wants to stop.

"Hey, you know what we should do? We should buy ridiculous t-shirts to wear from every place we stop," she says, grabbing onto my arm and holding it.

My pulse feels like it gets faster as her arm is on me. I like it.

"Deal. I'll find you one, you find me one. And we have to wear them. No matter what. The more ridiculous, the better."

"Alright. No peeking until after we pay," she says, grinning mischievously.

Minutes later, I have found the perfect shirt for her. It's

bright green and reads: "I am kind of a big dill," and has a dancing pickle on it. I smirk as she walks up to me, a navy T-shirt shirt rolled up in her hands. "Okay, let's see it. What did you get?"

She can barely contain her laughter as she hands it to me.

I unroll it and it reads: "I Love Hot Moms."

I snort and can't help but smile. "Really?"

She laughs. "Hey, you said the more embarrassing and sillier, the better."

"Well, you're a hot mom. I guess it works." I wink.

Our eyes lock for longer than usual and she fidgets nervously. She turns, but I don't miss the smile on her face as she glances down the street at some of the passersby.

I clear my throat nervously at her reaction to me flirting and say, "Here's yours," and hand it over.

She opens it excitedly and laughs as she looks at it. "It's perfect, we can wear these tomorrow."

I smile and shake my head. This is just what I need—silly and fun times. I need this distraction.

"Come on, Ace, let's get you set up somewhere." I slide my hand in hers and pull her along, her guitar slung over my shoulder. She doesn't seem to mind me holding her hand as we walk together and I have to admit, her hand feels good in mine.

We find a spot for her to set up and I tell her, "Okay, you do your thing."

I stand in a position where I have a clear view to take pictures and videos, close enough to step in if someone tries to mess with her. This is Vegas, after all, and I am not letting anything happen to her.

Allie confidently slings her guitar over her neck and launches into a pitch-perfect rendition of Jewel's "Who Will Save Your Soul." It doesn't take long for her to get the attention of a few people walking by who stop to watch and toss cash into her open case.

One guy lingers and leers. He spots me and I give him a murderous look, which makes him walk off, not looking back. *Good. Keep it moving, jerk.*

I lean back and cross my arms over my chest. I'm so proud of Allie. I can't wait to send pictures and videos to Beth and Evan. But right now, I'm just enjoying watching her sing.

Allie's next number, "Brighter Than The Sun" by Colbie Caillat, garners even more applause and cash. I can tell Allie's delighted by the attention and accolades. Watching her come alive and smile and laugh is worth it. People even join in singing with her.

"Thanks, everyone," she tells the crowd. "Just one more today," she says with a casual nod in my direction, then starts to sing "Fly" by Maddie and Tae. When she's done, the audience, which has grown tremendously, claps and tosses more cash into her case.

When the crowd clears, I approach her and take a look at

the proceeds. There must be a hundred bucks in there. "Holy shit, Allie!"

I turn and she gives me a big hug, wrapping her arms around my waist and pulling me tight. I lean in and hug her back, holding on for maybe a second or two longer than I normally would.

She pulls back from the hug. "Did I do okay?" she asks, her face pure excitement.

I clear my throat. "You did better than okay, Ace. They loved you." She looks like she's about to fall over; I reach out and grab her by the arms. "Are you okay?"

As I touch her, energy surges through me. Did she feel that electric current, too? I have been attracted to the women I've dated, sure, but Allie makes me feel different. Being with her thrills me and scares me at the same time.

"Yeah, I just got dizzy. That was exhilarating but exhausting. I think I just need sleep."

"Alright, let's call it a day. You can buy me dinner tomorrow, Ace," I tease. I wrap my arm around her shoulders and give her a gentle squeeze as we walk back to the car.

"Thanks for scaring off that creep, by the way. I almost laughed when I saw you do that."

"You think I'd let anything happen to you on this trip? No way. If Evan didn't murder me first, Beth would kill me."

"You're not wrong."

"He scares me with that Marine background of not taking

crap and protecting the ones he loves, and I surely would not want to cross him. But we both know deep down he'd probably never hurt a fly."

Allie stops laughing and becomes serious. "I could have handled that guy, you know."

I don't doubt that, but I'll let her go with this. "Sure, I know."

"But I'm glad you were there."

My gaze on her softens and I smile at her tenderly. I like that she wants me here.

"Let's get some good rest tonight and hit up Moab tomorrow. Sound good?" I ask.

"Sounds good," she says as she yawns. "Logan?"

"Yeah?"

"Why do you call me Ace?" she asks softly, looking at me.

"I don't know. It just kind of came out and you feel like an Ace. Why? Is that okay?"

"My dad used to call me that," she says quietly. "It's perfect."

And that's when I start falling for her.

CHAPTER 7

~

Allie

It's grey sweatpants
season.

I wake up feeling disoriented, not sure where I am. I stretch my tired legs and take in the room—light hardwood floors and open ceilings with the light wood rafters exposed. Clean and calm. I'd love to have a home like this someday. My brain catches up and I remember where I am... I'm in a big white bed overlooking the Red Canyon in Las Vegas, in a gorgeous home that Beth rented for Logan and me.

I have never stayed in a place like this. I took pride in my trailer, always keeping it clean for Caleb and myself. I decorated shabby chic because that was all I could afford, but it was easy and cozy.

This place is not shabby chic. It's contemporary and modern. The entire house is white with black accents, bright pops of color show on the tapestries that hang on the walls and throw rugs that feel strategically placed throughout the home. It has boho charm that I realize is cozy in its own way.

Smelling coffee, I take a big stretch, then head into the bathroom in my suite. It's so luxurious, with a huge, white, modern, clawfoot tub. I quickly brush my teeth, pull my hair up in a messy bun, and wander downstairs to the kitchen.

Logan is there, pouring coffee into two mugs. He's wearing only grey sweatpants that hang low on his hips, showing off his lean, muscular body and deep V dipping under his waistline. His shoulders are broad and sexy. Just as I'm thinking I could stare at him for hours like this, he sees me.

"Good morning." He hoists his mug and takes a sip. "Coffee?" he asks.

"Yes, please."

Logan hands the other mug to me. I carry it over to the kitchen table that faces out over the red clay of the canyon. I take a sip and close my eyes, relishing how good this coffee is.

"Why didn't you wake me earlier? I thought the plan was to head out around five or six?"

"You needed your sleep, Ace. I could tell. I did, too. Besides, this doesn't need to be a sprint. There's no need to stress about meeting a timeline. You've been through a lot," he says quietly. "It's okay to take some time to rest and get Allie back."

Ace. He keeps calling me Ace. That's all I can think about. I love it so much.

He's right. And even though I just woke up, I still feel exhausted. There's a level of mental and emotional exhaustion that sleep can't fix. I have been through a lot in the past few months—so much has happened, I haven't really had rest or time to process anything.

I swallow a big gulp of coffee and try to compose myself. I don't want to think about any of that now; I just want to live in the moment.

I change the subject. "I could get used to this view." I sip my coffee and take in the vibrant colors of the canyon. Terra cotta rocks and moss green cactuses form a rich and vibrant landscape against electric blue skies with puffy clouds.

"If you love this, I think you'll love Moab," he says. "I'm going to get ready. Take your time. It looks like there's some eggs and juice in the fridge, but I'm sure with our habits we'll be stopping for donuts and coffee later." He grins, then strolls to his own suite across the hall from mine. I take in the view as he leaves. And let me tell you about that view. Grey sweatpants, a muscular back, and his butt is… Chef's kiss. Perfection.

Ugh. Get it together, Allie. This is not the trip to catch

feelings for someone. I need to focus on getting home to Caleb. I have a lot to do to kickstart our lives in Freedom Valley and that's what I should be worried about. Although that Logan view... You'd have to be a nun not to appreciate that.

Yesterday, when we were walking on the Strip, he held my hand. *Held my hand.* And I thought I was going to trip over my own two feet it made me so nervous. It took me back to sixth grade when a boy named Frankie made my heart pitter patter when he grabbed my arm, linking our fingers together on the way to class. The feeling was just that pure.

Nope. Moving forward, I have to stop thinking about Logan in this way. I have to focus on my new life in New Hampshire and all of the exciting and overwhelming things I have to look forward to.

I'm worried about setting up my bakery. I've never run my own business before, so I know I have a lot to learn, but I'm looking forward to all of it. I'm also still worried about Caleb and his health, and I need to make sure that he stays my top priority.

I refresh my coffee and carry my mug upstairs to my room. I quickly shower and decide not to bother with makeup, get dressed in comfy jeans and a t-shirt, and tie a hoodie around my waist. I repack my bag and head down to the living room, where I see Logan sitting on the couch.

"I feel like royalty staying in a place this incredible," I tell

Logan.

He stands up and as he walks to the door, I notice he's dressed comfortably like me, in blue jeans and his "I Love Hot Moms" t-shirt, wearing Nikes and a New York Yankees hat. He looks so good my heart skips a beat.

All I can think about is seeing him without his shirt on. Those muscles. So many muscles. Like, more than a human male should have. My mind wanders to what it would feel like to trace them with my fingertip. With both of us lying naked in bed. Just after the hottest sex either of us has ever had...

I shake myself back to reality. We have a mission, and sex is not on the agenda.

"What are you shaking your head at?" he asks.

My mind races and I start to stall by grabbing my bags when my eyes land on his hat. "Well, first, I know you lived in New York previously, so that's probably why you are making the unfortunate mistake of wearing that Yankee's hat. But, being that you're now living in the land of the Red Sox, we'll have to add a new hat to our shopping list."

Good catch, Allie. Phew.

"Oh, and nice shirt." I smirk.

Logan looks at me and chuckles. "Let's see how many people look at me and laugh today."

"This is serious, Logan. Does Evan know you're a Yankees fan? He won't be happy about this," I tease, trailing behind him with my bags. "At this point, I'll have to offer you *my* protection on the streets of Boston if you continue to wear that hat around town. You know how Bostonians are... Very serious about their baseball. You're not safe." I shrug my shoulders at him.

I don't miss the playful eyeroll Logan gives me. "I'm sure it'll be fine."

I laugh. "Right, we'll see how that pans out for you."

We load our bags back into the cab of the truck and Logan re-hitches my car to the back. And just like that, we're leaving the fancy Airbnb and getting back on the road in no time.

"Looks like we need to re-fuel," Logan says, turning on his blinker to exit.

"Wait, already?" As I mentally start to add up what we've already spent in just one day and think about how much further we have to go, panic starts to creep in.

Logan quickly says, "This one's on me. No big deal."

But it is a big deal. I don't want to owe anyone anything, especially not Logan. I am not his responsibility.

"No, I'm going to pay for the fuel. I am going to keep track and take notes and we will settle up at the end."

"Sure, that's fine," Logan says as he slides out of his seat and fuels up the truck.

We go inside for donuts and coffee, as promised, and Logan says, "I get to pick them out today and surprise you."

"Okay, we'll see how you do," I tease.

He comes out with a box of donuts and two coffees. I head over and take the coffees from him, and we walk back to the truck.

"What did you get?"

He opens the box. "Ta-da! What do you think?"

I peer at his selections. They are all chocolate of some sort. S'mores topped, chocolate on chocolate frosting, chocolate glazed. It's a chocolate lover's dream.

He looks alarmed. "Wait, do you not like chocolate?"

I look at him and shake my head. "No. I don't like chocolate."

He looks crestfallen.

Then I say, "I *love* chocolate. These look amazing."

He breathes a sigh of relief. "You're going to pay for that," he says.

I snort. "Oh, yeah?"

"Yeah, you're picking next time," he says.

"Okay. I'll surprise you next time. If we get sick of donuts, we can find bagels or something."

He narrows his eyes at me, then playfully says, "We don't need that kind of negativity on this trip. We'll never get sick of donuts."

I take a big bite and smile at him as I wipe my mouth with a napkin, trying not to laugh at his pretend scolding.

I set up our playlist to make sure we keep going with good music. I open my phone to a missed call and text from an unknown number with a northern California zip code.

619-555-5465: Allie, it's Chris. Did you move? I want my son.

Oh my God. What the hell?

I'm speechless. First of all, how did he know I moved? Second of all, why does he care? Caleb is four, and he's never been interested in seeing him until now.

I am seriously pissed. I slap my phone down and my body tenses as the heat of anger pulses through my body. He has some nerve. I look down at my hands as they shake. I know I need to take a deep breath, but I can barely see as I blink back angry tears and stare out the window, trying not to get Logan's attention. He doesn't need to worry about any of my drama. He's doing enough.

I need to talk to Evan—he'll know what to do. I really can't believe this… Talk about great timing.

I feel as though my breath is cut off and a panic I've never known before begins to fill my body. Logan looks over at me, concern spreading across his face.

"I-I think I need to pull over," I say, grasping at my chest and leaning into the truck door.

Logan signals and turns off the highway at the next exit. "What's going on? Are you going to puke?"

"No, I think I'm having a panic attack." I get out, feeling the color drain from my face.

Logan reaches over to hold my arm. "It's okay."

He pulls into a gas station and parks. He gets out and comes around to my side of the truck. As he opens the door, I all but slide out, gasping for air. He sits with me and worry lines his forehead.

Panic boils up in me like it's going to swallow me whole. "Breathe, just breathe," he says. He stands and leans in over me to nab a bottle of water from the console. He unscrews the lid and hands it to me. "Here, take a sip. Let's try to stand up so you can take deeper breaths."

I stand and sip the water, my hands still shaking as I drink. "It's okay, you're alright," he says, rubbing my arms. "Let's walk for a minute." He turns off the ignition and takes me by the arm. I can feel myself calming down as we take a few steps. I take a few more sips of water.

"I'm so sorry," I tell him, but I'm so embarrassed I can barely look at him. "You didn't sign up for this, you didn't ask for any of this." My voice hitches a little as I speak.

"Hey, it's okay. Kat gets panic attacks sometimes, and she calls me to walk her through them. I would hope someone would help her out and make her feel better if she couldn't get ahold of me," Logan says as he looks into my eyes and smiles.

I can't help it, I reach out and hug him. He puts his arms around me and hugs me back, both of us content to stay like that for a while.

"You want to talk about it?" he asks.

"Not yet. I need a distraction."

He pulls me tight, then pulls back to look at me. "You're alright, Ace. Come on, let's look up a good lunch place. You still owe me a meal," he teases with a sexy half-smile.

"Tell me more about Kat," I say as we get back in the truck and buckle up.

Logan starts the ignition then coasts back onto the road. "Well, I already told you that she's like me, a black sheep that didn't conform to my family's expectations. She teaches middle school in Montreal. She's probably about your age. What are you, twenty-five?"

"Twenty-six."

"Also, Kat is a lesbian and lives with her partner, and my toxic family doesn't condone her choices."

"I'm sorry they're like that. I hate to hear when families do that."

"Kat's incredible and is changing kids' lives; I'm so proud of her. She works at a poverty-stricken, inner-city school and she organizes outreach programs and does so much to give back to her community. I think you'd like her."

"I definitely think I would. But your parents seem like a lot to handle." This conversation makes me really grateful for my parents. My mom and dad haven't always agreed with my choices, like moving to California in the first place, but they still loved and supported me. I know I'm so lucky to have had such a great family.

"You have no idea," he says.

"What are your other siblings like?"

He looks sad for a couple of seconds then says, "My older sister Sarah works in finance with my dad. My brother Tanner is finishing college and going into finance, as well. Kat and I are the unsuccessful ones, if you ask my parents."

"Success isn't always measured financially. What your sister is doing—changing kids' lives—is priceless." I reach over and put my hand over his for a few seconds.

"I'm sorry," I say. "That doesn't sound like a very fun childhood."

I'm appalled hearing this. I honestly want to scoop him up and declare him an honorary Harper family member at this point; he's too good for people like that. No wonder he loves the inn so much.

"It is what it is, Ace," he says quietly.

"Okay, I'm going to look up some restaurants, I'm hungry."

"Sounds good, just tell me where to go."

We find a rest area where we can grab lunch but decide to eat our Philly cheesesteaks in the truck because it's cold. After a while, he says, "Can I ask you something?"

"Sure," I say, looking over.

"What triggered that panic attack?"

I finish my sandwich and stuff my wadded-up trash into the bag before I answer, taking time to think about what I want to say.

"Remember when I said Caleb's dad never acknowledged him? Well, he had just texted me out of the blue asking me if I've moved, claiming that he wants his son."

He puts his sandwich down, his eyes stormy. "Seriously? How did he know you moved? Does he secretly keep tabs on you?"

"I don't know. That would be creepy," I say.

"What do you think he wants?"

This is the part that triggers the panic and fear. He ignored us for over four years, and when we needed him— when Caleb needed him—he refused to help us. Now it just so happens that *right* when we move, he wants to reach out?

"I honestly have no idea. I mean, he was fully aware that Caleb just went through major surgery. I reached out to him and his parents as soon as we found out, asking about their family medical history and if they'd be willing to test for a kidney donation for Caleb. I got no reply from any of them."

"The fact that they don't even bother to know such an awesome kid is tragic. But to further ignore him when he was so sick is just plain cruel."

"I agree. I don't understand them at all."

"How did you get through that, knowing that they just didn't care enough to help?" Logan asks.

"It sounds bad, but it didn't really surprise me that they didn't even bother responding to my pleas. Luckily, Evan was a match for him and gave him one of his kidneys. Caleb probably wouldn't have made it otherwise. He was too far down on the list."

"I know. Evan is the real deal. You hit the jackpot with a brother like him."

"I owe my brother everything," I say honestly.

"He'll probably never let you repay him anything," he says.

"He says he's going to make me bake him cinnamon rolls anytime he wants them. I said he had a deal." I grin. "But he's the best."

"So, they knew he was sick and possibly dying?"

"Yes, they knew. I begged. Our surgeon's office also sent certified letters requesting their help. Everything and everyone went unanswered."

"And now he randomly texts you? What a strange thing to do after all this time. You have to be more than upset. You must be furious, all things considered."

"Yes. I am angry. Where was he when Caleb's life depended on him? He has never offered any support or asked to see him even once. In a way, I have been relieved they haven't shown interest. They have money, and if they wanted to take me to court for custody, they could. I can't afford a custody battle. I know it's probably not likely, but I could lose simply because I couldn't afford it."

Logan crumbles up his sandwich wrapper. "I wouldn't worry about it until you know for sure what he wants. Leave him on read. You're supposed to be on a life-changing and fun road trip. Put it out of your mind for now."

I take a deep breath and exhale with relief. It definitely feels better to talk it out.

"Thank you for everything you're doing, Logan. Beth is lucky to have you as a friend."

"I hope you consider me your friend now, too." Logan glides back onto the road.

"Want me to take a turn driving?" I offer.

"No, I'm good for now. You know what we forgot?"

"What?" I ask.

"To find more t-shirts."

"Okay," I say as he gets out to top us off and sends me in to use the restroom. When I come out, he's looking at t-shirts. "Found mine," he says with a playful grin.

I look through until I find a ridiculously funny one. I smirk back as I find his size and nab it off the hanger.

We check out and then grab our shirts and head out to the truck. "Okay, here's yours," he says.

I unfold mine to see, "Mom Balls: The things you develop when someone messes with your kid." I lean my head back and laugh. "Perfect."

"I know, cheesy. But things will be okay with Caleb. No one is messing with a Harper kid. Things will be okay, you've got your mom balls."

I laugh. "Thanks."

He unfolds his and chuckles. "Really?" he rolls his eyes when he sees: "I'm running for a cause. I have to poop."

"Imagine making a blanket out of these shirts. It'd be known as the greatest road trip blanket. You could hang it over your couch or something. Hopefully it will be a trip full of fun memories. Try not to let Caleb's dad ruin this for you."

"You know what? You're right. I can't let him ruin this trip. We're going to have fun." I climb into my side of the truck, feeling super tired. "I'm just going to rest my eyes for a while." I curl up on my side and drift off, not waking up until we coast into the hotel parking lot near Moab.

~

CHAPTER 8

Logan

You're a catch.

I pull into the parking lot and gently nudge Allie's shoulder. She's out cold and has been for hours. She finally stirs and opens her eyes, peering up at me.

"Hi," she whispers sleepily.

"Hello, sleeping beauty. You're sleeping away precious daylight."

She lifts her hand to shelter her eyes from the sun streaming in. "What time is it?"

"We started out just after eight and now it's almost four; we're already in Utah."

"I can't believe I slept so long."

"You've had a long couple of months. Your body probably needs to catch up on rest."

"I didn't think I was that tired."

"Have you had any time to think about it?"

"You make a good point." She smiles weakly at me. "Let me pull myself together a minute and I'll come check in with you."

"It's no problem. I'll go get our rooms figured out. Take a minute to wake up. I'll be right back." The driver's door gives a squeaky yawn as I open it and step out. It feels good to stretch.

I took two boring conference calls while Allie slept. Even on my time off, I'm always working. I don't usually notice because I'm always alone, but taking this time to be with Allie has made me realize I don't take enough breaks or set up enough time boundaries with work. I enjoy what I do, but there is more to life than work.

The walls in the lobby are covered in white shimmery wallpaper, with a huge gold sputnik light fixture. The place is gleaming, with the setting sun reflecting off every surface, including the polished marble floors. I head toward the woman at the front desk to check in.

"Do you have a reservation?" she asks with a smile as she looks at my "I Love Hot Moms" t-shirt.

"Yes, under Logan Nolan for two guests."

She types my name into the computer. "Perfect, Mr. Nolan. You'll be in our executive suite on the top floor." She reaches over to grab two key cards and scans them. "Here are your keys. If you need anything, please let us know."

"Thanks," I say. "Have a good day."

When I get back to the truck, I find Allie leaning up against the side, sunglasses on, face pointed up at the sun. I'm relieved seeing her so relaxed, because honestly, her panic attack was scary; I hated seeing her so upset.

"We're good to go, Ace. Let's get our stuff and check out our rooms."

We walk side by side across the parking lot. As we enter the hotel, Allie slows her gait and looks at me when she sucks in her breath.

"This place is gorgeous," she says as we head to the elevator. "I want to do something nice for Beth and my brother to thank her."

"I'm sure they wouldn't mind your cinnamon rolls if you aren't tired of making them."

"I'm never tired of baking. I could bake them in my sleep."

"Well... You practically did," I tease.

We get to the top floor and enter our suite, clearly the best in the hotel based on its stunning Moab views.

Allie steps in. "This is... a dumpster."

She's joking. Because it's perfect and I'm just as stunned as she is. "Wow," I whisper. "Nice."

In silent awe, we take in the floor-to-ceiling windows offering stunning views of Moab with its terra-cotta-covered rocks. I place Allie's bag inside one of the rooms and mine in another.

"I'm going to get changed and go for a quick run," I tell her as I nod to the desert. I need to unwind after all that driving. My body is screaming for a nap, but my brain knows a run with be better for me.

"Okay, I might take a soak in that giant tub. Did you see it? You could fit four people in there!"

I laugh as I head into my room to change. Now I can't get the vision of her in the bathtub out of my mind. Great. This woman is taking up so much real estate in my brain, and not in the sisterly, drive-your-friend-across-the-country way. She's making me feel things. And I have to say... I like it. I like *her*. Unexpected, but here we are. I mentally remind myself to pretend that Beth wasn't right, but she was. Allie is great, and we're having a good time so far.

When I get back, I find Allie wrapped in a towel, with another towel wrapped around her head. She's sitting on a chair in the common area of our suite, scrolling through her phone so she barely notices me approach.

"This is bad," she mutters, reading messages.

"What is?" I walk over and look at her phone.

"While I was in the tub, my phone kept going off. When I got out, I found out it was Chris, texting over and over.

His messages started out short but demanding, then got downright scary. He told me he is coming after me for full custody of Caleb, then demanded the address of where I'm moving and my plans for work."

I look through the messages, which go from bad to fully threatening.

Anger swirls in my chest and heat burns my cheeks. I carefully think about how I want to respond because I know if I show I'm getting worked up, Allie will probably just get more upset.

"Okay, let's just think about this. Don't respond. Stop reading them and get ready. Let's go grab something to eat and talk it over, okay? No need to panic. Let's make a plan."

She nods and stares blankly while chewing the inside of her mouth. She must suddenly realize she's only in a towel because she suddenly pulls it tighter around herself and races into her room, shutting the door and leaving her phone with me. I laugh as I set it on the table and head into my room to shower and get ready quickly.

While I wait for the water to heat up, I send a quick text to my friend, Preston. He's a lawyer and recently helped Evan when his inn was having trouble with a banker. I figure it can't hurt to reach out.

Me: When you get a minute, I think we need to retain you for another Harper. This one has a deadbeat ex.

Preston: What is it with the Harpers always needing

lawyers?

Me: I don't know, man. How are you?

Preston: I'm good. Where are you?

Me: In Utah, driving Evan's sister back to New Hampshire.

Preston: What is this girl to you?

Me: Evan's sister.

Preston: You didn't answer the question.

Me: Friend.

Preston: What's deadbeat's full name?

Me: Christopher Carson out of California. Probably mid-twenties.

Preston: Okay, get me as much information as you can and I'll get on it.

Me: Thanks, brother.

I shower quickly and get dressed. I come out of my room to find Allie wearing a hunter green maxi dress and sandals, her long wavy curly hair draped to one side. She sits with her legs tucked under her while she texts on her phone.

She looks up and smiles. "You look nice." She watches me for a moment until her eyes quickly drop back down to her phone.

She looks worried.

I try to distract her again. "You ready to head out? I read the hotel restaurant has a great view," I say. What I want to say is that she's the great view...

"I'm ready." She stands, smoothing her hands down the

front of her dress.

When we enter the restaurant, I ask the maître d' if they have tables and the host immediately acknowledges me. "Of course, Mr. and Mrs. Nolan. Right this way," he says, motioning for us to follow him.

I glance at Allie and she stills mid-stride when he says that, but she doesn't say anything.

I just shrug and motion for her to go first and walk beside her to the table. I have to admit, I didn't hate hearing us referred to in that way. When I think of Mr. and Mrs. Nolan, I think of my parents and their dysfunctional mess, and I can't help but wonder what it would be like to break the cycle and have a healthy marriage. I'm not even sure what that would look like.

We get to our table and I take the seat across from her as the maître d' hands us menus. "Your server will be with you shortly," he tells us, then walks off.

I glance over the menu and dramatically raise my eyebrows. "What will you be having tonight, Mrs. Nolan?"

Allie's face gets red and she laughs nervously. "Oh, Logan," she sighs as she looks over the menu.

"What?" I ask.

"Nothing. You're a catch. You'd make a great husband or partner."

"I'm a catch, huh?" I decide to let that one slide. Maybe I'll tease her about it later.

We order and sit in silence for a bit before Allie jokes, "Do you think we can ever go back to mediocre dinner views?" she asks playfully. "I'm getting spoiled."

"Well, you're going back to one of the most beautiful places I've ever stayed," I say.

"That's true. I can't wait to see it all decorated for the holidays. That's my favorite time."

She seems to be in a good mood and a good headspace, but I also know that if we don't figure out what to do about Chris quickly, that situation could possibly escalate. I take a breath and gently ask, "So, do you want to talk about what's going on with Chris?"

"Not really, but like you said, I probably should just make a plan and stick to it."

"It's not a bad idea. What did he say?"

"I'm sorry to lay this all out for you; I don't mean to. Honestly, this is coming out of nowhere and it's shocking to me."

"It's okay. I know it's upsetting, especially when you've been going through so much already."

"He never so much as gave us the time of day, and now he wants my attorney's information? I'm still drowning in hospital bills. I can't afford an attorney on top of that." She looks out the window and crosses her arms across her chest.

"One day at a time, Allie."

I think about what she's up against and how it would

destroy her if she was ever separated from her little boy. I've only just met them, but even I've grown attached. I worry if Chris's actions have any validity. Whatever happens, though, I know I'm going to be there for her and Caleb. As a friend to both of them. I will help them fight.

"How's Caleb today?" I say, somewhat changing the subject. I'm trying to think about how I can tell her about Preston without her being offended or stressed out. I'm trying to make a good impression with her, not upset her.

"He's doing great. He misses me, but everyone's been keeping him busy. He really likes The Golden Gable." Her tone softens and I see her shoulders relax. I know how much family means to Allie.

"I'm sure he does. What's not to like? And how about Kase? How are they getting along?"

I've met Kase a number of times. He's the son of Mellie, the housekeeper. We all sort of take turns watching him while Mellie works.

"They're getting along so well. Evan says they are inseparable and take turns doing sleepovers at each other's houses."

"It's nice that they have each other."

"I miss him so much."

I put my hand over hers. Worry creases her brow, but even though she looks upset, she's so pretty. Her momma bear love is intense. I never had that growing up, and I love that she cares so deeply for her son.

We eat our dinners and head back to our suite to rest up for tomorrow's drive to Denver.

As we walk, I tell her about Preston. "I texted him today. I don't know if he can help, but he's a good guy, and I'm hoping he can give you some good advice at least, if you're interested."

Allie's eyes flash with disappointment. "I can't afford that right now. Besides, I don't need you to call a lawyer for me. I can take care of myself."

I put my hands up. "Okay," I say. "I'm sorry. I was just trying to help."

"I need to go to bed. I'm sorry, this is just a lot for me. I need to think," she says as she heads to her room. "Thank you, Logan," she says quietly before softly shutting the door.

I take a deep breath and sigh. I don't know where this need to protect Allie is coming from, but for some reason I feel like I have to help her. I've always been a lone wolf, but now here's this girl who has me roped in.

I grab my phone and text Beth.

Me: You up?

Beth: Yes, how's the trip going?

Me: It's good, but I think I like her. Evan would kill me, wouldn't he?

Beth: LOL, probably. What's going on?

Me: She's confusing, she's fun, and she's beautiful. Too beautiful for me.

Beth: Not true. You're a catch, Logan. Any woman would be lucky to have you.

Me: I don't know. How's New Hampshire?

Beth: Can't complain. Love being here, love these people, love this place.

Me: Can't wait to see everyone again. Only a few more days...

Beth: Thanks for doing this. I'm going to bed. Talk soon!

Me: Good night.

I answer a few work emails and set up a few meetings for when we have our stopover in Chicago. I like her. Maybe if I make this trip as fun as I promised, she'll see me as more than a ride home and more of a possibility.

~

CHAPTER 9

Allie

Get a grip, Allie.

We make it to Denver and check into another hotel. This time it's just a basic lodge, with two rooms side by side. Logan refuses to let me pay, and despite my attempts to try, I give up and log the cost in my notes to reimburse him later. The list of expenses keeps growing and it stresses me out.

Logan wanted to drive again, and I was okay with that. I'm so worked up about the situation with Chris, it would be hard for me to concentrate on the road anyway. But it also gives me an opportunity to scroll through job listings around Freedom Valley. There isn't much to choose from, but I plan to work on my resumé after dinner tonight and send it to a few places anyway.

I finally text my brother to let him know what's been happening with Chris.

Evan's a former Marine, he's a total alpha and can be a little bossy, but he's just protective of the people he loves. He has that whole, "I'll break you in half if you mess with me or my family" vibe.

I text my mom as well. To know they're all supporting me through everything makes me feel not so alone. I tear up with relief thinking how it will feel to have my family close to me again. I was so busy in San Diego, I didn't realize how alone I'd felt.

Chris can try to mess with me, but he better be ready for a fight. The shirt Logan bought for me was meant as a joke, but it's partially true. I am a bulldog for my family. Nothing could make me stop fighting for them. I am Caleb's mother and I'll decide where it's best we live. I can't wait to see how Chris explains to a judge why he hasn't bothered with his son for the first four years of his life. What scares me is that his family has money, and unfortunately, sometimes people with more resources win, even if they don't deserve to.

I glance over at Logan. He's so freaking hot, but that doesn't mean I'm not still mad at him for reaching out to an attorney for me. How much is that going to cost? I'm so stressed I could throw up. He must think I'm a helpless loser.

I can't even take care of myself and my child.

My phone rings and I let it go to voicemail. When I listen, I find out it's Preston, Logan's attorney, requesting I call him back. I put my AirPods in and call him.

"Hello, this is Allie Harper," I say after he answers.

"Hey, Allie, it's nice to meet you. I worked with your brother so I already feel like I know your family."

"Nice to meet you, too."

"Listen, I want to get some information from you. We have an investigator who is going to do a full work-up on your son's father and his family. Surprisingly, there are a lot of Christopher Carson's in San Diego, so we want to make sure we have the right person. What's his date of birth and middle name?"

I sigh. As much as I don't want to accept the help, and as much as I don't think I can afford it, he is going out of his way to help me.

"I'm really sorry, but I'm not sure I can afford to hire you, Preston. My financial situation is not the best right now."

"It's okay. Evan traded me a room at the inn for a while to cover legal services. I actually just moved to Freedom Valley and I'm staying at The Golden Gable while my home is undergoing renovations. I'm pretty much the inn lawyer now," he says then laughs. "It's truly my pleasure to help you out."

I exhale a sigh of relief knowing it's not total charity. "Oh, well thank you so much. I am so grateful."

"It's no problem. So, full name and date of birth?"

"May fifth, '95, and his middle name is Todd."

I give Preston some additional details about the situation and provide the information he requests. As we are talking and I realize Preston really is a good guy just trying to help me, I feel bad about the way I went off on Logan, knowing he is just trying to help, too.

Things are going to be different now. Moving forward, I am going to make sure I'm in the driver's seat. Chris is not going to hurt us.

We carry our bags to our rooms and Logan goes in with me to look around mine. "Alright, I'm going to go down for a workout and then grab a shower before dinner. Meet in the lobby at six?"

"Sure."

"What are you going to do? Want to come workout with me?"

I laugh. "Nope, but thank you. I'll get my exercise in the form of a nap or long hot bath."

"Um... Yeah, those are not forms of exercise, but good luck with that," he quips as he gives me a sideways grin and takes off.

I catch myself thinking about his workouts and wonder what he does during them. Muscles pumped and flexed. Sweat glistening. I can think of a few workouts I might possibly enjoy doing with him, but none that involve weights or the gym.

Get a grip, Allie.

I decide to take a nap and set the alarm for five p.m. I pass out the minute I hit the sheets and I don't so much as stir until my alarm going off at five wakes me out of a sound sleep.

I take a quick shower and put on dark jeans, boots, and a sweater. Denver's cold, and I know it's only going to get colder as we get closer to New Hampshire. I'm not used to the brisk weather, but I have to admit I've missed the change of seasons. Yet another reason to look forward to being back in Freedom Valley.

I apply some light makeup and blow-dry my hair, styling it with its natural curls down my back. I put on some lip gloss and check myself out in the mirror. *Not too shabby.*

When I hear Logan's shower turn on next door, my heart leaps. My mind wanders as I start to imagine how good he looks naked. I shake my head but can't seem to stop my vision of him lathering up all those taut muscles. I imagine standing before him, dragging my fingertips over his hard pecs, down his eight-pack abs. Water pelting down on us as he wraps his huge biceps around me then pulls me towards him, picking me up, my legs wrapping around his naked waist.

He probably doesn't think the same about me. And why would he? He's just being a nice guy and helping me in my time of need.

I finally pull myself together and head down to the lobby where I sit by a big fireplace and scroll through social media to pass the time while I wait.

I hear some boisterous laughing and I look up to see there's a group of guys sitting down across from me, looking like they are waiting as well. They look about my age.

A tall, broad-shouldered guy with a neatly trimmed beard and wavy dark hair apologizes to me then tells his friends, "Keep it down, guys. There's a lady present." He turns to address me, saying, "Sorry, we're hockey players. Some of them are lacking a few brain cells."

A red-haired player with a matching ginger beard nudges him and says, "Speak for yourself. I have all of my brain cells. I think Lackey knocked yours out in the last practice."

I smile innocently at them. "Hockey? Is that with the egg-shaped ball or the round ball?" I deadpan.

They freeze and it's clear they're trying to figure out if I'm serious, but my face gives nothing away. I have a four-year-old; I have perfected my poker face. Finally, I crack up, putting them out of their misery.

They exhale and roar with laughter. "This one has jokes," a blonde Viking type says, looking at me. "Where are you from, darling?"

"New Hampshire. You?" I ask.

"Upstate New York, originally," he says. "What brings you to Denver?"

"Just passing through."

"Well, I'm glad we got to run into you here."

Noticing they all have a good amount of facial hair, I joke, "So are beards now required by the NHL?"

The ginger-bearded player admits, "Nope, but it keeps our faces warm."

"What team do you play for?" I ask.

"That depends. Who is your favorite NHL team?" Ginger Beard asks. I can tell he's teasing but he's also trying to not tell me.

"Well, I'm from the Northeast, so hockey is a big deal. I'm a Bruins fan, but I'll watch all the teams. Actually, my dad enjoyed hockey a lot."

The dark-haired player nods but still doesn't offer who their team is.

"What's a stunning girl like you doing in Denver without a date?" the Viking directly asks, leaning forward, his blue eyes twinkling.

"She's waiting for me," Logan interrupts. He comes from up behind me and places his hands on my shoulders. "Ready, gorgeous?" he says, then leans down and kisses my cheek.

Flames shoot up my face and all of a sudden, the room is hot. *Really hot.* I try to play it cool and smile, shaking myself back to reality, "Right, yes, let's go… honey."

"Awww, bummer, Shetty! She's taken!" Ginger Beard says as he jabs the Viking in the ribs.

"Have a great evening, guys. I hope you hit a touchdown!"

I accept Logan's hand as we walk out into the cold evening. Once we're out of earshot of the hockey players, he peers at me. "Touchdown?"

"I was just messing with them." I laugh.

"Do you know who those guys are?" he asks as he opens the door to our waiting rideshare.

I slide in and he gets in on the other side. "Hockey players," I say, grinning.

He snorts and says, "They're Predators."

"What? No, they were nice," I say, buckling my seat belt, confused.

"No, *Predators*. As in the Nashville Predators hockey team," he says.

"How do you know?" I ask.

"I'm from Canada. Hockey is pretty much a religion for us," he says.

The driver takes us to Ruth's Chris Steak House. I've never

eaten at this chain before, but I know it's expensive. I'm feeling nervous because my funds are maxing out. I have kept detailed notes of our expenses, but I'm worried I won't be able to cover everything. If Logan senses my worry, he doesn't let on.

"I love this place," he says. "I've eaten here all over the country. I think you're going to love it, too."

I'm probably not going to love paying for it, but I decide not to worry about that for now. "How was your workout?" I ask instead.

"I'm not used to sitting so much and tomorrow will be a long stretch, so it was good to get a long run in. I'm sure I'll just want to crash when we get to Chicago."

"I hope you don't mean literally," I tease.

"I haven't let you down yet with my driving. Plus, Evan would tear me limb from limb if anything happened to you. Then he'd probably set me on fire."

"You're probably right," I muse. "He'd also kick your ass for what you said about me in front of those hockey players. Evan has always hated all my boyfriends. Even pretend boyfriends."

"Have you had many pretend boyfriends?"

I snort. "No. I also haven't had many *real* boyfriends."

"I can't understand why not," he says, his hand on my lower back as he guides me to our table. My back is tingling where he has his hand. I feel like a teenager on a first date.

Except this is not a date; I only wish it was. Just like I wish he felt the same way about me as I do about him.

We get to our table and open our menus. Logan orders a bottle of red wine and the server returns quickly with the botte and two glasses.

"Let's talk about those boyfriends," Logan prods. "Why haven't you dated much since Chris?"

I laugh. "I haven't dated at *all* since Chris. I haven't had time for anything other than working and taking care of Caleb."

I wouldn't change things for the world, but I do feel like I've missed out sometimes. I would *never* regret Caleb, but there are times when I wish I had found someone who could have been my forever *before* I had a child. Now that I have Caleb, there's a lot more to consider. If I did find someone, he would have to accept both of us, because we're a package deal.

Logan takes a sip of his wine but keeps his eyes trained on me.

"What about you?" I ask.

"I travel a lot. Most women get bored of that."

Honestly, to me, Logan is the least boring guy. I can't imagine anyone getting bored of anything about him. He clearly has never met any woman who could truly appreciate him. But again, I don't want my mind wandering down that path, so I deflect again.

"Where do you typically travel to?" I ask him as our server brings our appetizers.

"I have places in LA, New York, and Boston," he says, then puts his napkin on his lap. "Boston is new, and I'll be selling the one in New York soon and primarily staying in Boston. Sometimes I stay in Chicago, but I don't have a place there."

That is a lot of homes, especially in big, expensive cities. *Holy cow.* I had no idea just how successful he was, but now I'm starting to understand. We truly do come from different worlds, and the realization has me feeling a little self-conscious.

"Where will you be living after we get back to New Hampshire?" I ask, then take a bite of crab cake.

"Boston is either a make it or break it type of situation."

"How do you mean?"

"I'm up for a big promotion at the agency. If I get it, I'll head up the entire eastern side and be in Boston permanently. If not? I might have to go somewhere else."

"Do you want to stay in Boston?"

"Yes, I do. I want to be near Beth, and I like it there."

Now I'm really rooting for his promotion. Selfishly, I want to keep him in Boston, where it's closer to us at the inn.

"I think you should work on the Yankees fan thing. That might be a problem if you stay in Boston."

Something feels like it's different now. The energy has shifted. His eyes are on me more, he's sitting closer. He even reaches out and holds my hand for a while before the seafood tower we order comes. *Interesting.*

"In any case, I'll be staying at the inn through the holidays." He swipes a jumbo shrimp and takes a bite. "I was so hungry."

"Me, too," I say, looking around and taking in the space.

"So, I know you like to bake. What about cooking?" he asks.

"I'm actually a bit of a foodie. Though you'd never know it with what I usually make for Caleb. Do you like to cook?"

"Sometimes. With how much I work, I usually don't have time."

"I do love to try different recipes. Unfortunately, Caleb doesn't appreciate my efforts. He likes kid food." I grin and roll my eyes. "Chicken nuggets, macaroni and cheese, and applesauce."

"I would appreciate your efforts," Logan says, that sexy half-grin turning up his mouth again.

Oh my God, is he flirting with me?

My face gets hot and I take a sip of my wine, which only makes me feel warmer. I lean back and fan myself. "Is it hot in here?"

Logan casually replies, "Maybe it's just you."

For a second, there's a tension in the air between us. Not a bad tension, but a current of something all the same. It's almost too much to bear and all I can do is laugh. Thankfully, he also laughs. Does he feel it, too?

"You're a flirt," I say and roll my eyes playfully at him.

He says nothing, just levels his eyes on me and literally drinks me in with his eyes. It's the most seductive thing I've ever seen. I want more.

After stuffing ourselves on porterhouse steak for two with garlic mashed potatoes and crispy onion rings, we request an Uber and lumber back to our hotel. When we reach our rooms, I'm not ready to say goodnight. We're having a good time. Logically, though, I know tomorrow will be a long day for both of us.

He walks me to my door and softly tells me, "I'm right next door if you need anything." When I open the door, he steps in and checks it again. My heart is pounding and I really wish he'd just stay, even in the separate bed. I just want to be with him because I haven't felt this close to someone before, and judging by the way he looks at me, I think he might feel the same way.

Even still, he heads back out the door. "Ready by five, okay? We'll stop for donuts and coffee before we hit the interstate."

I nod. "I'll be ready. Sleep well."

"You too, Allie."

He closes my door and then I hear him close and lock his own, and now I know he's safe, too. I can't help but wonder who makes sure he's safe when he's traveling? Probably

Beth.

But I wonder if he wants more from someone. Maybe from me…?

I fall onto my bed and stare at the ceiling. Do I really believe a successful literary agent would give even a passing consideration to a single mom who has debt, no money, no home, and no job? I'm not a catch. I have nothing going for me. Who in their right mind would want to take this on?

I fall asleep wishing things were different. That we lived in a different world, one where it would be a possibility that someone like Logan would want someone like me.

CHAPTER 10

Logan

She wants to
know me...

I barely slept last night because I couldn't stop thinking about Allie. She's gorgeous, smart, and amazing, but I have to keep reminding myself she's off-limits. How am I going to get through the rest of this trip without messing things up? I thought if I kept myself busy by continuing to drive, that would help.

But it doesn't actually. It just gives me more time to think. Yesterday I caught myself dreaming of living in Freedom Valley with Allie and Caleb, in a house with a white picket fence, helping her set up and run her bakery.

I am screwed. I want something I can't have. What do I have to offer them? Sure, I could support them financially, but what about being the husband and father they deserve? I don't have that in me.

Today's a fifteen-hour drive, but it will be worth it when we get to Chicago. As a surprise, I booked Allie a day full of spa treatments at the hotel there. Something tells me she hasn't had a spa day in a long time—if ever—and this will be a great way for her to unwind while I take a few meetings.

When Allie comes down at five, I already have the truck warmed and ready with coffee waiting.

She climbs into her seat and pulls her coat around her. "Okay, it's really cold out there," she says, then notices the mug waiting for her. "Oooo, coffee!" she says with an adorable smile then warms her hands with her cup.

"And..." I say, as I hold up a bag of pastries and kolaches.

"You really know how to treat a girl, Logan Nolan," she deadpans.

I hold her eyes steady but tease her back, "I aim to please."

She reaches inside and pulls out a kolache, then hands the bag back to me. When I reach in and take one, she asks, "Are you going to let me help drive today?"

"Probably not, but thank you for offering. I really like driving," I say. I take a bite. "These are really good."

"Yeah, they are. Treat me like this every morning and you

might just never get rid of me. I can be bought with kolaches and coffee."

If only that was all it took. I would buy her the moon if it would make her smile.

"Good to know," I say. I put the truck in gear and we take off.

"I'm looking forward to getting to see Chicago," she says before taking a bite of her kolache, crumbs spilling down her shirt. Even at her most awkward moments, I'm so attracted to her. She's different from all the women I've dated. None were nearly as down to earth as she is. I knew that from the first night I met her at her trailer in California that she was something special. I knew when I made those cinnamon rolls that I was screwed. She had me.

"Good, because I have a surprise for you there."

"Oh, boy, you know I love surprises," she quips, playful sarcasm in her voice.

We drive for a few hours and as soon as we stop for lunch in Omaha, Nebraska, Allie's phone rings.

"Oh, it's Preston," she says. "I'm going to take this before we go in, okay?"

I nod and decide to give her some privacy as I fill up again with gas. I stand outside the truck with my hands in my pockets, watching her face and her shoulders sink. She finally pushes the button to end the call. She glances up at me and her eyes fill with tears.

"What happened?" I ask as I jump back into the truck.

"It's not good," she says, in anger and frustration. "He and his wife have found out they can't have kids, so they're going for full custody of Caleb."

"Wow. Did you know he was married?"

"I haven't talked to him in years. I had no idea."

"What else did Preston say?"

"He says they'll likely try to dig up dirt on me and paint me as an unfit mother."

"That's bullshit. Nobody would ever believe that." My blood feels like it's boiling as I hear this. "What did Preston say to do?"

"He wants me to get a solid job as soon as possible... And..."

"And what?"

"And get married as soon as possible."

I feel somewhat surprised as I take in what she's saying. I'm not sure that what Preston is suggesting is the best legal advice, but it's probably the best at getting what he wants for his client. He is good at what he does, and if he is suggesting something so off the cuff, he must have his reasons.

She rolls her eyes. "Like that's going to happen. I don't even have a boyfriend."

Allie mentioning a boyfriend and husband makes feelings stir in me that I don't recognize. *Jealousy?* Just thinking about her with another man makes me unhappy. What is going on and where are these feelings coming from...

Maybe I could help her. It would just be on paper, right?

"We could get married." The words tumble out of my mouth before I can take them back.

She gapes at me. "Are you nuts? I'm pretty sure if we come back married, Evan really *will* kill you. And what would Beth say? You can't marry someone you just met."

"People do it all the time, I'm sure. And it's just on paper, right?"

"I think you have lost your mind."

"I don't mind helping you. I'm always up at the inn anyway, so we could make it look legit."

"Well, too bad we missed our shot at eloping in Vegas," she says dryly. "This could have been a done deal *and* we could have taken our picture with Elvis."

"Allie, I wasn't ready for marriage in Vegas," I say, trying to keep a straight face. "That was only a couple of days ago. I didn't know you well enough."

"And you do now?"

We both laugh for a while, then get out of the truck. I put my arm around her. She doesn't shake it off but leans in. *Interesting.*

As we walk through the truck stop to get lunch, Allie stops and points at a wall of t-shirts. "We'll have to pick some up before we leave," she says. "What about this one?" She holds up a black t-shirt that reads, "This is my crop top" with corn on it. I laugh and she puts it back. She links her arm in mine again as we make our way to the diner.

"I was being serious, Allie. We could do it."

"And I was being serious. I couldn't do that to you. That's a huge commitment to someone you just met. That's a lot more than just helping out a friend."

"It's not a problem. Not for me. I have the money. I can more than provide for all of us. It wouldn't even be a big deal, trust me."

"Oh, yeah. Are you like a secret millionaire or something?" she asks as she slides into the booth.

I cough a little and avoid the question. I know she's joking, but she's about to find out real quick that it's a lot more than that.

Allie leans in, relentless. "Logan?"

"Well, yeah, but it's not really a secret," I say, grabbing a menu and looking it over. She's quiet, so I look over the menu at her and her jaw drops.

"I do okay," I whisper, my eyes darting around to make sure no one can hear us.

She looks shocked. "Oh my God. You're totally serious right now." She leans back and swallows. "Are you joking?"

"That depends. Do you snore?"

She scoffs and picks up a menu. "I'm hungry, and this is not happening."

We order burritos and chips and queso and sit quietly for

a while until finally she says, "Are we crazy if we do this?"

"Probably," I say, then take a sip of my water. "But we're grown-ups, and we're allowed to do crazy things."

"All joking aside, I don't even know that much about you. Maybe we should spend the next few days getting to know each other, in case there's a quiz or something?"

"And who would be quizzing us?" I ask, trying not to laugh.

"I don't know, the marriage police? Our family? Okay, maybe I just want to know you."

She wants to know me...

I'm thinking maybe she's feeling me, and I *know* I am definitely feeling her.

"Not a bad idea. Let's start with you. Tell me everything."

"I've already told you everything there is to know about me. It's you I don't know about."

"What are your dreams for you and Caleb in New Hampshire?" I ask, dipping a chip in some queso.

I continue to dodge her questions. I need to stay in the driver's seat.

"I already told you I want to open up a bakery and coffee shop in town," she tells me.

"But what will you do there?"

"What I love most, I guess. Feed people and create a future for my family."

"I like that. What will make this stand out in Freedom Valley?"

"Maybe create custom cakes? Not exactly sure, but I definitely want to have a cozy home for Caleb to grow up in that is close to my family. Maybe one day, eventually, get married for real and have more kids. What about you?"

I swallow. *Damn.* All of that sounds so good and I didn't even realize anything like that would ever interest me. I thought I had my whole life planned out as a perpetual bachelor, but now, being with Allie, seeing the joy having a family brings her... I'm not so sure.

"I want to get this promotion in Boston. I like my life. It's predictable and challenging. I like my clients, and I like negotiating deals. I like finding new books that are gems and making them wildly successful. Outside of my career, I haven't really thought about any other dreams."

Until now.

"What was your childhood like? Tell me more stories about you," she says, changing the subject.

"Not that exciting. I went to boarding school from the age of eleven through my final year, and in the summer months I went to camps. After I graduated, I applied to NYU and got in, much to my parent's dismay. They're still disappointed in me, and if they get the chance, they are quick to remind me."

"Okay, that is kind of exciting. Boarding school? I don't know many people who went to a boarding school."

"It wasn't as exciting as you would think," I muse. "It was lonely. But not as lonely as growing up in a family where I was raised by nannies and parents who were never around. In some ways, boarding school was probably the better option."

"Then what happened..." She anchors her attention on me.

"After college, I got a job in a literary agency and worked my way up from intern to full agent in a matter of a few years. I've been successful, and I love what I do." I shrug.

"But your parents can't see that."

"More like they won't. They just don't care about anything unless it's their own agenda."

"What is on their agenda?"

"I honestly don't know anymore. I'm out of touch with all of that. I keep to myself and only stay in touch with Kat."

"So you're basically Canadian royalty and you're sitting here in this diner, casually eating a burrito and driving a girl you just met across the country?"

I roll my eyes and laugh. "I'm *not* Canadian royalty. I never was that pretentious guy. That's my family, not me. That's why I made my own way and built my own career."

"What made you agree to drive me home to New Hampshire?" she asks.

I think for a minute. How *did* I get here? I wanted to help Beth. But now? Now, honestly, I feel like I'm doing this for me. I want to spend time with Allie and have fun on this trip too. In some ways, Allie and I aren't that different.

"I made a deal with Beth," I tell her. "It was before I met you, before I realized you'd become my future fake wife."

Just saying that out loud, even jokingly, felt exciting and not at all scary. Just a week ago, I never dreamed I'd be sitting here in a diner in Nebraska with a woman I really like, thinking of marriage—even a fake marriage.

"What was the deal?" she asks.

"She agreed to do a *People* magazine interview for me driving you home." Just saying this out loud makes me feel kind of gross, but it wasn't like that. Beth has an incredible writing career and people want to know her better—both as an author and as a person. She has a tragic story she isn't sure if she's ready to share, and if this was what it took to get her to push herself, then of course I was quick to agree.

She chokes on a chip and says, "Um, excuse me? Like the *actual People* magazine? Does my brother know this?"

I shrug. "I don't know. All I know is that it's a big deal for her and will give the inn great exposure."

"Sounds reasonable," she says.

"It's... good for everyone."

"What are you thinking?" she asks.

"I'm honestly not even sure where to begin. This trip... It's been wild."

"What do you mean?"

"It's just that I met you and realized..."

She raises her eyebrows at me. "Go on..."

"That I really like Evan, and that if you were related to him, chances were good that you'd probably be cool, too."

"And...?"

"And the jury is still out on that," I tease.

She rolls up her napkin and throws it at me, smiling. "Hey, now."

"I'm joking. Of course! This has been a fun trip, I'm glad we're doing it."

"Me, too," she says. "So, are we really doing this?"

"The trip or the marriage?"

"Well, we're already on the trip. And we still have quite a ways to go to get home, so we have plenty of time to plan out our fake future."

But does it *have* to be fake? Because I have from now until we get home to get her to make it real.

"Do you need a prenup or anything?" she asks quietly. "I'll sign anything you need me to."

My heart dips as she asks this. The fact that she is even considering this makes me feel like she would never take advantage of me. "I know you would. I'm not worried about it. You're a Harper. I've learned you're good people. I'm pretty sure my sneaker collection is safe."

"Exactly how many sneakers are we talking about?" she asks. "If we have to share a closet, will there be room for *my* sneaker collection?"

"I've seen your sneaker collection. They'll fit."

~

CHAPTER 11

Allie

The next morning...

"You booked me at the spa?" I feel like my jaw hits the floor when I say this. "What does that even mean? What do I do at a spa?"

Inside, I'm starting to freak out. I've gotten an occasional pedicure at the mall before, but this? For me, this is like next level, Julia Roberts getting spoiled in *Pretty Woman* type of treatment.

"It means you are going to relax and get pampered while I take a few meetings with clients," he says.

I can't even try to hide that I'm body scanning him. I

mean, he looks so hot. Smoking steamboat hot in his navy pants and crisp white button-down shirt, like he just stepped out of *GQ*. And here I am in a t-shirt that reads, "Mountains aren't funny. They're hill-areas." I'm feeling extra frumpy right now next to him. Our t-shirt game has been fun, but seeing him in his real-life work outfit of a suit that makes me drool on my t-shirt? Wow. Definitely feeling more and more out of my league here.

Where did this side of him even come from? And how big of a deal is this guy? As soon as I get a minute, I'm googling him so I can figure out what I am getting myself into.

I smile at him. "You look like a completely different person dressed up like that," I tell him. "That outfit really, uh, *suits* you."

He groans and I giggle. "Thanks," he says. "It's just a few meetings. I'll be back in our t-shirts by tonight."

I can't help but imagine unbuttoning his shirt, one by one. Then pulling it down over his massive biceps, running my hands over his pecs.

Okay. That's enough, Allie. Focus.

Logan opens the door for me. "Come on, I'll walk you downstairs."

Standing next to him in the elevator, I suddenly feel very plain and out of place. I smile at him. "Thanks for this. Maybe you'll come back and I'll look like I belong next to you."

His eyes move over me approvingly and land on my lips before his gaze travels back up my face to my eyes. "You definitely belong next to me, Ace."

I shiver.

We enter the spa and the lady at the front desk straightens up and smiles, no doubt at Logan, as we approach.

Same, lady. He has the same effect on me.

"Good morning," he tells her. "Allie Harper has an appointment for the next several hours. I want her to have every service available. Anything she wants," he specifies.

"Of course, Mr. Nolan. We'll take good care of her. Jen is preparing her room right now." She looks over at me and smiles. "Welcome. Is this your first time at our spa?"

"Thank you, yes, it is." This is so far out of my comfort zone.

Logan puts his hand on mine. "This is all part of the 'Allie finding Allie and having fun again' mission. You have my number. I have two meetings across town and one over dinner tonight, here at the hotel. I'd like you to join me at the dinner, if you would? I might have jumped the gun and assumed you'd want to join, so I ordered a dress and shoes to be delivered to your room."

"Okay," I croak out, meekly. I feel like Cinderella, but at the same time, it does feel fun to get pampered and dressed up. I've gone so far out of my comfort zone on this trip, I don't even know where I am at this point.

Logan grins and his dimples are deep. "It'll be great, Ace. You relax, dream about your new bakery, order whatever you want. Herbal tea, mimosas, whatever. I'll see you back in the lobby at six-thirty for drinks before dinner. Okay?"

"Okay, sure," I tell him. He gives me a light, tender tap on the arm before heading out.

When he leaves, I can finally breathe again and turn to the woman at the desk. "Did that really just happen?" I ask her. "I mean, is this real?"

She looks at me and bursts into laughter. "Yes, this is real."

"He's *really* hot, isn't he? I mean it's not just me. He's really smoking hot, right?"

She gives me a look that lets me know beyond a shadow of a doubt that it isn't just me. "Mr. Nolan has been coming here for years, and yes, he is indeed very attractive."

"With other women?" I inadvertently squeak, worried she'll tell me he's *always* here with other women.

"No, he comes in by himself for a massage or quick haircut."

Relieved to hear this, I look around at the spa and take in the calming area. It's like I stepped into a new lifestyle, and I have to admit, I could get used to this. I bet it feels amazing to be pampered.

She pulls a leatherbound, menu-type book out from behind the desk and lays it out for me. She must sense that I'm overwhelmed because she immediately steps in to make some suggestions.

"Okay, I think we should start with a ninety-minute deep-tissue massage along with a facial, then order you a full spread of breakfast and coffee. Then we have Nala who is going to do your manicure and pedicure. Afterwards, Samantha will do your hair and makeup. How does that sound?"

"I've never done anything like this before, it all sounds so amazing. Thank you." She leads me back and shows me where to undress and get ready.

I've just finished my facial after my massage and I have never been so relaxed in my life. I feel amazing, and now I'm sitting here with Meg, the receptionist, eating breakfast. I convinced her to eat with me so I wouldn't have to eat alone, and we've become fast friends. I told her all about my big cross-country move and showed her pictures of Caleb. She's been telling me about her upcoming wedding to Josh, a professional hockey player here in Chicago. She's probably the coolest chick I've ever met.

The food here is so fancy and beautiful. I could get used to this, I think, remembering the thrifted, chipped mugs I drink out of at home and my inexpensive store-brand coffee. I have been so spoiled on this trip.

By the time I've had all of my services, it's already four and I feel like I've wasted an entire day, but I feel so good I don't give it another thought.

My nails are done in a deep burgundy, and my hair gets a much-needed trim and a deep condition. Just as Samantha is ready to style it, she asks, "What does your dress for tonight look like?"

"I don't know. It was supposed to be delivered to my room. I haven't seen it yet," I say over the hum of the blow dryer.

She turns off the dryer and calls out to Meg, "Can you go get Allie's dress and shoes for tonight?"

"The spa closes at six, but you can finish getting ready down here then have a big reveal," she says, rubbing her hands together with satisfaction.

A few minutes later, Meg comes back carrying a garment bag and a fancy department store bag under her arm. She unzips the bag and pulls out a shimmery purple lace cocktail dress with a high neckline.

"Oh my God, it's beautiful." My breath hitches as I say this out loud. This dress looks like it costs more than I make in a month. I can't believe Logan did this.

She then produces a pair of nude heels that aren't too high, which is good because I haven't worn heels in so long and I think I can handle these.

"You're going to look incredible in this dress, Allie," Meg says.

"What if it doesn't fit?" There's only one way to find out. I slip it on and hope for the best.

I wonder how he knew my size. Oh my God, how did he know my size?

"It looks perfect," Samantha coos. "You're stunning." She spins me around and finishes my hair, pulling part of it up and allowing my curls to fall down my back in dark chestnut waves. "Girl, people would kill for your hair. They'd pay top dollar for this color and buy extensions for these waves. And you just *have it.*"

"Aww, thanks."

She pulls over her makeup cart and says, "Now tell me, what's your makeup routine?"

"Routine?" I ask, feeling awkward again.

She smiles. "What products do you usually use?" she asks.

"Whatever's in my makeup bag," I say, realizing I have no idea what's even in there anymore or how old or expired it must be.

"Lip balm," I try again, keeping a straight face as I look at her. "I don't really have time or money for makeup or a beauty routine," I say. "I wish I did."

"That's okay. I'm going to show you a few inexpensive tips and you can make a list of what to buy."

When they're done with me, I step out feeling like an absolute queen. I've never felt this beautiful in my entire life. I take a spin, and the women look frozen with delight.

"If Logan doesn't put a ring on this one, then I can't even…" Samantha murmurs to Meg.

I look in the mirror and still see myself, just a different version. I'm Caleb's mom, unemployed and essentially homeless for now. But this girl? She's a future businesswoman who will own her own bakery and her own home. That's who I see now. No more pity parties. No more wallowing in what I don't have. I'm going to focus on what I do have. One foot in front of the other.

I hug them all. "Thank you, thank you, thank you SO much! I have had the most incredible day of my life."

I go up to my room quickly to refresh my deodorant and lipstick and switch out my purse to a tiny clutch. Nothing fancy, just a black zipper wristlet I thought would look better with my dress.

I snap a quick selfie and send it to Beth.

Me: Going to dinner tonight with Logan for his work dinner. We're in Chicago.

Beth: Oh my freaking GOSH. You look incredible.

My phone rings and I see it's a FaceTime from Beth. I immediately accept the call.

"Momma!" Caleb holds the phone in one hand and snuggles with a black and white puppy in his other. "I'm holding Bossy, Momma."

"Hi, baby! I miss you so much! She's so cute."

Beth looks over and murmurs, "Allie, you look like a showstopper. What does Logan think?"

"He hasn't seen my makeover yet," I say.

"Um, well, he's going to love this," she says.

"Thank you. Logan left this dress for me and asked me to attend his work dinner with him tonight. I feel so pretty."

"Well, you are. Enjoy it. Logan is a really special guy, and he means the world to all of us. I'm so glad you two are having fun," she says as her eyes twinkle.

I look at my watch. "Oh no, I have to be downstairs in five minutes. Thank you for everything, Beth. Bye, buddy, I love you!"

"Tell me how everything goes later!" she says. "Oh, and take pictures!"

I quickly walk to the elevator and pass a few people who stare at me. When people look at me, I think about who they used to see—a worn-down, haggard mom in old thrift-shop clothes. And not the cute kind. The bottom of the barrel kind.

Now, I feel like a vital, successful woman ready to take on the world. I could get used to this feeling. This is how I want to feel all the time.

Logan texts that he's running ten minutes late so I sit at the bar and order a glass of wine, hoping it will calm my nerves as I scroll through my texts. Chris has been surprisingly silent the past two days. Not sure if that's a good thing or not. Preston texted when he made contact with Chris's lawyer to let him know his firm will be representing me, so now we just wait and see.

"I'm waiting for a young woman," I hear Logan tell the host.

"Mr. Nolan, I believe your young lady is waiting for you at the bar."

I look over to see the host motioning to me. Logan pulls back and freezes, then he breaks into the biggest smile and walks over and kisses my cheek.

"Wow, Allie," he whispers in my ear, sending chills through me. "You look..."

"Thank you," I whisper back, locking eyes with him. His stare is smoldering. I am feeling so many butterflies in my stomach right now, it's hard to breathe.

"I have no words," he says. "Just... wow."

Heat rushes to my face as I step down off the barstool and reach for my wine. Logan beats me to it, picking it up with one hand and putting his other hand on my lower back, guiding me to the front of the restaurant. We walk to the back to a private area and sit at a table.

"Who are we meeting?" I ask him as he pulls my chair out for me to sit down.

"A client and a publishing house representative. Just work, nothing big, but I'm so glad you're here." He continues to stare at me and grins.

"What?" I ask nervously.

"That dress was made for you." There's a curious, deep longing in his eyes.

A vaguely sensuous light passes between us. I can feel it, and from the way he is looking at me, I think he can, too. I can feel the sexual magnetism bouncing off him, in his crisp, white dress shirt, now unbuttoned at the top. And he smells so good. Like cedar, spice, and manly man.

"Do I look good enough to stand next to you now?" I tease.

He laughs as he takes a sip of his water. "You always look good enough to stand next to me. I think you could wear a paper bag and make that look good, Ace. You truly don't realize how lovely you are." He reaches over and takes my hand. Inside, I'm melting. This room feels hotter.

Confidence radiates off him; he's in his element. This is a side of Logan I haven't seen before. I have been hanging out with traveling Logan, who eats donuts and chooses cheesy t-shirts at roadside stands and poses for random ridiculous selfies every time I ask.

This Logan? He exudes power and strength. I like both versions. He pulls this off effortlessly. Me? I still feel like I'm playing dress up, but I kinda like it.

I look over and find him gazing back at me and my heart flips. This man is so hot. Stick a fork in me, done. I know I shouldn't want him. Who am I to want him? I'm Allie, a single mom, jobless and pretty much homeless. He is Logan, a successful businessman who has his stuff together. I have nothing to offer but ex-drama and a mess.

No, I shake my head. That's not my narrative anymore. Future businesswoman and homeowner. I refuse to believe anything else. I am not weak. I am Allie. Strong. I keep repeating this to myself every time the imposter syndrome threatens to creep in.

"Why are you shaking your head?" he asks.

"Just repeating my new mantra," I say.

"And what is your mantra?"

"I'm a businesswoman and homeowner. More like affirmations, manifesting what I want."

"I like it," he says as he smiles.

Two gorgeous women walk in and nod when they see Logan. They head over to our table. Logan stands to greet them and shakes both of their hands, introducing me as his friend, Allie. *Friend.*

Sara La Casta introduces herself as an editor for Berkley publishing house and Marion Landon, a best-selling author, who is a client of Logan's. Sara is petite and blond, with warm brown eyes, and wears a black dress that exudes classiness and confidence. Marion is tall with high cheek bones and whiskey-colored eyes framed by stunning long eyelashes. Her dark hair falls down her back in braids, and she wears a white romper that's a total power outfit. These women are girl bosses.

Listening to them talk over dinner about books and future projects and catching up on past books, I love their conversations. Their excitement and passion for Marion's projects pull me in. I make a mental note to buy every single book this lady has ever written because if her books are even slightly as cool as her, I know they'll be amazing.

"So, Allie, what do you do? Are you in publishing?" Sara asks, taking a sip of her wine.

"I used to work in marketing, but now I'm opening my own bakery."

It feels really good to say this out loud and actually own it. I am going to be a business owner, doing something that I love that makes me feel good and provides for my son.

"Ah, that's amazing. What do you specialize in for baking?"

"I love to make specialty cakes, but anything really. I love trying new recipes."

"You wouldn't believe her cinnamon rolls," Logan says. "They're to die for."

My chest swells with pride and gratitude as he says this. I look over at him and put my hand on his.

"How did you two meet?" Sara asks, looking between us.

Logan fields this question. "We actually just met. She's a close family friend of another client, Beth Markwell."

"Oh, how is Beth doing?" Marion asks. "I heard about her story... Tragic. What is she working on now?"

"Beth's doing well. She's actually staying up at an inn in New Hampshire while she's working on her next book. Allie's family owns the inn she's staying at," Logan says.

"Oh, I love the idea of a New England inn. It sounds so dreamy. How long has it been in your family?" Marion asks.

I immediately relax when talking about the inn. "It's been in my family for three generations now, going on four with my son. It's a pretty great place."

"It's become a second home for me. Very peaceful there," Logan agrees.

"Maybe that could be my next writer retreat getaway. I'm always looking for inspirational places to write," Marion responds.

"We'd love to have you anytime," I say with a smile.

Our food arrives and the others discuss book business while I eat my pasta and listen. Logan laughs when Marion says something, and the way he throws back his head, I fall for him even more. This is dangerous. I can't stop looking at him, he's so happy and engaged. He makes this look fun and easy. His hand reaches over the table and covers mine to keep me included as they talk.

These little things… I sigh.

Sara steps out to take a call, and Marion and Logan strategize a few details for Marion's new book coming out.

As the restaurant begins to clear out for the night, I excuse myself to go to the restroom. On the way back, I start chatting with the musicians in the main room, because let's be honest, they're my people. Musicians and bakers? I'm in.

"Do you play?" one of them questions, gesturing toward the piano.

"Yes, since I was little. I sing a little, too," I say, running my fingers over the beautiful piano keys.

"Play a little if you want. We're just packing up."

"Okay," I say as I sit down on the bench and kick my heels off before setting my feet on the pedals. I position my hands on the keys, doing a few warm-up chords as a song comes over me. I start singing "Like I'm Gonna Lose You" by Jasmine Thompson. I get lost in it, absolutely abandoned. I pour into that song, forgetting that we're in a restaurant with a few tables lingering.

My fingers glide over the keys as my emotions pour out of me right into this song. Then I think about Logan and how I don't fit in with his world and how I can't take things from him that I don't deserve.

I stop playing and look up, realizing where I am. My face is hot when I realize what I've done. I've gotten lost in the moment and played that song for this entire restaurant. Which, granted, was three tables, including the one where Logan is still sitting with his clients. *Oh my God.* I probably embarrassed him. I look out and shield my eyes from the light to see if he's even paying attention.

Shit.

He's staring at me in what looks like shock, along with Marion and Sara. They begin clapping, as do the other two tables. Someone in the room whistles.

I look over at the long-haired piano man whose piano I'd just hijacked. His eyes are wide and his mouth drops open.

"You said you could play a *little*," he mumbles.

"I do play a little," I say as I stand up and slide my heels back on.

He gives me a sidelong glance as he wraps up a cord. "No. That was more than a little. What's your name?"

"Allie. Yours?"

"Tom. Take this if you're ever serious about playing more than just a little. You have a gift." He slides a card across the piano top.

"Thanks," I tell him, but I'm a little surprised at his reaction to say the least. "I played in a band in high school."

"That kind of talent is a lot more than high school talent."

I think about what he's saying and how he doesn't even know me, and I realize he isn't just saying that to make me feel better about myself.

Singing, playing music, and writing songs make me happy; it's time I started to make time for it again. Maybe I could set up an open mic night or something in the cafe part of the bakery I want to open. I have so many exciting ideas.

I take my time making it back to our table, nervous to go back and sit down. I keep my head down but as I get to the table, Logan stands and pulls me to his chest. "That was incredible, Allie."

I pull back, breathless, and look up at him. "I don't know what came over me."

He pulls back, searching my eyes. "You're so beautiful and talented."

"I just... I just got caught up in everything."

He leans in, kisses my cheek, and murmurs in the same gentle tone. "Incredible. Come on, let's go wrap this up and head to bed, Ace."

Head to bed. If only.

I take his hand and lazily follow him, my mind again wandering to places it has no business exploring.

We walk back to the table and Sara and Marion both stop chatting and look at me in awe.

Marion says, "Girl. Where did you learn to play and sing like *that*?"

I smile. "I took piano lessons when I was younger, but mostly just self-taught. I love music."

Sara smiles. "That was beautiful. You were great. You're very talented, Allie." She looks at Logan and adds, "Hang onto this one. She's a powerhouse."

Hearing these compliments from these successful women makes me feel good. I look over at Logan who's grinning ear to ear. He looks proud of me. I'll take it.

We say goodnight to Sara and Marion, and Logan holds my

hand as we walk through the lobby. The glances we get as we walk through to the elevator aren't lost on me. We look like a power couple, only I don't hold any power.

Yet.

I also don't want this night to end. It was fun playing Fancy Allie and Logan. Tomorrow, we go back to Road Trip Allie and Logan.

~

CHAPTER 12

Logan

Strictly on paper, right?

My phone rings at 5:07 a.m., which sounds early, but Beth knows I'm already up and running. I watch my breath steam as I stop to accept the call. "Good morning."

"You're up early. Are you running?"

"I was," I tell her. "And now I'm talking to you. What's up?"

"Just finished up some writing before the busy day starts around here." There's a smile in her voice that hasn't been there before. "But that's not why I'm calling."

No. Of course not. I wait a beat for her to ask, "How was

last night? Allie sent me a selfie and she looked gorgeous! Who did you guys go to dinner with? It looked important if you needed to bring a date."

"A client and an editor. No biggie. We had a great time."

"Ooh, what publisher?"

"Berkey."

"Cool."

"Has she, err... talked to you about anything?"

"Not really. Just about Caleb, and told us about your fancy dinner. Why? Is the trip going okay?"

"Yeah, it's been good. We've been having fun. I can't believe we're almost halfway done."

"You're the best for doing this, Logan. I can't wait to see you guys."

"Hey, has Allie talked to you about what Preston recommended?"

"No, what's going on?"

I'm so nervous to tell her this. I'm not even sure what she's going to say.

"Preston thinks she should get married to prove she has stability and can take care of Caleb."

"Okay, I'm confused. Who is she supposed to marry?"

"We were thinking me," I say quietly.

Then there's nothing. Like, not even crickets. Did she not hear me?

"Beth? Are you still there?"

"Are you kidding me?" she finally unleashes. "You two just met. *Just met.* Are you together? Is there something I don't know? You know what, never mind. Don't tell me. Evan is going to lose it. Like *lose* it. Do you want to *marry his sister you just met*? What is going on?"

"Listen, it's just on paper. It makes sense, Beth. I can more than take care of her and Caleb, you know that. Plus, I really do like her. I want to help her."

"Helping her, liking her, and marrying for love are all very different things. Don't you think you both deserve to marry because you actually love each other?" she stammers. "Dammit, Logan, I asked you to give her a ride to New Hampshire. Not MARRY her!"

"I know. I know. But I'll be helping her. I think this custody stuff with her ex is really serious. You know Preston wouldn't even put that on the table if he wasn't concerned enough to be playing it this way. What if she loses Caleb? Are you going to be okay with that if we don't even try? I can support them. She'd never have to worry. He'd have good medical insurance and stability and the threat of him taking Caleb could go away."

After a long pause, she asks, "Why are you *really* doing this?"

I put my face in my hands, leaning on the bench where I stopped my run. "I'm not cut out for real family life, Beth. I can't really be together with her, but I can still be there for her. I can help her. And at least… At least that's something."

"If you really do like her, why do you think you can't truly be with her?" she asks, showing no signs of relenting.

"You know why. I'm a workaholic. I've never had a family other than you and Kat, and I would make the most horrible husband and father. I can't be like him." My voice breaks.

"You're not your father," she says firmly. "I've known you for a long time, and I've seen you at your best and at your worst. And let me tell you, your worst is not even close to his worst. You're an incredible man and you have so much to offer. You deserve love. The kind that Evan and I have. I can see that you don't believe that right now, but I see you, Logan. You just need to see it, too."

I hear what she's saying, but it's so much to take in right now, I feel overwhelmed. I know hiding behind a fake marriage because I don't think I can hack it in a real one is childish and irrational, but I do like her. A lot. I want to help her, even if it's all I have to give.

"Thanks."

"Just don't do anything you'll regret, okay? I love you, Logan. I'm here for you anytime."

"Thanks, I know. I'm here for you, too."

I don't need anyone to be worried about me, but if I'm being honest? I'm scared. This got deep, quick. It's crazy to think we haven't known each other very long and I'd do anything for her.

"To be honest, I'm surprised at how much fun we're having and how quickly we've connected. It's like I've known her all my life."

"These Harpers will pull you in," she says with a chuckle. "I don't know how I did life before Evan. I can't imagine not having him in my life right now. I truly love him so much. I feel like I have a family again."

It was so hard watching Beth be so sad and closed off for so many years. Seeing her find her forever in New Hampshire with Evan makes me so happy for her.

"It's what you've always deserved, my friend."

"You deserve that too, you know…" she says.

"I don't know, Beth," I say. "I'm doing my best."

"I know."

"It's going to be okay," she says. "Just enjoy your time with Allie."

I think about all our fun t-shirts, jokes, music, and we *are* having a good time. It has been more fun than I've had in a long time.

"We've been decorating the inn this week for the holidays and Caleb and Kase are having a blast playing together non-stop. It's so great to have him here."

"Caleb seems like such a great kid."

"You made quite the impression on him before he left. He talked about you after he got here."

"He did?" I ask, surprised.

"Yeah. I guess that's a good thing since you'll be his stepdad," Beth says dryly.

"Ha, ha," I quip. "But I guess you're not wrong. Allie and I have a lot to talk about."

"Yeah, you do."

"I just feel like I'm in a really good place right now, sounds like we both are," I say honestly. "I guess we are lucky to find Harpers."

"You can thank me for that," she teases.

"Whatever," I laugh.

Giving up on my run, I start to walk back to the hotel while we finish our chat.

"Alright, I have to get ready so we can hit the road. It's going to be a long day of driving ahead."

"Drive safe."

"I will," I say, knowing how she worries about us on the road. "We're very careful."

"Can't wait to hear how this next leg of your trip goes. Maybe you'll be planning a baby shower?"

I pinch the bridge of my nose, "Why would you say that?" I groan.

"Oh, I don't know, buddy," she jokes. "You already planned the wedding. Can't wait to hear stories of what's next."

"We definitely have some stories to share."

"Is she sharing a room with you?"

"No, of course not," I scoff. "She has her own room, and

I've been a perfect gentleman. Do you think I *want* Evan to kill me?"

Beth laughs, but we both know he's incredibly protective over the people he loves, and I'm not a hundred percent convinced I've earned his trust and loyalty yet.

"Wait until he hears this marriage stuff…"

"Are you going to tell him?" I ask.

"Nuh-uh. No way. You can tell him that when you get here."

"We'll figure it out," I say, taking a deep breath. "Alright, later, Beth," I say as I enter my hotel room to get ready.

Allie and I definitely have a lot to talk about today.

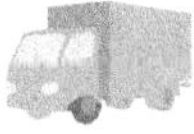

"So, you really want to do this?" I ask as I slide into the driver's seat and start the engine.

"Why would you want to help me? This is a big deal, Logan," she asks, putting the question back in my court.

Why *am* I helping her? I like her. A lot. I don't know how to put that into words. It's like pretending to do what I could never do, because that's all I have to give. I can never measure up to the husband and father she deserves.

"You need to look stable for the court. It makes sense."

"This is strictly on paper, right?" she asks, looking over at me.

"Do you want it to be strictly on paper?" I ask her.

"I like you. I know we just met, but I like being with you, and I want to know you more."

I glance back over at her, my breath hitching. "I like you, too." I reach over and squeeze her knee.

"So where does that leave us?" she asks. "I don't want this to cost you any money. I will cover everything I can."

I know I need to explain this, but I don't know how to make her understand besides being blunt, and I really don't want to sound like a jerk.

"Okay, if we're going to do this, we're going to have to be honest with each other, right?" I check my mirror then shift to the middle lane.

"Of course," she says, then pauses briefly before adding, "What do you mean by that?"

"Okay, well, I have a lot of money. Not saying that to brag, but I have a substantial trust fund I've never even touched. I've also made my own money. A lot of it. I have more than I could ever spend in my lifetime. I have no children and no immediate family. So, I can afford to take care of you and Caleb. I need you to understand that, okay?"

She reaches over and turns down the volume on the radio. "I'm sorry, did you say trust fund?" She tilts her head at me, her eyes blinking with bafflement.

"It's not that big of a deal. I'm only telling you this to put your mind at ease that once your ex and his lawyer see what they're up against here, they *will* back off. I think he's trying to manipulate you, probably because he thinks you have no money or support. This is a surefire way to make sure Caleb stays safe with you in New Hampshire. I think this is the best thing for you both."

She looks at me for a long time before saying, "I don't want to take advantage of you or take your money, Logan."

"I already know you wouldn't. If I thought that, I would never have agreed to help you. Allie, you are the kindest and most sincere person, and I really want to help you and Caleb."

"You've already done so much for me. I appreciate..." She stops and sits back in her seat.

"What?" I ask.

"This just seems so farfetched, doesn't it? I mean, who does this? Who gets married on a whim like this?"

"I guess we do. And it happens probably way more often than you realize. We can think of it as a business agreement, if that helps."

After a minute, she pulls out her guitar and asks me if I mind if she plays something. "I have nervous energy and need to play to think."

"You killed that song last night on the piano. You know that, right? What else do you have up your sleeve?"

"That's actually one of my favorite songs," she says as she begins to strum and sing "Everything Has Changed."

Listening to her play is calming and soothing. We might be crazy for doing this, but as we've been on this trip, it just feels strangely right. I want to know her, know her son, and be around them—even if it isn't real. I'll take what I can get.

She finishes, and I say quietly, "How you're not a professional musician, I'll never understand. You have such pure talent."

"Thank you. But have you heard Evan play? He's the real talent of the family."

"No, but listening to you, I find that hard to believe."

"We definitely both enjoy it," she tells me. "And who knows? Maybe we'll do live music at my bakery coffee shop if I ever get to open it."

"I think that's a great idea, Allie. You're a great baker, and with your marketing experience and tenacity, I know you can pull it off."

It's important to me that she knows I believe in her. She gives me a shy smile, and it feels like a reward. I want to keep the good vibe going so I ask her, "What would you call it?"

"I don't know," she says, still strumming her guitar. "I'd have to think about it. I just want to bring people together, you know? A place where people can meet up for coffee. A place for kids to come for after-school treats."

"You'll find the perfect name."

She looks over at me and changes the subject. "Okay, so you're staying in Freedom Valley over the holidays. What about Kat and her partner Maggie? Won't you miss seeing them?"

She puts her guitar in the back and turns to face me, tucking her feet under her.

"They'll do Thanksgiving on their own. I do miss them so much; I haven't gotten back to see them in a while."

"What about the holidays, though? Do they ever come to see you?"

"No, they usually stay in Montreal."

"What if we invite them down?" she asks.

"I'd love that. I can ask them. It would be really nice to see them," I admit, pleased that she thought of it.

"Do you ever see yourself moving back there?" she asks as she scrolls through her phone.

Her long, dark, wavy hair falls over her shoulder and I resist the urge to run my fingers through it. She's so pretty and the crazy thing is I don't think she even realizes it.

"I've tossed around the idea of getting a cabin and some land up there for summers and getaways, but I don't think I could live up there permanently. Not when my work is mostly in the States."

I try to hide my yawn but I can't. I'm struggling to stay awake after such a long drive, and I know I need to stop and get some more coffee.

Allie notices. "Are you ever going to let me drive?" she says. "Why don't I take over for a while and let you get a little nap in?"

I can't even argue with her; I know I need a nap. I switch places with her and I'm out so quickly, I don't even remember falling asleep.

~

CHAPTER 13

Allie

That was so hot, Ace.

Okay, so I might have messed up. I played around with the routes on my phone when we were talking earlier to see about going up through Montreal and back down to Freedom Valley. It only added on a little bit more time. I grew up not far from the border, and I've still never been, which feels like a crime. Especially that I haven't visited Montreal. It sounds like such a romantic city.

So, I changed out the route he had set up in the GPS and took a slight detour. He might be mad when he wakes up, but either way, here we are now just crossing into Canada.

Luckily, he left his wallet in the console with his passport tucked into it.

He stirs. "How long was I out?" he asks, sounding groggy.

"Six hours."

"You have got to be kidding..." He sits up straight and reaches for his phone to check.

"I'm just joking. Only about two." I laugh. "Don't kill me... but I took a different route."

He slides on his glasses and looks out the window. "Wait... Are we in Canada? Oh my God, what did you do, Allie?" He turns toward me and looks panicked. I need to chill him out.

"Don't get mad." I smile and grit my teeth. "I just thought it would be fun to see your sister. It wasn't that far of a detour, and I've never been to Canada before even though I've always wanted to go. And I know you haven't seen your family in a while, and I know how I feel when I haven't seen my family in a while. So, here we are..." I bite my lip, stopping my nervous rambling. I don't know how I thought he'd react, but I didn't think he'd be mad.

He sighs. "Okay." He pinches the bridge of his nose and looks tired.

"Okay?" I ask. "Are you mad?"

"No. I just wasn't expecting this. I'm going to book us a hotel for tonight."

"I'm sorry," I say quietly. "I just wanted to surprise you with something nice."

"I just need a minute."

"Okay. I'm going to stop at the next exit so we can get something to eat."

As I drive to the next rest area, the silence between us is killing me. Logan is texting on his phone and barely looks up. He says he's not mad, but he is eerily quiet and I'm worried I upset him.

I park and brace myself for him to be upset with me. I hope he can forgive me when he gets to see his sister and visit his hometown.

Logan puts his phone down. "I booked us a room at the Four Seasons. It looks like Kat and Maggie are free to hang out with us tonight and tomorrow morning before we head out. And they are delighted," he says dryly, a smirk on his face.

"So you're not mad?" I ask.

"No. In fact, we're ahead of schedule. And to be honest, I'm excited to see them. It's been a long time."

Relieved, I sigh. "If we're ahead of schedule, why don't we stay tomorrow night, too? I can't believe I've never been to Montreal. It's not even that far from Freedom Valley."

"Are you sure?" he asks. His phone buzzes with a text and he beams when he reads it. "Kat is so happy right now. I didn't realize how much she probably needed this, too."

Of course I'm anxious to get home to Caleb, but I want this trip to be about Logan, too. *For* Logan, too. It's obvious having time with his sister and her partner matters to him, and I'm also excited to meet them and see this part of his life. "Why not? Let's make the most of this."

I deeply exhale the breath I didn't even realize I was holding. I'm relieved that he's not mad right now. This could have easily gone a different way.

"I still can't believe you did this," he says slowly, shaking his head, "but I am excited to show you around Montreal. Just wait till I take you to the best donut shop in the world. It's called *TDB* and it will blow your mind."

I tilt my head at him. "Really?" I challenge. "In the *entire* world?"

"In the entire galaxy," he retorts.

"Well, in that case, how can I refuse."

"You can't refuse a great donut. You can't even refuse a crappy donut."

"Oh, so true. It's like you know me."

"I think we've already established that donuts and coffee are the way to your heart, Allie," he says lightly.

I give an overly dramatic fake sigh and decide to prolong the drama. "I'm going to be the best fake wife you've ever had, you know. You're never going to want to get rid of me."

He doesn't say anything, only giving me a pensive gaze. His mouth turns up like he's trying not to smile.

As I turn into the hotel parking lot, he says, "This was a long drive today. I need a long swim, a soak in a hot tub, and a good dinner."

"I second that." We grab our bags out of the back and I make sure everything's locked. "Except for the swim part."

"You don't want to swim?"

"I don't want to exercise," I reply.

He just laughs and shakes his head.

"There's many different ways to exercise, Allie."

Oh. My. God. What does *that* mean?

"Oh, really? Well, maybe you can show me one that isn't boring sometime." I flirt back and watch his face. His mouth twitches and his eyes darken, but we keep walking.

We make our way to the hotel and I can't help but notice this place is on another level. The lobby looks totally futuristic, right out of *The Jetsons.*

"It's so chic here," I whisper to Logan. I suddenly feel very insecure in my sweaty black leggings and my t-shirt that reads, "We're a perfect pair" with a noodle and a block of cheese on it. Logan seems unphased in his "Save the neck for me, Clark" t-shirt, with that funny line from the movie *Christmas Vacation.*

"Why don't you wait here?" He motions to a sofa that probably costs more than my car.

"Sure," I say and sit, crossing my legs, feeling nervous and out of place while he confidently strides to the desk to check-in. The woman helping him smiles and clicks away at her computer. She appears to be making conversation, and I can tell whatever she just said to Logan, he isn't happy about. He stuffs his hands in his pockets as she stares intently at her computer monitor, then she slides two key cards across the counter to him.

As he starts walking back to me, his body goes rigid when an older gentleman and a much younger woman, probably about my age, in a short, tight, white dress, approach him. They stop and talk to him. His eyes dart to mine and back to them. I stand to make sure everything is okay, but he shoots me a look that says, "Stay."

Who are these people?

Logan folds his arms over his chest and stands rigid but taller, clearly looking uncomfortable.

The older man then says something that makes Logan cringe before they walk away from him. Logan watches them until they're out of sight, and then heads back over to me.

"Who was that?" I ask.

"I'll explain upstairs." He grits his teeth, obviously upset.

"What about our bags?"

"Already on their way up to our room."

"*Our* room?"

"They're all booked for a conference. They only have one room left. It's fine, I'll sleep on the floor. I'm so tired, I could sleep on a pile of sticks right now."

I gently grab his hand and lean into him. "It's okay. We're practically married. We can share a room as friends, right?"

I keep it light, trying to coax a smile out of him.

Only he's not smiling. He's frustrated, and I don't know how to make it better.

Logan stays quiet as we make our way to our room. He opens the door to find... one bed. Well, this just got even more exciting. And the best part? The glass shower wall separates the bathroom and the bedroom part. It's an open hotel room. My heart flutters. Now I'm nervous, but in a good way. I can tell he's upset, but I don't know if it's from the room situation or the people in the lobby. I decide to keep quiet so I don't add to his bad mood.

We fall back onto the bed simultaneously and sigh. Our rhythmic reaction to this day would be funny if he wasn't so upset.

"Are you mad about the room?"

"I'm exhausted," he says to the ceiling. "It's not about the room. I'd prefer to share a room with you." My stomach fills with butterflies. "I just didn't need the drama in the lobby."

I think I've already figured out the answer when I directly ask, "Who were those people?"

"That was my father." He rubs his hands over his eyes.

Now I feel terrible. Coming to Montreal was my idea, and the first place we stop, it immediately put him in a position to run into his family, who I know he didn't want to see. "I thought so. It looked like you didn't want me to see him."

"I most definitely didn't want you to see him, and I don't

want you to meet him. He's toxic, and I don't want him knowing about anyone in my life who's important to me."

I'm important to him...

I try to let that sink in for a bit, but he quickly adds, "Anything he touches, he destroys."

My heart sinks. Logan doesn't deserve this. I can't imagine having these feelings about my own father.

"And the woman? I'm guessing that wasn't your mother."

"Likely one of his mistresses."

My whole body goes stiff. "One of?"

"It's no secret in my family. He always has a side piece or two. I'm telling you, Allie, he's garbage."

It's no wonder Logan wants nothing to do with his family—and that he seems to fear marriage and fatherhood—if this is the kind of man who has been his example.

Logan pulls himself up off the bed. "I have to take a shower, but then we're going over to Maggie and Kat's for pizza, okay?"

All of a sudden, I feel exhausted. "Sure," I tell him through a yawn. "Can I just close my eyes and nap for a minute, though?"

"Of course," he says.

"What should I wear?" I ask, barely able to get the words out.

Logan looks at me blankly for a second or two then laughs. "Leggings and a t-shirt, Ace. You're going to love Kat and

Maggie."

He takes his bag and heads into the see-through bathroom to shower, not even caring that it's right next to the bed. I turn away and face the window.

The next thing I know, he's shaking my shoulder gently. "Wake up, sleepyhead. It's time to get ready," he says.

He lays on the bed next to me and turns to face the window to give me some privacy. I get up quickly, grab my clothes and toiletry bag out of my backpack, and jump in the shower.

I watch Logan, still facing the window and either playing on his phone or sleeping, I can't tell. When I'm done, I quickly blow dry my hair, put on some mascara and lip gloss, and tie my hair in a messy bun.

I check on Logan and find him still asleep. *Damn.* Even asleep, he's hot. I sit on the edge of the bed and gently rub his arm. "Hey, I'm ready…"

He mumbles and opens his eyes. "Okay." He stretches and yawns, exposing his six-pack abs. "I'm so hungry. Let's get going."

We take an Uber to Kat and Maggie's brownstone, which seems probably as old as the city. It's as bohemian and eclectic as the neighborhood they live in.

"Do you think we should have brought a bottle of wine or something?" I whisper quickly after we ring the bell.

"Nah, they are totally chill," he says. I can see his breath as he speaks.

"Canada is so cold!" I put my hands in my pockets.

The door swings open and a petite woman with bright blue glasses answers. "Logan!" she squeals as she hugs him and then turns and hugs me. "Hi, Allie, it's so nice to meet you. Come on in. Maggie is making homemade pizza. I hope you're hungry."

I feel mostly at ease but with a twinge of nervousness. I want them to like me, I realize. I'm falling for Logan fast. I need to pull back, but I may already be in too deep.

We follow Kat inside and toss our coats over the back of one of the chairs. Just like the outside, the inside is casual and comfortable. The oversized couch has a knitted afghan tossed over the arm, and there's art everywhere. Vintage glass candle holders line the shelves. The bookshelves are crammed. Like brother, like sister; they love books. Their home is beautiful, cozy, and warm.

Maggie comes out of the kitchen, wiping her hands on a dishtowel, and the way Kat's face lights up says it all. "This is Maggie," Kat tells me before turning to Maggie and confidently stating, "This is my brother's girlfriend, Allie."

I glance at Logan. He shoots up an eyebrow but says nothing. *He says nothing!*

I shake Maggie's hand. "It's so nice to meet you. Thank you for having me."

I'm surprised at how much I really want them both to like me. Although, I guess it makes sense seeing as they are Logan's family, the only family he gets along with, so if they're important to him, I want to make a good impression.

Damn. I'm falling hard.

Logan looks oblivious as we enter the kitchen, with its gorgeous butcher block island, vintage mid-century-modern light fixtures, boho rugs, and bright plates.

In the middle of the island is a charcuterie board that's a literal work of art. Vegetables, fruits, nuts, meats, hummus, olives, and bread crisps grace the board. The part of me that loves food and baking has such an urge to take a picture, but I don't want to make it weird.

I sit next to Logan at the counter and help myself to a small plate of snacks. He smiles at me as he spears a cherry tomato and shoves it in his mouth. He puts his arm around my shoulder and pulls me in for a quick hug.

"Red wine or beer?" Kat asks.

"I'd love some wine, please."

Logan says, "Beer for me. Thanks."

Kat gives Logan his beer, then pours my wine into a beautiful glass. Maggie selects music from her phone that plays on a hidden speaker. I already love them both for being so welcoming and keeping things casual.

"Is this your first time visiting Canada?" Maggie asks me.

"It is. Montreal is gorgeous. I can't wait to explore the city tomorrow."

Logan draws his beer to his lips and my stomach dips. I can't explain it, but I really wish I was that beer bottle right now.

Stop it, Allie.

"So, Logan tells us you're a fantastic baker," Kat says.

I take a sip of my wine and set it down. "Well, that's high praise. Thank you. I've loved baking since I was a little girl and could reach the oven at my family's inn in New Hampshire."

"That sounds straight out of a Hallmark movie," she jokes.

"It sort of is. It's one of my favorite places," I tell them.

"It really is special. I'm glad I won't be living too far from The Golden Gable." Logan says.

"I hear you're a chef. How did you get started?" I ask as I select some snacks from the charcuterie board. I take this moment to slide in closer to Logan even though my brain is screaming to put some space between us.

"Actually, it's not that glamorous. I worked on the line, cooking part-time in high school and college. Then I dropped out of college and went to culinary school, much to my parents' dismay."

What do their parents have against supporting their kids' dreams?

"I've been cooking professionally for five years now. I'm a chef at Evolve here in Montreal."

She gets up and opens the oven. "I hope you like pizza."

"I love pizza." I take a sip of my wine and look over at Logan. His gaze meets mine and my stomach flips again. He's just devastatingly handsome.

"So, how did you and my brother meet?" Kat asks.

"Logan's friends with Beth, my brother's girlfriend."

"Wait, you're Evan's sister?" Kat exchanges a look with Maggie, who's busy cutting up pizza and laying out the slices on another big board.

"Yep, he's my older brother. Beth asked Logan to help me move from San Diego to New Hampshire."

"What a trip! How has the drive been?" she asks.

"Pretty epic," I admit, smiling. "We've seen some beautiful places."

Maggie walks over with the wine and tops off my glass. "So, you two just met this week?" I can tell they're both still trying to figure us out. "And you're dating?"

Logan walks back into the room at just that moment. "We're not dating," he says.

Kat and Maggie look at each other, confused.

"We're getting married," he says casually as he pulls his chair out and nonchalantly sits back down at the counter. He snags a slice of pizza, but just as he's about to bite into it, he looks up and realizes we're all gaping at him.

I cover my face with my hands. Way to really leap there, Logan. I can tell he's still being feisty after the whole encounter with his father earlier. He's on another level now. Here I am, trying to make a good impression with his sisters, and he's blowing it.

"What?" he asks.

I want to crawl under the counter.

"I need more wine, babe," Kat says, and Maggie tops her off. She then looks at me and says, "Just so you know, he's never even introduced us to a girlfriend before, let alone a future wife." Then she turns to Logan. "Our parents are going to flip out," she tells him. "You know that."

"I'm not going to tell them."

I must look as uncomfortable as I feel because Kat pulls up a chair next to me and sits, pulling the pizza closer to us.

"I'm going to share this with you two, but it doesn't leave here," Logan says. "Not to anyone, okay?"

They both nod and pause, waiting for him to go on.

"Allie is going through a custody dispute with her ex. Preston suggested we get married. If Allie and Caleb have me and my insurance, things will look more stable for them, and her dirtbag ex won't be able to take Caleb from her. So, obviously, no one can know it's a ruse."

"Got it," Kat says.

"Also, we've become great friends," Logan says, as if he just explained something so basic. He shrugs his shoulders, then takes another bite of pizza.

"Um, are you nuts, Logan?" Kat says, looking to Maggie for confirmation, who quickly returns a look to say she agrees. "I mean, I know you love pissing off our parents, but this is going to be a really big deal to them. You know how they are. This will be in the papers. Allie will get shredded in tabloids. Did you tell her that we're unfortunately kind of on the radar up here?"

Tabloids?

"Wait, what?" A tense silence envelopes the room. All I can see now is pictures of me and Caleb that may end up somewhere on the internet. I didn't think about that.

"I thought about that, and of course I don't want that for you, Allie," Logan says. "Things are complicated enough with your ex. But I've thought it through, and I honestly think it's fine. It's Canada. We don't even live here. I'm not worried about it, and you guys shouldn't be either. What I do with my personal life is none of anyone's business."

He pauses for a beat before he continues, "Oh, speaking of minding their own business, I saw dear old Dad with one of his flavors of the month this afternoon at the Four Seasons. He was pissed I didn't tell him I was coming to town. He said I should have made an appointment. Can you believe that? He actually scolded me like one of his employees."

"The blonde or the redhead?" Kat asks before taking another bite of pizza.

"Blonde. Younger than you. Classy, huh?" he takes a sip of his beer and sits back.

I can't believe how casually they talk about their father's affairs. They grew up in a different world than me, that's for sure. It's sad and hard to imagine. I would never speak of my parents this way.

"So, he saw you, and you know what that means? Sarah will be coming by, mark my word," Maggie declares.

"Great, you've awoken the beast." Kat groans, but continues, "In our last conversation, she asked me when my 'gay phase' would be over because it's embarrassing the family."

"I'm sorry, what?" I ask. "Your sister said that to you?"

Kat and Maggie nod solemnly. "Yep, you have no idea what kind of shitshow you're stepping into. How these two came out normal is beyond me, but I'm grateful," Maggie says.

Kat leans her head on Maggie's shoulder and says, "Thanks, babe."

I squeeze Logan's thigh under the table and lean into him. I'm feeling really bad for them both right now. I can't believe their family has treated them this way.

"Anyone up for a game of gin rummy?" Maggie asks. She starts to load our plates into the dishwasher and wipes down the counters.

"I am. Just need a quick stop in the restroom," Logan says then heads down the hall.

When he's out of earshot, Kat asks me, "Do you really like my brother, or is this all fake?"

I am not at all surprised Kat's asking me this. I can tell she wants to protect her brother, and she just met me. I would do the exact same for Evan. "I really do. He's kind, protective, gentle, and so much fun to be around."

She pulls a deck of cards from a drawer in the island and begins shuffling. "He doesn't give his heart over easily," she says. "Give him a chance. No matter what he says or does, just remember he didn't start life with the tools he should have. Relationships and trusting people don't come easy to him."

I nod and sip my wine. "I'm so sorry."

"I've been through six years of therapy after the childhood that we had. My family is so damaged, and it took years to repair the way that impacted me. Unfortunately, Logan hasn't really done the work yet. But, I must say, he seems different around you."

I try to imagine what it must have been like to have been used and manipulated his whole life by the people who should have encouraged and loved him. It's so foreign to my own experience with my family, I'm not even sure what to say. I decide to change the subject.

"So, I know you're a middle school teacher. What do you teach?" I ask.

"Seventh-grade English. I love writing, and I love working with kids. Especially the hard kids. Those are the ones who need love the most." She deals the cards into four piles.

"That's amazing. Have you read any of Beth's books? I'm so excited to finally meet her."

"You'll like Beth. She's so personable. We used to tease Logan that they were a secret couple, but they never actually were. Just super close friends."

"She's really great," Maggie chimes in. "Quirky and funny."

"And she'll love it that you bake," Kat adds. "She has quite a sweet tooth."

"Oh, honey, you'll have her heart. She wants Logan to be happy."

Logan walks in at just that moment and sits in front of his cards. "I'm happy," he says, scooping up his cards and looking them over.

"So, when do you guys think you'll get married?" Kat presses. "And are you having a big wedding? How far are you going with this?"

"We haven't really decided," Logan replies. "I was thinking we'd maybe go to the courthouse when we get to Freedom Valley and do it there. What do you think?" he asks me.

I would rather talk about this later, privately, so I just murmur, "Mmhm," and look down at my cards.

A loud knock at the door startles us.

"Right on time," Logan quips with an eye roll as he heads to the door to answer it. He looks out the peephole and swears. "Just as we called it."

Kat sits back in her chair, her forehead creased in worry. "I knew she'd slither by sooner or later. You know she's his snake in the grass, always ready to pounce and do his dirty work."

He opens the door and says, "Sarah."

"Logan," she says as she pushes her way inside. Her light blond hair is perfectly styled, no hair out of place. She's wearing a suit tailored specifically to her body and she's carrying a clearly expensive designer handbag, possibly valued at more than I made in my former annual salary. "Kathryn."

She doesn't even bother to acknowledge Maggie, which is not lost on me.

Bitch.

"I see I wasn't invited to this little... family dinner, or whatever it is." Her critical gaze lands on me. "Who are you?"

"What do you want, Sarah?" Logan says, squaring his shoulders. Kat remains seated and Maggie stands in the living room.

"Dad said he saw you today at the Four Seasons and we wondered what you were doing in town. Are you moving back?" Her eyes fall back on me, clearly still trying to figure out where I come into play here in this dynamic.

"And you?" she circles around me, her glare burning through me as if she's trying to intimidate me.

I'm not about to let her scare me. "I'm Allie," I say as

anger knots through me. I know her kind. She reminds me of Chris's family—the way she looks at me, the way she talks to me like I'm not good enough. I've had enough of people like her.

"Sarah, why don't you just go home," Logan says, trying to diffuse the tension in the room, which seems to be getting hotter by the minute. I can tell he isn't going to acknowledge who I am—I'm sure to protect me, just like with his father.

She glares at him reproachfully. "It must be nice to run off and play with books all day while I'm here taking up the slack on the family business that *you* should be helping with."

Logan stares at her with indifference, saying nothing.

"You have responsibilities, Logan. It's time to man up. Dad says it's time to come home or lose out. He's done with your games."

"Leave now," he tells her, a chill in his words like I've never heard from him before. "You weren't invited here."

His tone triggers me, and I decide I'm done.

"I think your siblings asked you to leave," I say, walking over and holding the door.

"I don't think anyone asked you, *Allie.* You don't belong here, and you better not be *with* Logan. He doesn't need to explain to the board or anyone else why he went slumming for the likes of you."

Oh, now it's on.

"Are you okay?" I ask, staring at her intently, waiting for a response.

You can hear a pin drop in the room. Maggie, Logan, and Kat are frozen in amusement.

"Are *you* okay?" she lashes back at me. "I asked repeatedly who you are, and no one will answer me."

None of us respond, which seems to make her even madder.

"Dad is going to be so pissed," she says smugly.

"I was asking if you were okay because I can't imagine walking into my own brother's home and treating him the way you are treating Logan right now, with this disrespect and classless bullshit. So, let me ask again, *are you okay?* Do you need to step out into the hall, compose yourself, and try this again?" She's not getting out of this one.

"You have no idea who you're even talking to, you little peasant. You probably just saw some dollar signs and thought you landed yourself a Nolan." She laughs maniacally, like she's just made the best joke.

I look over at Logan. He's clearly starting to enjoy this. He pulls his lips into a thin smirk, seeming not even remotely bothered by my statements. I take this as permission to keep going.

I knot my fingers through his and stand close to him. "Calling someone you don't even know names and judging them when you know absolutely nothing about them? I guess what they say is true: Money can't buy class, Sarah."

"And what would you know about me or money?"

"You may not know who I am, but I'm aware of who you are. And I don't take too kindly to people treating others the way you're treating us right now."

"Are you kidding me, Logan? You're a Nolan."

Logan just grins and pulls me closer, throwing an arm around my shoulder.

"This won't be happening, honey," she says condescendingly.

Maggie and Kat are still frozen, taking this all in.

"What makes you think you're good enough to be with a Nolan? You aren't even on the same planet, little girl."

"Well, you know what they say?" I say, holding up my free hand. "Every toxic family needs someone to call them out on their bullshit. Looks like a job for me."

Sarah seems speechless. She's fuming, at a loss for words, and the others seem to be enjoying it.

Ready for her to leave, I wrap up with, "It was so lovely to meet you, but you're going to have to go now. We're just in the middle of something, and you're not invited." I pull Logan closer and kiss his cheek.

"Yes, time for you to go," Maggie says, holding the door open.

Regret, or something else I can't read, passes over Sarah's face, but it's gone almost as quickly as it shows up. "You're trash," she says.

"Better watch how you talk to people," I remind her, cocking my head to the side and giving her a firm smile.

"You're in so much trouble, Logan." She shakes her head then stomps out.

Maggie shuts the door and bursts into a mixture of snorting and laughing.

"Logan. If you don't wife this one up, I will. She just took down a Nolan on her first bite. I can't even…" she teases.

I try to get a read on Logan. Was that too much? "I'm sorry," I stammer. "That was probably taking it too far. I just couldn't stand the way she was judging you all."

Logan smiles brightly. "You just smashed my sister, Ace. I don't think I've ever seen anyone take her on like that. She deserved every minute of it." He grabs my shoulders and steers me back into the kitchen. "Maggie, please tell me you made dessert."

"I did," she says. "A pudding chomeur with a chocolate raspberry sauce."

"I don't even know what that is, but with that French accent, it sounds irresistible," I say.

I'm filled with relief that Logan isn't mad at me for telling his sister off. When he grabs my shoulders and whispers to me, "That was so hot, Ace," I melt.

Logan

This changes
everything for us.

I can't believe Sarah just showed up like that. Actually, I can. She's just awful. I used to get so mad and argue back. Now, the more irate she gets, the calmer I get.

I'm nowhere near as wealthy as my father, but I've carved a solid path for myself. My biggest goal when I became a literary agent was to make it on my own. I'm really proud that I can say I successfully achieved that milestone.

I live simply, like Kat does. She was smart enough to cash out her trust fund and invest it on her own before she came out to the family. My father's still bitter and angry about that. He's mostly mad he now has no way to control my sister, and sadly, I think he's just given up on her. He never sees or talks to her. She's won awards for her teaching, and she's incredible for all the work she does in her community, but he'll never see it.

My mom never stood up for me when my dad would berate me and tear me down, which he did every chance he got. I've always thought of her as cold and spineless. She's never been a mother to me, and she definitely showed me the kind of parent I would never want to be.

I watch Allie chatting with Kat and feel like they seem to be genuinely enjoying each other. Despite the fact that I'm still feeling frazzled by Sarah, I'm happy that Allie is getting along with my sister.

No one has ever gone to bat like that for me before. For a minute there, I was convinced she really was my wife. It makes me feel like maybe we can make this work. For *real*. I've had so much fun this week and I definitely don't want it to end. Any of it. Her crankiness in the morning before she's had coffee. Her soft snores as we drive. Our easy banter. Her laughter.

Maybe this doesn't have to end.

I think about her ex and can't help but wonder how did he not see her, not want her? How could he ever give her up? She's phenomenal.

I notice she's grinning at me and I realize I must have missed something. "I'm sorry, what did you say?" I ask.

"We're making official plans for Christmas. At the inn. You'll be with us, too, right?"

"Yes, I'll be at the inn," I say. I turn to Kat and Maggie and continue, "Of course you guys should come. I'd love to spend Christmas as a family."

I'm playing it cool right now, but inside, my heart has swelled so much I feel like it could pop out of my chest. I love this. I want this.

The scariest part is that I didn't even know I wanted this; I don't think I would want this if it weren't for her. For Allie.

"You look tired. You want to go?" Allie asks, tilting her head. I'm freaking exhausted, but I don't want to admit it to her because I love watching her have a blast with Kat and Maggie.

"We better order a ride, babe," she says casually as she goes back to discussing Christmas plans with my sister.

Babe?

I pull up my app and order a car before tuning back in to their conversation and beginning our goodbyes.

"So, you're meeting us for lunch tomorrow, right?" Allies asks them. At their in-sync nodding, she continues, "Then let's go exploring. I want to see all of your favorite Montreal spots. I need to find some souvenirs for Caleb. Maybe when he gets stronger I can bring him up here to visit," she says.

We put on our coats and I hug Kat goodbye. "Thanks, sis."

When I hug Maggie, I tell her, "You are the best chef in the world. Love you," I say, pressing a kiss to her cheek.

Maggie blushes and she backs up, her head down. I love her for Kat. They're perfect together.

We head downstairs and get into our ride. I sink into the seat as we drive to the hotel. "I'm sorry about Sarah. Most of my family is a mess."

"Are you kidding me? That was the most fun I've had in forever. I mean, yes, Sarah is horrible, but Kat and Maggie are *amazing*. Besides, have you met Evan?" she jokes. "All families are a little nuts." She pulls her scarf around her neck and shivers.

I pull her closer to me, tucking her back into my chest, and I realize I've never had this. This natural intimacy with someone. She didn't freak out about most of my family being so awful—dysfunctional on a silver platter, really. *Literally.* And she didn't run away. In fact, it's the opposite. It's like she's running *toward* me.

I hold her closer and she snuggles into my chest. We stay like that, just watching out the window, the rest of the way to the hotel.

Yeah. I can see myself with this girl. Dammit.

When we get back to the hotel, we make it upstairs quickly, both of us exhausted.

"I'm just going to go change real quick," she says as she heads into the bathroom. The glass between us is lightly frosted but I can still see her silhouette changing. She even makes that look sexy.

I put my phone on the charger, grab my clothes, and change quickly into a pair of shorts and a t-shirt. There's this elephant in the room with only one bed. I want to say something. Anything to make this feel less awkward.

When she comes out, I say, "I can make a bed on the floor."

She jumps into the bed. "Do you want to sleep on the floor?" she asks me.

"No, but I don't want you to be uncomfortable."

She tilts her head and says, "I'm uncomfortable with you sleeping on the cold floor. Hurry up, you can keep me warm." She pulls the blankets up under her chin.

I take a deep breath and exhale when I get into bed.

"Night, Logan," she whispers.

"Night, Ace," I murmur as we both drift off to sleep.

When I wake up the next morning, Allie's pressed up against me. Her dark chestnut hair falls across her pillow. I carefully shift so as not to wake her and grab my phone from the nightstand. I order donuts and coffees to be delivered from TDB, then set my phone down and fall back asleep holding her.

A while later, I wake up to a soft knock at the door. Allie

stirs and I slide out of the bed to get our breakfast. I walk back in and set hers on her bedside table. I sit up in the bed and eat my donut while checking my email. Oh, great, one from my dad.

Dad: I want an appointment immediately.

That's all it says. I hit delete. Whatever. I'm not letting him ruin my day, or my time with Allie.

Allie stirs. "I smell coffee. Logan, is there coffee? If there's coffee, I'm going to marry you *right now*."

"Well, I'll prepare my vows," I say, chewing a mouthful of donut.

She sits up and looks at me. "And donuts? I'm going to have your babies, too." I choke on my donut, and she laughs. "Just kidding. But seriously, you are the best. I'm glad I got to lock you down before some other girl discovers how freaking awesome you are, even if it's not real. No babies. I wouldn't be opposed to a dog, though." She sits up and takes a sip of her coffee and leans back against the headboard, sighing appreciatively.

I grin at her and set my phone down and grab my coffee. "Are you opposed to having more children?"

"I'm not. But I thought you were."

"I like kids, I just haven't found the right person to have them with."

"Really? I thought you wanted to focus on your career?"

"I don't know. I like to keep an open mind. I could have both."

"You surprise me," she says. "I'll miss this time I had with you when it's over."

"We don't have to miss it," I say. Just having her lying here next to me makes my senses spin. She's become a best friend, and deep down, I do want more. If I'm being honest, I am terrified I'll mess it up.

"What do you mean?" she says as she turns to face me.

"Well, it doesn't have to end. I'm coming with you, and as an employee of the Boston office, I'll be working remotely in Freedom Valley for the holidays. I'll be going back and forth to Boston a few times, but you and Caleb can come there with me, too." I stretch my legs out in front of me.

A soft and vulnerable expression washes her face. She exhales, looking like she's about to deliver bad news. "We've gotten close," she says carefully, looking at me. "I have loved this time with you, every second of it, and I would be interested to see where this goes. If we tried for real, if we were for real."

"For real?" I say quietly.

"Yeah. For real," she murmurs, tracing her fingers down the pillow next to me and looking up at me with her big green eyes. I can tell she's nervous, and my heart pounds as she comes to a halt inches from my face.

Her last words are smothered with my lips as I pull her close and move my mouth over hers, her lips warm and sweet on mine. I take my time kissing her deeply, softly, slowly, and moving across her ear lobe and down to her neck, swinging her into the circle of my arms.

She moans softly, sinking onto my lap, and our eyes lock, hers darkening in desire, and I can feel her heart beating in unison with mine. Our bodies feel like magnets together, pulling us closer and closer, like we can't get close enough.

"I can think of several reasons not to do this, but then I think of a million reasons why we should… And that matters more," she murmurs.

"You matter more," I murmur into her ear.

"You matter more, too," she whispers, pulling my shirt up and over my head.

I kiss down her cheek and pull out her scrunchie, then run my fingers through her hair as I kiss her deeply. Our connection together is undeniable. Less than one week of knowing her, and I know she's meant for me and I'm meant for her. We need this. We deserve this.

Her arms wrap around me and she kisses me deeper, her hands running down my chest, all over me, pulling me closer. Both of us can't get enough.

I pull her shirt up and over her head and she's left in white lace panties and no bra. I kiss her breasts slowly, taking my time as I look up into her eyes and she melts under me, with me.

"I need you…"

I reach over for my wallet and pull out a condom. Her eyes never leave mine as she tugs my shorts down, her hands finding my length, and I take a deep breath as I lean in to kiss her.

I don't stop kissing her as she reaches down and pulls me inside of her, ready for me as much as I'm ready for her.

Our bodies move together in the most natural rhythm I've ever experienced, and being underneath Allie, being *inside* of Allie, is my new favorite place. The heat between us is intense as we move in sync, in and out, up and down, slowly enjoying this first time together.

For as nervous as Allie can sometimes be around me, her eyes never leave mine during this intimate moment. I move in to kiss her, making sure to be gentle and go slow.

"More..." she murmurs, and it's my undoing. I flip her over, pushing into her with more speed, more umph, more feeling, and it's both not enough and too much. As we come together, she grips my shoulders until her legs relax from around my waist.

I lay my head next to her and pull the sheet over us, bringing her close. "I've wanted to do that my whole life with someone."

"Have sex?" she laughs, confused.

"No, be with someone and feel that connection," I say. "I can't explain it, but it's different with you, Allie."

Her eyes soften and she lays her head on my chest. "This

changes everything for us."

"For the good, definitely," I say.

"Because I can't imagine going back to a life without you in it. Every day that I've gotten to know you more, I can't imagine not talking with you and laughing with you. I loved meeting your family... Well, most of them. And I want to know you more."

"Allie," I say hoarsely, "I'm not sure how to do this. What if... deep down, I'm an asshole just like him? I can't hurt anyone like he hurt me and Kat."

I run my hand down the stubble of my chin and peer out the window at the cold and foggy city.

Allie stares at me for a while, then finally blinks and says, "Well, you're not like him. Everyone has their moments. He's... on another level. You can't punish yourself because of how someone else has been." She's confident when she speaks, and I like that it's a matter-of-fact issue for her. I see her take a deep breath before continuing, "If you feel the same and want to see where this goes, then that's great. But if you don't, I need to know before I fall any deeper here."

I stare down at her as she lies against me. "I do want to see where this goes, but I'd be lying if I didn't tell you that I'm scared. I don't know if I can be enough for you and Caleb. I don't know how to be a real husband, much less a real parent."

"Caleb doesn't need you to be his dad. You can start by

being his Logan. I've done this on my own for years now; we don't need to be saved. I've learned to save myself time and time again when I've been let down. I'm willing to try here. And I hear you that you're scared and hesitant and wondering if you could really do it, so if you're not all the way in, that's okay. I'll respect that, and we can try to go back to where we were—before now."

"I don't think we can go back to the way we were before today," I whisper softly.

She wraps her arms around me and lays her head on my chest, pulling me into her. I close my eyes and lean back. I need her, I need this. I've kept myself alone for so long, feeling like I'm protecting others, but maybe I am punishing myself for the way my family is.

"Are you going to go workout?" she asks, tracing my arm muscles with her fingers.

"I was," I say.

"Was?" she asks.

"Yes, but now I don't want to leave. What were you going to do?"

"I was going to take a bubble bath in that giant tub," she says as she grins. She reaches over for her scrunchie and wraps her hair up in a messy bun on top of her head.

"You're so beautiful," I say, gazing at her. No makeup, messy hair, and pajamas, and she's just perfect. She's who I want to see and be with every day.

CHAPTER 15

Allie

An intervention?

Even after the bubbles are gone, neither of us want to get out of the huge tub. I know I'd like to spend the whole day in the room with only him, but we have things to do. "Okay, I'm washing my hair so we can get ready," I tell him. "I'm excited to see Kat and Maggie again. And to see some of Montreal."

Logan groans but agrees and gets out to join me in the shower. He presses me up against the wall and we kiss for a long time until the water runs cold. We quickly get out and dry off, and he shaves while I dry my hair. It's like we've done this every day for years. I sneak a few glimpses at him and catch him doing the same.

"Where are we meeting them?" I head out of the bathroom and grab my clothes to get dressed.

"Schwartz's Deli at noon. They have the best smoked meat and poutine," he says excitedly. "Then we're going to hang out on Saint Laurent Boulevard, and I think Maggie wants to hit up Jean-Talon's Market to buy something to cook for dinner. It's a big outdoor market with lots of shopping, so I think we can find some fun stuff for Caleb there."

Logan walks confidently to his bag with a towel wrapped around his waist and I can't help but stare. His shoulders are sculpted, his body is lean. This man is a work of art.

My head's down, focusing on my clothes and getting ready, when in one motion, I'm in his arms, my soft curves folded into his hard body. Logan tips my chin up and covers my mouth in a kiss that makes me whimper. He stops and says, "Did you hear what I said?"

"Sounds good," I murmur, breathless as my heart hammers my ribs. I have no idea what he said. But with that kiss, I'd agree to probably anything.

"Just wanted you to remember I didn't forget about this morning. I meant what I said. For real." His eyes lock onto mine.

His phone starts ringing and he looks down. "It's Sarah." He ignores the call and slides the phone back into his pocket. "She's not ruining my morning. You about ready?"

"I just need ten minutes." I slide on my jeans, sneakers, and an oversized off-the-shoulder red sweater.

We walk hand-in-hand to the lobby and freeze when we see his dad, Sarah, and another woman standing there. Waiting.

Logan's mom looks like an older version of Sarah, and she treats me in much the same way her daughter did last night. With indifference.

"Logan," she says as she walks forward and hugs him awkwardly.

"Hi, Mom." Logan stiffly hugs her back. His hand slides back into mine when she backs up to stand next to his father. It's almost as if a line in the sand has been drawn. His dad and Sarah just glare at him.

"Aren't you going to introduce me to this woman?" His mom's voice finally breaks out. "Sarah says you're *with* her," she hisses angrily. "Do you even know where she comes from?"

These people are talking about me like I'm not here when I'm only a few feet away from them. Like I'm a dog and they're discussing my pedigree, or whether I came from a shelter or not.

I watch Logan's face. He simply stares at them all and says, "What do you want?"

Sarah starts to talk but his dad puts his hand up and says, "We need to stop you from making a huge mistake. Can we talk to you? Privately."

"What mistake, Dad?" he says calmly, ignoring Sarah's question. His hand twitches in my hand briefly. They wouldn't have caught the movement, but I can feel it all right now. I can feel his heartbeat pounding next to my arm, despite his cool and calm business demeanor.

"Associating with... this woman." His mom glares at me.

Logan blinks at all of them and says, "Have a great day." He starts walking, pulling me around them, out the front door and onto the street.

"Oh my God, what was that? An intervention?"

He nods. "I'm surprised they didn't just get a key from the front desk and barge into our room to pack up my stuff and drag me home."

"Well, they might have barged in on some things they wouldn't want to see," I say, trying to lighten the mood.

It works, because Logan snorts out a laugh. "For sure."

"Would they really just come into your room, unannounced and uninvited?" I ask. My family can be overbearing at times, but they wouldn't do that to me.

He looks at me and says, "Yes. They have no boundaries, and they think they can control me by always dangling money over me. What they don't understand is that money is not my currency. It's not what motivates me, and I am sick of them always doing that."

I look at him and say thoughtfully, "Well, what *does*

motivate you?"

"Family. Happiness. Laughs, jokes, being with someone who just gets you and loves you for who you are, not who you could have been."

My face softens into a sad smile. "Well, I think you're pretty great."

"Thanks. I think you're pretty great, too."

"Why does Sarah stay there and put up with that? Does she like that life?"

"My dad thinks we all belong to him and he can tell us what to do with our lives. He micromanages Sarah, too. He picked out her husband, her house, everything. He controls everyone around him with puppet strings."

Ugh. Hearing this is hard, but seeing it firsthand is even harder. Maybe I made a mistake making him come to Montreal. I thought I was doing something good, but now I'm not so sure.

"I'm really sorry," I tell him.

"What are you sorry for?"

"Making you come here."

"No, it was good. I liked seeing Kat and Maggie."

"Do you need a hug? A donut? What do you need?"

His mouth turns up. "I'm good, thank you. I'm not letting them ruin this for us. I've been looking forward to sharing this last part of the trip with you before we go home."

Home. I love the sound of that. Home with Logan.

Together. Now that we've decided to try for real, I want more time with him before I have to share him with everyone else.

"I've learned to just ignore them," he continues. "It makes it worse in some ways, but it keeps my peace, and that's what matters. It still haunts me when I think about the family I should've had, but there's nothing I can do about it."

Hearing this crushes me. My family is everything to me. The fact he doesn't have a solid family makes me want to give it to him, to *share* it with him.

"You have me and my family. My mom loves you. Beth is your best friend, and Evan... Well, Evan might kill us both when he finds out what we're doing, so we'll have to work on that." I laugh nervously.

"Yeah, I'm really not looking forward to that conversation."

We spot Kat and Maggie walking toward us bundled up in coats, hats, and scarves. "Hey, you two!" I smile and wave.

"You just missed the family reunion at the hotel." They don't look surprised by Logan's comment. Probably relieved they weren't a part of it. "Mom, Dad, and Sarah came to ambush me about my life choices," Logan says, rolling his eyes.

"I've been through that, but now they finally leave us alone." Maggie cringes.

Part of me will be relieved when we're back in the safety of Freedom Valley and away from them.

"Kat and I definitely want to join you in Freedom Valley for Christmas, if that offer still stands," Maggie says.

"Absolutely!" I say. "It's going to be great. I hope you like big family fun and tons of food."

Logan squeezes my hand and his eyes meet mine. I know this makes him happy, and I can tell he's looking forward to it, too.

"That sounds right up our alley," Maggie says with a big smile.

"I'm looking forward to it. Let's go eat. I've been craving this place," Kat says.

"Definitely hungry," I say as we walk into the deli together.

Logan seems so at ease and happy with his sister and Maggie, so unlike his rigid stance around his parents and Sarah. I'll be damned if they're ever around my kid.

The thick roast beef sandwiches on warm bread, complete with spicy mustard and crunchy pickles, are delicious. "Now I know why you love this place," I say, wiping my mouth.

"Right? I hope you'll come back in the summer because that's when it's really pretty here," Kat says, taking a sip of her drink and pushing her plate away.

"Next stop, Jean-Talon Market," Kat says.

As we walk, I hold Logan's hand, then lean in and hug him.

"What's that for?" he asks, smiling.

"I just like you. Plus, you fed me. I'm always happier when you feed me."

"That is true. You do tend to get hangry," he says, grinning.

We walk and occasionally stop to shop so I can buy a few things for Caleb and Kase. I can't wait to get home and give them a few little souvenirs.

My phone rings and I see Preston is calling. Logan looks over and nods. "Let's take that. Guys, we'll be right back."

We step into an alley and I answer on speakerphone. "Hey, Preston. Logan and I are both here. How are you?"

"Hey guys. Glad you're both here. So, unfortunately, I don't have good news. This family has a lot of connections and money. They've filed a motion in New Hampshire to move forward for full custody. He's got a date set up for mediation for the beginning of December, and we need to be ready."

My heart drops. Logan puts his arm around my waist and pulls me close. "What do we need to do?"

"Did you get married yet?"

"Not yet, but we will when we get into town. What else can we do?" I ask.

"Make it look legit. He has several private investigators looking into this. If this doesn't look legit, he will tear that apart in court. Keep your heads down, don't tell anyone that this isn't real. As far as everyone knows, you're love birds. Got it?" Preston says, then sighs.

"What?" Logan asks, pensive. His arm tightens around me.

"I wouldn't say he doesn't have a chance. He does. He has money and resources, and he's using them. I don't know these judges, so I don't know which way this could go. In the worst case, he'll get Caleb. Or, he'll get 50-50 custody and Caleb will get shipped from one side of the country to the other—which can get extremely expensive, not to mention, it would be incredibly hard on Caleb. He knows he has the upper hand on that one. In the best-case scenario, the judge gives him visitation. That's reasonable. I just want you both to be prepared."

Logan sucks in his breath. "Can we hire investigators to dig up dirt on them?"

"Already in the works, man. You know I wouldn't leave you hanging. When do you guys get into Freedom Valley?"

"Tonight, late," Logan replies.

"You haven't said much, Allie. Are you okay?" Preston asks.

"I'm just processing. I can't lose him. It's just not fair. I'm not opposed to them being in his life, but the way they're trying to take him from me when they never even wanted to know him just feels wrong." I start to cry, wiping hot tears of anger away.

"I know. But we're doing everything we can. The fact that you and Logan are now a family and can show that Caleb is well cared for will go a long way. You've done a great job,

Allie. Even if Logan's a formality, it'll help. You're a good mom. Caleb's lucky to have you," Preston says.

"Thank you," I whisper.

"Okay, I'll see you both soon. Safe travels."

We hang up and Logan pulls me close. "It's going to be okay," he says.

We head back in and say our goodbyes to Kat and Maggie. On the way to the hotel, I look out over the view of Montreal. "Thank you for showing me around your beautiful city. I love Kat and Maggie."

Logan replies, "The first of many trips, I'm sure."

This warms my heart. We've had this trip together, which has been nothing short of magical. Now, we're going back to reality, which means a job hunt, finding housing, battling a custody case, and general motherhood. I have a lot of baggage that he didn't sign up for and yet here he is, walking alongside me, helping me carry it.

When we arrive back to the hotel, we head upstairs and quickly get everything packed up to head out. Both of us are quiet, and it's obvious we've both got a lot on our mind.

"What are you thinking?"

"I'm thinking about how hot you look in those jeans." I walk over to him and kiss him deeply, moving backward until we fall back onto the bed.

"Allie, as much as I want to stay, we've got to get on the road. If we don't get up now, I'm never getting out of this bed."

I nod and sit up. "Let's get back to reality."

"New reality," he says.

I like that. New reality.

CHAPTER 16

Logan

I even got a wife
out of it.

I haven't told Allie this, but my parents and Sarah are on the warpath. They're not happy with my choices, and my dad has let me know he'll be speaking to his financial advisor about my trust. As if that would change anything, as if I want anything from them.

I don't.

I can see myself buying a home in Freedom Valley with Allie, opening a bakery together, and making a life there with her and Caleb. I'll travel for work, but we'll be together as much as we can be. It won't be perfect, but it'll be right, and we'll be happy.

Something I think about a lot is how could my parents and Sarah ever be happy? They sure seem miserable, and they want me to be miserable with them. That life is not for me; it never will be.

When we get on the road, Allie calls Evan.

"We need to talk when we get there, okay? No, everything's okay. All of the custody stuff is heating up. We're going to court with him in a few weeks. Yeah. Preston is helping." She runs her hand through her hair and leans against the window.

"Yeah, it's not going to be easy," she continues. "Yeah, I know." She sighs. "Okay, kiss him for me and tell him I'll be there to cuddle him in the morning. See you soon." She hangs up.

"They had a pretty long day and he's going to bed, so we'll see him in the morning," she says. "I've had so much fun on this trip, but I miss him."

I'm looking forward to getting settled in, but I'm also nervous. Things have changed between us and I'm wondering how her mom and Evan are going to take it. Beth didn't seem too keen on us as a fake couple when I talked to her about it. That was only a few days ago, but it feels like weeks. Now I wonder how she's going to take it when I tell her it's real.

"I didn't realize how badly I needed this trip. Just to be me, Allie, not just a mom," she says wistfully, looking over at me.

"I had fun, too. I even got a wife out of it," I deadpan as she bursts into laughter.

"And a kid," she says softly.

"And a kid." I look over at her and smile, squeezing her hand.

"What if we don't work out in real life?" she asks worriedly.

"Don't think about that. We're good, Ace." I pull her hand to my lips and kiss the back of it, reassuring her.

"Just focus on the here and now. That's all we can do, okay?"

"There's just so much going on, so much transition."

"I know, but we have to make sure we're enjoying what we have and not letting outside stressors like your ex take over."

She leans her head on my shoulder.

"It's going to be good. Tomorrow, after you get everything you need, Pete, Evan, and I are going to unload your truck into the storage unit they rented. You and I are going to the courthouse as soon as we can to get married. I think we should just go do it quietly and not make a big deal out of it. We can do a redo later if you want, but it's a small town and people will talk. So quietly, quickly, and we don't say anything. Do what Preston says."

"Okay," she says sadly. "This isn't how I pictured getting married. I thought my dad would walk me down the aisle, I'd have a big reception at the inn, dancing in the barn. And I always pictured a fall wedding. A big, white, simple cake, amazing food, and dancing."

"One thing at a time," I tell her. "Eyes on the prize. We'll be able to breathe after we get through this court stuff. Chris has to learn that he can't bully and manipulate you just because he has money. I have plenty of money to fight him, Allie. You're not in this alone, okay?"

It's funny how you can meet someone and spend time a little time with them, then not be able to imagine them not being in your life anymore. We haven't known each other for very long, but there is definitely something between us.

We get to Freedom Valley around 10 p.m. and we're past the point of exhaustion, both of us just wanting to sleep. Tomorrow is Thanksgiving and I'm hoping there's a lot of food and napping involved. I park in the back and we walk into the main building. Beth and Evan are sitting on the couch in the front area, her legs across his, head on his shoulder. They look up when we come in and jump up to greet us. It makes me so happy to see Beth happy and content like this.

"Allie," Beth breathes as she pulls her into a warm hug.

"I'm so happy to finally squeeze you in person."

Allie hugs her back and says, "Thank you for everything, Beth. And for taking such good care of Caleb this week. I'm so grateful for you both." She hugs Evan. I didn't realize how much these two look alike. Evan is tall and broad-shouldered and lean while Allie is petite with curves, but there's no denying they're related with their dark hair and piercing green eyes.

Beth pulls me into a big hug and whispers, "Thank you, Logan. I'm so glad you're here."

"Me too," I say as I hug her back.

"Thank you for all that you've done," Evan says. "I appreciate it, man."

I nod but can't help but think about what he's going to say tomorrow when we explain to him that I'm going to be his new brother-in-law. *Surprise.* We have a plot twist here. I look to Beth to see if she's told him anything and when she shakes her head slightly, I know she hasn't.

"Mom's already in bed," Evan says to Allie. "I reserved a two-room suite upstairs for you guys. We'll work things out tomorrow."

"I'm so glad to be home," Allie says. "How's Caleb adjusting?"

"He's been fine," Evan replies. "He loves playing with Kase every day. He gets tired easily so he naps every day, but other than that, he's loved playing and having a friend."

"I can't wait to see him. Where is he?"

"He's having a sleepover with Kase," Beth says. They're pretty inseparable now, like little buddies. And they even tag team up against us for snacks and staying up later."

"Alright, well we're exhausted. Tomorrow is a big day with Thanksgiving and we're getting up early to cook," Evan says. He turns down the lights, locks the front door, and heads over to his cottage with Beth.

~

Allie

Yeah, she's mine.

I still haven't figured out how to tell Caleb about Logan and me getting married. How do I explain to him that his dad, who never met him, now wants him, and oh by the way, here's a new stepdad and stepmom, too? Is this fair to do to Caleb? What if we end up divorcing and then Caleb has to deal with the aftermath? I didn't think this through and it's keeping me awake. I glance over at Logan who's out cold and snoring softly. I gently slide out of his arms. It's too soon for Caleb to see us together and I want to talk to him as best I can.

He stirs. "Where're you going?"

"I'll be back," I whisper. It's early in the morning, but I head to the bathroom then quickly dress for the day in jeans and a sweater. I open and close the door ever so quietly, then make my way down the stairs.

As I get close to the kitchen, I hear voices. Even though it's Thanksgiving, we're open and usually have guests for the holidays. My parents have always strived to make everyone feel welcomed and loved, especially those who might spend holidays alone if not for us. That's the heart of the inn right there. People generally leave feeling happier than when they arrived.

Everyone is in the kitchen but Caleb's first to spot me.

"Mommy!" he shouts. He runs over to me and jumps into my arms. "I missed you," he says as he starts to cry.

"Oh, baby, I missed you, too. So much."

His little arms wrap around my neck and he pulls me close. I breathe him in, a mix of his lavender bath soap and sweaty boy hair. I love this little boy so much. My precious boy. My whole life. My everything.

I don't let him go as I tell him, "We get to live here in New Hampshire now with our family."

"And Kase?"

"Yes, baby. And Kase." Poor Caleb has been sick most of his short life, so he's never had the chance to make a close friend. Yet another benefit of being back home.

He pulls away to ask, "Logan's here, too?" He looks behind me. "Where's Logan?"

My heart warms. He's only met Logan once and for a short time, but he already seems to like him. That's got to be a good thing. I mean, if things work out…

"He's sleeping. How have you been feeling, buddy?" I ask, smoothing his light brown hair around his face.

He looks up at me with my same green eyes and says, "Kase and I are building a fort, Momma. I want to show you."

"Let Momma get some coffee and something to eat, then you can show me everything. I can't wait to see."

My mom comes in and gives me a big hug. "Good to have you home, honey."

"Thanks, Mom."

"Where's Logan?"

"He's still asleep."

"Logan helped Momma make all the cinnamon rolls when I was sleeping," Caleb reports.

The memory warms my heart. The man had just met me and gave up an entire night's rest to help me out. He's a good man.

Evan looks at me quizzically. "Cinnamon rolls?"

"I had a cinnamon roll sale in the neighborhood to make money for the move and sold forty-three pans. On the night before we left, Logan finished baking the last six pans after I fell asleep," I admit, finally coming clean. It feels like months ago that I did that, and it's crazy to think it was just a week ago.

Evan's face softens but his eyes still search mine. "Well, it's good you can bake in bulk, because Mom tells me you're taking over the baking here now," he says, putting his arm around me.

"I have so many ideas," I tell him.

"Logan's up, by the way," he tells me. "I just saw him duck out the front for a run."

"That does not surprise me," I say. "He does that. A lot."

Beth comes in, her hair still wet. "He says he gets his best ideas on his runs. Whatever." She grins. "If you ever see me running, you should probably run, too. Something is chasing me."

"Same." I laugh. "I'd rather be doing almost anything other than running."

"If I could burn calories reading, I'd be more fit than Logan and Evan," she says.

"Right?" I say. "It's just not fair."

"How did you sleep?" she asks as she pours herself a mug of coffee.

Now is not the time to talk about all the things that kept me tossing and turning all night, so I tell a small lie. "Great, but I couldn't wait to get up. I had to get in my snuggles with Caleb this morning."

No one needs to know that I'm still working out all of the

details of our crazy life right now. We can talk about that later... Maybe.

"Thank you for taking such great care of him."

"He's such a good boy. Such a pleasure to spend time with him. And he's so cute with Kase," she tells me.

"Where is Kase?" I ask, anxious to meet my little guy's new best friend and his mom.

"He's out with Mellie," Evan tells me. "They should be back in soon."

"So what are the plans for today?" I ask as I load plates into the dishwasher.

"Logan, Pete, and I are going to unload and return your truck, and Mom and Sasha are cooking Thanksgiving dinner. Beth will watch the kids. Why don't you just get yourself settled in?"

I missed this so much. In California, everything fell on me and me alone. Having others be close enough to be there for me when I need help means so much to me. Even small things like helping me with my truck... I don't take anything for granted anymore.

"So, what's really going on with you and Logan?" Evan asks slyly. "What happened on this road trip?" A worried expression mars his face.

I know Logan told Beth about our plan because he tells her everything, but I don't know if he asked her not to tell Evan yet. I glance at Beth for a clue, and she shakes her head.

Now is as good a time as any.

"I was nervous when we left California because I didn't know him. I was naturally hesitant to make the long drive with a virtual stranger, but we actually ended up having so much fun. Logan is a really great guy. I even got to meet his family, and I really love his sister and her partner, Maggie."

His green eyes peer at me as I continue.

"So, well… I didn't plan to fall for him, but I did. So, we're going to go to the courthouse and get married soon."

Evan is quiet for a while, then says, "What did you just say?"

"It's complicated," I tell him.

"That's an understatement. You're marrying a guy you just met."

"Honey, let her explain," Beth says gently, making Evan relent.

"When I talked to Preston about the custody situation, he actually suggested it," I say, biting my lip. "He says that if I'm married and settled down with a job, it will go better for the custody dispute with Chris. So, Logan is helping me."

"I like Logan," he says cautiously, "but you have to admit, this is nuts. So just give me a minute to process what's going on here."

"What's going on is that Logan, who's a good guy, is trying to protect me and Caleb from Chris, who isn't."

"I get it, Allie. I saw firsthand what Chris did to you guys…

I can't watch you go through that again."

Before I can ask Evan what he means by that, the door opens and Logan picks the perfect opportunity to step in.

He nods at me and I stare at him, not sure what else to say but, "How was your run?"

"Good. You guys look serious. What's going on?"

"We were just discussing your impending marriage," Evan says.

Oh, crap.

Logan looks at me. "I thought we were going to tell them together."

"Hey, you told Beth." I give him a small smile. "I had to come clean. It was eating at my conscience."

Evan turns and looks at Beth. She diffuses him with a grin and a wave. "I mean... He's a catch," she tells him. "Like you're a catch." She shrugs her shoulders. "And I agree with Preston."

"Does Mom know about any of this?" Evan asks.

I cast my eyes down. "Not yet."

"This will be fun." He chugs the rest of the coffee in his mug then turns his attention to Logan. "You're really marrying my sister, who you just met last week?"

Logan inhales deeply then exhales. He reaches for my hand and says, "Yeah. I am."

Beth looks delighted. Evan shakes his head and looks up at the ceiling.

CHAPTER 18

Logan

She's definitely
a fighter.

"What are your plans for my sister?" Evan asks as we unload Allie's things from the truck. He's looking at me like he's trying to decide where to bury my body on his property if I don't say precisely what he wants to hear.

I can tell he's serious, but his voice is soft. I know he's probably just worried about Allie; I was the same way with Kat whenever she dated before Maggie. I've been expecting this conversation and I'm as prepared as I'm ever going to be. I take a deep breath and plant my hands on my hips, steadying myself for whatever Evan's reaction will be.

"You should know that I really like her, a lot. She's funny and smart, and we really connected on this trip. I want to help her." Evan doesn't intimidate me as he might some guys, but I respect him and it's important that we get along. He's Beth's future husband, and Beth is my best friend and top client. Not to mention I'm going to be *marrying* his sister within the next few days… So, yeah, his support matters.

"And you guys are really going through with this?" he asks, pushing a stack of boxes to the far corner of the storage unit.

Honestly, it started out as a sham idea, a way to help her out. But the more I get to know her, the more real it is for me. I want to be her husband and help her parent Caleb in whatever way she'll allow me to. I'm getting her a real ring. I'm all in."

I don't want to admit this to Evan, but I am scared as hell. For all of it: marriage, being a good husband while maintaining my career that is like my first love, navigating parenthood as a stepfather. At the end of the day, though, when I'm with Allie and Caleb, it feels right, and that's what matters.

"I don't know what Beth's told you about me, but I didn't grow up with much of a family. I think that's why I was so drawn to the inn when I first started coming here. I like it here. I like all of you guys, and I like feeling like I'm part of a family." I stop talking, realizing I may have said too much.

"You matter, Logan. I'm grateful for you and everything you've done for Beth over the years. You're always welcome here, brother." He picks up a few of Caleb's toys and puts them in the back of his truck to take back to the inn. "You don't have to marry my sister to have that, though."

I nod, unsure what to say. Having Evan accept me is a big deal.

We drop off the truck and as we drive back to the inn, Evan asks, "So, what's the status of the custody?"

"She has mediation with them in a week and a half. Preston says it's pretty serious and could go either way, so we have to get all of our ducks in a row and quick."

Evan's knuckles turn white as he grips the steering wheel. "You know who was in the delivery room when Caleb was born?"

"Who?" I ask.

"Me. That piece of shit left her alone that day and every other day she was out in California. He couldn't be bothered to support them financially either. And for that, I will always hate that guy. I'm so glad she's back home where she has us."

"It's weird he's doing this right when she moves," Evan says. "Where was he when Caleb was sick?"

"Preston says he's married now and they are struggling to get pregnant," I say quietly. "He's using the angle that he can provide better for Caleb than Allie can. And while that may be true at the moment, with her married to me, they will never want or need for anything. So that will hopefully rule out the provider role he's trying to play." I'm not telling him this to be a dick. I just want him to know that I'm doing everything I can to help.

"Good luck with that," Evan chuckles. "Have you met my sister? She's the most independent person on the planet. She tried to Venmo me money for her moving truck this morning. She doesn't like to take anything from anyone. It's great that you're able to make her look good on paper, but you should know she won't like taking anything from you."

"Oh, believe me, she's made that clear on our road trip. She wrote down every penny that we paid for things in her notes to try and reimburse me," I say. "Not like I'm going to let that happen, but believe me, I know."

"When she was in high school, our parents tried to buy her a used car. She left a pile of cash in their room that week. She emptied her bank account of everything she'd saved to pay them back. She doesn't like when people do things like that for her, she's always been like that."

"Why?" I ask.

"Who knows," he says. "She's just always been fiercely independent. She worked three jobs while going to college. She used to sleep in her car in between classes and shifts. Our parents got so mad when they found out, our dad made her quit one of her jobs on the spot. She was so pissed, but she did it."

"She's definitely a fighter," I say, thinking about how strong Allie is and apparently always has been.

He turns his attention back to me. "So, you can see this will be tough. Good luck, man." Evan chuckles as we pull up. "Let's go get lunch, I'm starving."

We pile out of Evan's truck and walk up the back steps. Caleb and Kase are playing on the back porch with the dogs. It's been a while since I've seen them, but they've already gotten so big. I kneel and pet them, scratching their ears as they wrestle over a toy.

"What are you guys up to?" I ask the boys as I rub one of the dog's bellies.

"We're going to build a monster truck with boxes. And we're going to hide from the goblins," Kase says.

"Goblins, huh?" I chuckle.

"Yeah. And Caleb and I are going to build swords!" He holds up his hand to high five Caleb.

"That sounds amazing. I can't wait to see it. Can I help?"

"Yes," he says. "You can be the goblin."

I laugh. "Okay, I'll be the gooey green goblin, buddy."

"Yes!" Caleb says excitedly.

Watching Caleb and Kase play, I can't help but think this is where I'm supposed to be. Hanging out with this group of people who feel more like family than my own blood. Making memories. Taking care of them. Living this dream with them.

"Did you guys have lunch?" I ask them.

"Not yet. Mom said soon."

I stand and stretch. "I'm going to help your mom, buddy."

I pat Caleb's back as I walk by. He's a good kid and I'm lucky to get to be in his life. I won't take anything for granted with this family. I know I'm with amazing people.

The kitchen has a huge island for food prep and serving and long counter space on the other three walls. Sasha has taken over one entire side preparing a turkey and a ham.

Margie comes over and hugs me. "There's my future son-in-law," she says, grinning.

I hug her back. "Hey, Margie, how are you doing?"

"I'm okay, honey," she answers. "Did you get the truck all situated?"

"We did," I say. "We came in search of lunch."

"Don't eat too much," Sasha says. "We're having our Thanksgiving feast in a few hours."

"We just need a little pre-game snack before the big feast," Evan says.

"Let me wash my hands and help you guys." I glance around the kitchen and spot Allie rolling out pie crust. I walk over and kiss her cheek. "How's it going?"

She grins and leans into me. "So good. It feels so good to be home."

"I see you told your mom?"

She shrugs. "That woman quite possibly loves you more

than me. She was over the moon. Better not break my heart or you might just break hers as well."

"Never gonna happen," I say, swiping a pumpkin scone from under a glass cookie platter. "What are you making?"

"I'm on pie duty. I'm making pecan, pumpkin, and apple. Did you see Caleb out on the porch?"

"Yeah, but they're apparently getting ready to battle goblins," I tell her. I reach into the cabinet and pull out a glass and get ice and water from the fridge.

"How can I help?"

She rubs her hands down her apron and looks around the kitchen. "Have you eaten? Let me make you guys a sandwich."

This girl. She's always thinking about everyone and taking care of them.

I circle my arms around her and hug her, leaning against her as we roll out the rest of the dough and lay them on the two pie plates.

"Let's get these pies in and then we can eat together," I say. Someone needs to make sure she eats, too.

We work together, side by side. My hand brushes hers and she glances up at me, a seductive look in her eyes. I don't know what's happened to me over the last week, but this girl gets under my skin more and more with every look. She's stolen my heart in this short amount of time, and I really can't wait to marry her.

Sasha asks me to take out the trash, so I gather up all the bags and take them out to the dumpsters behind the shed. Once I step outside, I notice a blond guy hanging out on the Adirondack chairs, watching Kase and Caleb. Something feels different about him, like he seems off somehow.

"Hi, are you a guest here?" I ask, trying to be friendly as I approach him.

He startles for a minute, then shifts his eyes. "Yeah, no. I'm just visiting."

"I asked if you're a guest here?" The hairs on my arms prickle. I'm not liking this.

He stands, shifting his feet. "I better get going."

"What's your name? I'm Logan," I say, putting out my hand, trying to keep him from running off before I can get more information on why he's sitting here watching Kase and Caleb before I destroy him.

"I'm just visiting. My parents and I are staying at Cranmore." He points at Caleb and Kase and says, "One of those boys is my son. I'm just trying to figure out which one. Neither of them would talk to me when I asked their names."

"That's probably because they've been told not to talk to strangers. And that's what you are. A stranger. You best be going," I tell him, not breaking eye contact. I have a feeling this is Chris, and there's not a chance in hell that he's going to intimidate me.

I watch as Mellie comes out of the garden shed, looking

alarmed. She pulls both boys inside. She's on her phone, I'm guessing with Evan.

I take a deep breath, thinking very carefully before I speak again. I want to go get Allie, but I don't want her around this guy either. I also don't want to say or do anything out of anger that I will regret because I will be under scrutiny in this upcoming custody case too, being Caleb's legal stepfather.

I sigh with relief as Evan comes down the back steps and walks toward us. Chris doesn't see him coming until Evan is right behind him.

"Everything okay?" he asks, his hands tucked in his pockets.

"This guy just told me that he's trying to figure out which one of these boys is *his* son."

Evan stares at him for a few moments until finally his hands come out of his pockets. He flexes his fingers, takes a deep breath, and says, "You're not a guest here. You're trespassing."

Chris glares smugly. "He's my son. I have rights."

Evan looks baffled. "You don't even know which one is your son. My sister has sent your family pictures and letters, begging you to be a part of his life. And you don't even know which child is yours?"

Chris doesn't say anything, he looks like he doesn't even know *what* to say. Evan is good.

He continues, "I don't know what's worse. That you don't know who your son is, or that you show up here sneaking around like a fucking creep around kids. Give me one reason why I shouldn't call the police right now."

"I came for what's mine," he replies, his tone cold.

Evan takes a step back. "You came for what's *yours*? Are you kidding me right now, man? You know nothing about this kid. When's his birthday?"

"Listen, I don't have to justify anything to you. I don't even know you. Who are you two to my son? Because his mother can't even take care of him. He belongs with me and my family. He's mine." His voice is inflamed and belligerent.

"Who is *we*?"

Chris's cold, angry eyes snipe at me, and I do my best to match it with calm.

"This man is Evan, Allie's brother. He was there when your son was born. He's the one who made the effort to be there and be the father figure in your son's life when you weren't. He also just saved your son's life and gave him a kidney. Me? I'm about to become your son's stepfather. So, us? We're his family. The only family he knows, because you bowed out when your son and his mother needed you." I stare at him, waiting for him to come back from this one.

"His stepdad?" he asks full of disbelief. "Allie is so… And you're so…" he says, looking confused, running his hand through his hair.

"Allie is so, what?" Evan asks, looking at him, trying to understand what he's hearing.

"Allie's a loser. She can't keep a job and doesn't take care of herself. How can she possibly take care of my kid?" he says as he holds his hands up in triumph.

"I think you need to leave," I say firmly. "Our lawyer's been in touch with your lawyer and that's how this needs to be handled. You aren't even named on the birth certificate. So go get in your car and stay away. If we see you here again, we'll be calling the police and filing a restraining order. We'll be passing all of this onto our lawyer, as well."

Evan's thunderous green eyes challenge Chris to make a move. Chris says, venomously, "I'll be back for my son. And he'll live in California, far away from this shit hole." He spits out the words as he shoves the Adirondack chair on its side and storms off toward a black Cadillac Escalade.

Mellie joins us, still holding her phone and showing us that she recorded the entire interaction. "Think we can use that in court?"

Evan nods and Mellie slides her phone back into her pocket as we watch Chris's taillights get further and further away.

"That was intense, wasn't it?" I ask.

"I'd been watching the boys, but I couldn't see the man sitting there in the chair. Then I heard you, so I came out," Mellie says. "I can't believe he just showed up here like this."

"It's pretty ballsy, that's for sure," Evan says. "How are the boys doing? Are they shaken up?"

"No, they're watching a show and playing with cars," Mellie says. "They didn't hear anything after they went in. You guys did a good job keeping that situation calm. Better than I would have done."

"I just didn't want him to see us lose it. We don't need to add to the drama," I say.

"You both did good," Evan says.

"We need to go get Allie," I say.

"Hold up, Logan." Evan walks toward me, holding out his hand. "Thank you for that," he says, nodding at me.

His approval matters to me. Not only do I want him to know I'm here for Allie, but I want him to trust me. They both matter so much to me.

"No matter what, I'm here for this family. You carry a lot of this yourself. I'm happy to help you in any way that I can," I say, shaking his hand.

"Okay, man. Let's not make it weird," he says, slapping me on the back.

We notice Beth and Allie watching out the kitchen door, grinning.

"Busted," I say playfully under my breath, thankful for a moment of levity. Until I remember that this situation is serious, and if Chris is willing to show up here unannounced and attempt to make a scene, we need to consider what else he is capable of. "She's going to be so pissed when we tell her what just happened."

"Yeah, maybe let's wait until after dinner. This is the first Thanksgiving we've all had together in years. I'm not messing this up." Evan pushes through the kitchen door and pulls Beth into his arms, kissing her deeply. He then takes a seat and says, "It smells so good in here."

Allie grins at me and whispers, "What was that?" as she nods at Evan.

I kiss her cheek and whisper, "Brotherly bonding at its finest. What are you up to?"

"Sneaking the kids some pie. Want some?" she says, smirking. "Basically, we're all just big kids sneaking pie at this point."

"Absolutely, I do," I say, leaning in and squeezing the boys' shoulders as they kick their little legs and eat at the counter.

"You know, we're not sneaking pie when we're all complicit," I say, laughing as I take a plate too.

"Dessert first... You know I like to break the rules on occasion." She laughs. "What have you boys been up to?" she asks as she arranges food on a charcuterie board.

"Just hanging out," I say, nodding to Evan. He nods back.

"Who wants to start a board game?" Mellie asks the boys. "I'll show you how to play Battleship." She heads over to the family room and pulls the game out of a cabinet.

As I look around at this family, doing all of these regular, everyday things, it hits me that this is what I've been missing in my life. I didn't have these family dinners, board games, or sneaking pie moments in my life before now.

I catch Allie looking at me, taking me in from head to toe.

Yeah, she's mine.

Allie

I love him.

After dinner, we put the kids down for the night and decide to mess around on the piano. I'm playing "All of Me" by John Legend while Evan and I are singing in harmony. His rich, bold voice pulls Beth in from the kitchen and she leans against the door frame, smiling at him. He sings the lyrics to her and she visibly swoons. He stops singing as he pulls her in for a kiss and I take over, my voice folding through the room.

Logan enters the room and stares at me with an unreadable face but his eyes are shining and locked on me.

I sing the sultry lyrics and look at him as I play, his arms folded over his chest as he leans in to listen.

As I finish playing and fold down the piano lid, Logan comes over and says, "That was beautiful, Ace."

Evan's head snaps to mine and he says, "Ace? I haven't heard you called that since Dad. Does he know he called you that?"

"When we first met, Logan randomly called me Ace. It kind of stuck, and when I told him that was always Dad's nickname for me, it felt special, and now it's sort of our thing," I say warmly, smiling at the memory.

"I love hearing it again," Evan says. "Pieces of him are still here."

"Of course they are. He built this place into what it is. He's everywhere, and I think he would be proud of all of us."

"Yeah, he would," Evan says quietly.

Logan and I settle in on the big comfy sectional sofa in front of the huge stone fireplace where Evan has a fire going. Beth is curled up across from us and Evan sits down next to her.

Mom carries a tray of cider in. "Thanks, Mom," I say, taking a steaming mug for us both.

"Evan gathered us here because he wants to talk to us. So, what's this about?" Beth asks, taking a mug and sipping it.

"I'm just going to cut to the chase here," Evan says. "So, earlier today, Logan and I caught Chris sneaking around outside, watching Kase and Caleb play."

My breath catches in my throat. "What? He's *here*? Why didn't you tell me?" I start to panic, my stomach clenching tight.

Logan pulls me close. "It's okay. He didn't even know which one of the boys was Caleb. It was pathetic."

"Logan and I told him we'd handle everything through the lawyer and sent him on his way. Mellie actually recorded the majority of the interaction on her phone. We're going to send it to Preston tomorrow."

"But he's *here*. He's in Freedom Valley. He came all the way here on Thanksgiving, and he tried to see my son. Where is he now?"

"The Cranmore," Evan says, murmuring over a sip of his mug.

"Ugh," I say with disgust. "Of course he's staying at Cranmore."

"Do you have that video of Chris? I think we all need to see his ugly mug so we can make sure we don't find him creeping around here again. I want Pete, Sasha, Mellie, and all of us to see it so we know," Mom suggests.

Evan nods. "Good idea."

Beth holds up her hand, looking mad. "Okay, rewind. He didn't even know which kid was his son? Kase and Caleb are not even the same age, and they look nothing alike. What the actual hell?" Anger lights my eyes.

"I would give *anything* to hold my Emmie. His kid is here,

and he doesn't even recognize him. That is devastating." Beth's husband and baby were killed in a drunk driving accident six years ago and my heart breaks for her. She's been through a lot.

"He's had almost four years to get to know Caleb. And he couldn't be bothered when his boy was sick and needed a transplant. He couldn't even be bothered!" Beth is shaking now. "So, no, he doesn't get to swoop in now and be a giant dick and just take him. Nope."

Evan puts his arm around her and pulls her close. "I know, baby, I know."

Hot tears stream down my face out of anger, and if I'm being honest, partly from relief. I'm trying to picture myself out in California, sitting in my trailer alone, trying to fight off Chris on my own. Now? I look at the family around me. My mom, Beth who is crying and mad for me, my brother who has always had my back, even from across the country. All rallying around me during this. And Logan holding me. I don't know exactly how all this will work, but I know he's here, and I feel better—stronger—when he's with me.

We sit for a while and then I take a deep breath. "I'm just exhausted. I think I'm going to go to bed." I stand up and Logan follows.

"Good night, everyone. Happy Thanksgiving," he says.

"Happy Thanksgiving," Beth says, weaving her fingers through Evan's, leaning onto his shoulder.

I make my way up the stairs, my legs feeling heavier than they should, making the steps hard to climb. We make it to the top and I quietly tiptoe into Caleb's room. I pull his quilt up around him then carefully step out of the room, closing the door softly behind me.

I walk into our room and sit on the edge of the bed. Logan sits next to me and puts his arms around me.

"I can't lose him, Logan. I can't. I love him so much. I begged the Carsons to be a part of his life for years. I've been nice, but I'm done now. I'm done playing nice," I say.

Logan nods. "We're going to fight this, and I'm in this with you. You're not alone. You have all of us."

"Thank you," I whisper. "I have no idea what I did to deserve you, but I'm so grateful for you. And insanely happy you're here with me," I say sincerely.

"Insanely, huh?" he says, pulling me close and kissing me softly.

"Yeah," I whisper, leaning into him. "I'm tired, Logan. So tired of fighting for someone who wouldn't fight for me. Fighting now for what's rightfully mine."

"I know. Let's get some sleep. Tomorrow is a fresh day."

I shower and get ready for bed. When I sneak in under the covers, Logan's already sleeping softly but stirs and pulls me into his chest.

I feel safe with Logan, and that's when I realize...

I love him.

The next morning, I wake up to Caleb dive-bombing into our bed.

"Wake up, Mom!" Caleb says, curling up next to me.

"Buddy, what time is it?" I ask, reaching for my phone. 7:53. I snuggle back under the covers, folding Caleb in, too.

"Are you hungry, buddy?" I ask.

"Nope, Logan fed us," Caleb says.

"Where is Logan?" I mumble.

"He went running," he says. "Can Logan be my dad now?"

I freeze, not knowing what to say. "I don't know, buddy." It just seems like the only answer I have at this time before my body is appropriately caffeinated.

My heart feels so full right now that I don't want this moment to end, but I've always been so independent and okay with being on my own. I worry about how things will change now that Logan is part of our new dynamic here.

"Do you want Logan to be your dad?" I ask, lazily running my fingers through his hair.

"Yes. Kase wants him to be his dad, too," he says. "We can be brothers."

My heart melts, and I smile sadly. These boys are so sweet. Both were dealt a hard hand of cards, but it brings me joy to know they are surrounded by so much love at the inn.

Caleb jumps up and bounds out of the room, full of way more energy than I currently have.

"I heard that." Logan leans against the doorway.

"You did? Think you can handle Mellie, too?" I tease.

"Pfft, I can barely handle you, Ace," he teases. When I throw a pillow at him, he adds, "Kidding. How did you sleep?" he asks as he lays the pillow next to me and leans in to kiss me.

"Pretty well," I tell him.

"I got the boys their breakfast."

"Thank you," I say as I turn and kiss him again.

Caleb comes back in. "Eeewwww, they're kissing!" he yells out to Kase and runs back.

Logan and I burst into laughter and I sit up in bed. "I'm going to get us coffee. I'll be right back," I tell him.

I slide my feet onto the floor and pad downstairs to the kitchen. I make a fresh pot of coffee and pour two mugs, then splash some cream into both. I carry them back to the bedroom.

Logan's sitting up, his back against the headboard, the blankets gathered around his waist, he reaches for the mug and smiles, "Thanks, babe," he says.

"I like when you call me, babe," I say, sliding into the bed next to him. "What are your plans for the day?" I ask, sipping my coffee and looking over at him.

"Going to hole up in your mom's cottage with my laptop

to work for a while. I'm also going to be checking in with Preston to tell him everything that happened yesterday with Chris showing up unannounced."

"Maybe I should call Preston about that?" I suggest.

"If you want, but I need to talk to him about a contract for work, so I can or you can, doesn't matter."

I nod. "Okay, you can if you want. I'm going to move us back to Mom's cottage and get us settled in. I need to find a place to rent here soon, and it's time to get my bakery business figured out with Evan since I'll be using the inn."

"For *us* to rent," he reminds me, sipping his coffee and peering over at me.

"Okay," I say, smiling.

"Now, how can I help?" he asks.

"If you can, just take our bags back when you go back to the cottage. I'm going to make up our beds and get us situated."

He looks at me and says, "I meant with the bakery and the house. What if I rent a place nearby for us so we can get really settled and make a home? Might look better for the court situation?"

"I thought about that, but I really want to be at the inn right now, especially through the holidays. It feels so magical here for Christmas. I really want Caleb to feel that." I look at him wistfully.

"Yeah, I get that, but I can't keep mooching a room off

your family."

"Okay, we can look," I tell him. "That gives me some time to save up money."

Logan rolls his eyes, smiling, "Allie. I am covering the housing. We'll work it out. Okay?"

I don't want him to think of me and Caleb as burdens or that I am just with him for support. I don't want to start a relationship off on that foot. It's important to me that he sees I can pull my share. It doesn't seem to matter to him, but it matters to me that I contribute.

"We'll see," I say.

Later that night, we all clean up the kitchen together after dinner. I grab Logan's hand, telling him, "Come for a walk with me."

It started snowing earlier and it's beautiful out. I slip my gloved hand into his. We walk without saying anything until he asks, "Allie, are you really going to marry me on Monday?"

"I am. Are you really going to marry *me* on Monday?" I ask, throwing the question right back at him as I kick a pebble on the dirt road, damp with snow.

"Yes," he says, pulling me closer and kissing me, my lips on his in the cold night air.

We come across a field and stop. "What is this place?" he

asks. "It's really cool here."

"This is the old Donegal Farm. It's actually for sale. Evan and my mom have talked about buying it because it borders the inn's property. He wants to put a hobby farm here with gardens, maybe add a farm-to-table restaurant in the old barn. Apparently Mellie is a huge gardener and she grows all kinds of things in the small garden at the back of the inn. It's just an idea at this point, they haven't actually done anything with it yet. I don't think Evan has the money for it yet."

I could see this being an extension of the inn and adding to the property. A perfect place for Caleb and me. *And Logan.* Just walking the grounds, it feels like it should be ours.

I stop. "Can I tell you something?"

"Of course."

"I don't want you to go through with this unless you're positive you're comfortable with it. Really think it through, and know that I'll be okay whatever you decide. Marriage is a big deal, and I don't want it to change things between us. Okay? I like us."

"I like us, too."

CHAPTER 20

Logan

We have a problem.

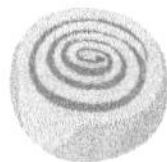

On Monday morning, Allie and I get ready and head to the courthouse at 10 a.m. Beth and Evan come with us to be our witnesses, and we're all quiet on the way there. Evan glances at us in the rearview mirror a few times, looking worried.

Beth turns around and says, "We're going to be in-laws. Our kids will be your nieces and nephews."

"Is there something I should know?" Evan asks, laughing looking over at her.

She grins and holds his hand across the console. "Yes, let's get to work on that."

Evan gives her a smoldering look and raises an eyebrow in agreement.

"Eww, get a room," Allie teases playfully, shoving his shoulder.

"You're getting married before we are, and we've known each other longer. Does anyone else find this weird?" Evan asks.

"It's only weird when you make it weird," Allie says, reaching over to squeeze my thigh. Heat and electric currents race through my body when she touches me. We've been inseparable since we've gotten back, constantly sneaking away to be alone together. We're like teenagers hiding our relationship from our parents—we can't get enough of each other.

"Nah, it makes sense when it's right," Beth says, getting out of the truck and throwing her purse over her shoulder.

We enter the courthouse, an old stone building with a faded "Freedom Valley" sign set in stone on the façade. An older woman at the front desk glances up from her computer as we approach.

"So, this is just the official wedding, but we get to have a big reception party with Mom and everyone else at some point in the future, right?" Evan asks.

"Yes," I say as I look over at Allie. She squeezes my hand and pulls me closer.

I greet the woman and tell her that we're here for a

marriage license and to do a justice of the peace wedding.

"Can we do that today?" I ask.

"Allie May. You've grown!" she says, ignoring me because she's so excited to see Allie. She circles the desk to wrap Allie in a big hug.

"Mrs. Matheson, what're you doing here? Did you stop teaching?"

"I retired from teaching, honey. I work here part-time now. You're getting married?" she exclaims, her hands on her hips, looking from Allie and back to me.

"Yes, this is my fiancé, Logan," Allie says, threading her arm through mine.

"Well, alright then. The judge has an opening at eleven. Let's get your license filled out." She hands us each a clipboard. This feels so impersonal. I look at Allie as she busily fills in the information on her clipboard. We switch and sign, and then Beth and Evan sign as our witnesses.

Allie looks down as we sit on the bench and wait for the judge.

"Having second thoughts?" I whisper. Evan shoots a concerned gaze.

"No, this just feels so *impersonal.*"

"I just had the same thought," I murmur.

Evan puts an arm around her and pulls her close. "We can still have that big fall wedding you want next year. You plan it and we'll do it."

Allie nods. "Yeah, that sounds good," she says, but the

look she gives me is skeptical, as if she's wondering if we'll still be together by then. God, I hope that's not what she's thinking.

I kiss her cheek and pull her close. "I'm going to make you happy," I promise. I whisper in her ear, "It'll be okay."

"The future Mr. and Mrs. Nolan?" Mrs. Matheson calls out. As we walk up, she says, "Ready?"

We nod and join the judge at the front of the courtroom. Beth takes pictures with her phone while Evan stands next to me, still looking like he's not quite sure about all of this.

So many thoughts race through my head. Mostly I'm trying to convince myself that this is the right move, that this is all going to be okay. I know doing this is huge—I'm helping her, I'm becoming a husband, and I'm becoming a *father*. The two things that terrify me the most.

The "ceremony" is quick and before I know it, we are saying our vows and I'm kissing her.

Beth is ecstatic, whistling and clapping, before she kisses Evan and pulls him close. "I can't wait to marry the shit out of you," she says to him as she kisses him again.

"Hey, you two could grab a marriage, too? Maybe they have a BOGO deal?" I joke as Evan glares at me.

"They're a mess," Allie says, shaking her head. "Well, husband, should we go home and celebrate?"

Back in the truck, Evan's phone rings and he answers. "Hey, Mom. Yeah, they did it. They're married. Wait, what?

Okay, we'll be right there. Don't let them in and put the boys upstairs."

He looks at us as he backs up the car. "We have a problem," he says. "Caleb's dad and grandparents are now at the inn, demanding to see Caleb."

CHAPTER 21

Allie

I can't.

I call Preston immediately to explain what's going on and get his advice on what we should do. He tells me that he's heading over and he will handle it when he gets there. It's reassuring that I don't have to deal with this on my own anymore, but I still start to cry. Logan squeezes my shoulder, telling me he's there and that it's going to be okay.

When we pull up to the inn, Chris and his parents are sitting in their Escalade out front. They get out when they see us.

Chris's parents are dressed nicely and his mom is carrying

an expensive handbag. Her hair is dark and styled in a perfect bob; not a hair out of place. She walks up to me with an attitude.

"Finally. You kept us waiting long enough. I want my grandson. Now." She snaps her fingers like she's willing him to appear before her.

"Who are you?" I say, addressing her and the older man with a salt-and-pepper comb-over standing next to her. Chris slinks back with a thin blonde wearing a coat with a belt. She looks embarrassed and looks away.

"You know damn well who I am. And I'm tired of you keeping my grandson from us."

"We've never formally met. And did you not return all of the letters and pictures I sent? Did you not get the text messages that I sent? The pleas when I needed you all to get tested because your grandson needed a kidney and almost died? Because he has a hereditary kidney disease caused by a gene that your family carries?" I cross my arms in front of me and wait for an answer. I am freaking pissed right now. Who does she think she is?

"He's a Carson, and I want him where he belongs," she says, ignoring my challenge. "You can't even take care of him. You don't have a job and you live in a motel," she says, waving her arm at the inn.

Logan steps forward. "You all need to get in your vehicle and leave. Now." His tone is so severe it even gives me chills.

Thankfully, Preston pulls up just that minute in his white Volvo SUV, with a police cruiser trailing behind him.

"You called the police?" Chris yells at me. "Why did you do that? You are even stupider than I thought, Allie." He shakes his head in disgust.

Preston comes forward. "I'm Mr. and Mrs. Nolan's, attorney. You are on private property and you're trespassing. You need to leave immediately. This is the second time you've trespassed and attempted to intimidate my client and her family. We'll also be filing restraining orders against this entire party this afternoon."

Sheriff Maxwell stands next to him, gripping his vest in his hands and looking perplexed. Chris's mom ignores Logan and turns to the officer. "Excuse me, sir, we just need our grandson and we'll be on our way."

His eyes narrow at her. "You'd best be on your way *now*, ma'am. You've been asked to leave," he says, unflinching. "This here's a matter of the courts."

I look up at the side of the SUV and notice Mellie is there with her phone tilted sideways, filming the whole thing.

"You *married* her?" Chris smirks in disgust at Logan. "Big mistake, buddy. She's trash. Not the type of girl you marry."

Logan's body jerks but he doesn't move, which makes me realize he must know Mellie is recording as well.

"Get on now." Sheriff Maxwell jerks his thumb over his shoulder. "And don't come back here again, or I *will* arrest you for trespassing."

"We're not done. We'll see you in court," Chris's mother says. "And we'll be taking our grandson home."

I say nothing. I know how to play this game. I'll help them make their bed by saying nothing, and then I'll win. I'm shook up, but I'm also running on a high that Logan just married me. Today is our special day.

They pile into their Escalade and pull out, spraying gravel everywhere, and Chris flips us off from the back window. Nice. Wow. What is he, five?

Preston nods at Mellie. She heads over to us.

"You get all that?" he asks her. She nods.

"Where's Caleb?" I ask her.

"Inside with your mom and Kase, playing Legos. She's keeping them distracted. I'm going to text her that they can come out now. Oh, and congratulations," she says, smiling while her fingers fly over her phone as she sends a text to my mom.

"Thanks," I say. "I'll be right back." I need to see for myself that Caleb is okay. I'm so shaken up and upset.

Mom brings the boys downstairs as I come in. "Hey guys, how's it going?" I say, ruffling Caleb's hair and leaning down to pull both into a hug.

"They're gone?" Mom asks.

"They're unbelievable, Mom." My chest feels full and anxious as I pace the room.

"We won't let them get near him," she reassures me.

"They are getting closer and closer," I say. "I don't like this. I just hope court goes the way we want it to go."

"How was the wedding?" she asks. I catch a hint of sadness in her smile.

"It was okay. Just a part of our plan. But we're still doing a real wedding this fall, Mom. I want Evan to walk me down the aisle. I need you there with me for the real thing."

"Okay, let's plan it," she says, smiling. "It'll be okay, honey," she says, running her hand through my hair.

The next morning we're still all on edge because of the Carson invasion, but we're trying our best to be normal. Logan wants us to go to Boston with him for a few days, and while he has work meetings, I'm going to take Caleb to the transplant center to do a check-in and establish care with his new team.

We borrow Beth's SUV because Logan's car is in Boston, and Logan is so cute trying to figure out how to install Caleb's booster seat in the back.

"Alright, buddy. Did you go potty? I want you to go potty before we go. Run inside and go real quick, okay?" he says.

The two-and-a-half-hour ride from Freedom Valley to Boston goes by fast.

Logan reaches over and squeezes my hand while he drives. I squeeze it back, wanting to pinch myself. Is this real? Is he real? Could we be a real family like this?

Doubt starts to creep in and I push it away. No. Not today. Today I'm going to pretend this is real and stay in the moment.

"Look at us, always in a vehicle together," I joke.

"Yep, feels right. Maybe we should quit everything and just travel the country in an R.V.," he says.

"I would actually do that," I say.

"Oh, yeah?" he asks.

"It would be a great adventure."

Before long, we pull into his driveway. His house is not what I imagined. I thought he'd have a modern, flashy home. This is more like a family home, even though it's insanely beautiful and expensive looking. It looks like a great place to raise children.

"Just how rich are you?" I whisper.

"It's just money, Ace. It's not a big deal. Come on, let me show you the house," he says proudly. He grabs mine and Caleb's hands and leads us inside.

The décor is clean, cozy, and comfortable, with white walls and trim and light wood floors. It's an open concept space, so I can see the white kitchen in the back of the house looking out over the backyard. It has butcher block counters and a huge fall bouquet of flowers on the center island. Caleb runs off to explore. Logan proudly escorts me around the first floor and to his office at the front of the house.

"Is that where you'll work?" I ask.

"When I'm here. I can work from anywhere, though," he says. "Boston was just where my home base was. Now it's Freedom Valley," he squeezes my hand and pulls me closer to him. "With my wife," he adds.

I like the way it sounds when he says those words. "It's really nice here. But can I decorate for you? Add some cozy touches?"

"You can do whatever you want to it, Ace. It's all yours."

All mine. A home for Caleb and me. Not in Freedom Valley, but home is where family is. I learned that out in California. I missed home. I want a home with the people I love. I want this.

He pulls me in and murmurs in my ear, "Let's go see the upstairs." Then to Caleb, he says, "Come on, buddy. Let's go see your new room."

"There's no toys here," Caleb says, disappointed. "Where are all your toys, Logan?"

"We'll have to buy some, buddy," he says, pulling him up into his arms as we head up the stairs. "Can you help me pick out some cool ones?"

"Yes. You need dinosaurs and Legos," Caleb says, looking quite serious and businesslike.

"We can do that." Logan laughs.

The huge master bedroom is contemporary, in dark and lighter grays. A king-sized bed with a big black headboard is set against one wall. His closet is the size of our bedroom in my mom's cottage, and it's meticulously organized by color. He has over a dozen pairs of expensive-looking leather shoes, belts, suits, you name it.

An entire side of the closet is empty, and he tells me that's my side. *My side.* Pray tell, what does this man think I'm going to put in there? My Walmart shirts and thrift store jeans that could take up maybe a fraction of that side? We live on different planets. I look around and my stomach sinks.

I don't belong here.

Logan's phone rings and he answers it. "Nolan," I hear him say as he heads down the hall.

I enter the room next to the master bedroom. It has a full-sized bed decorated in lighter, neutral tones. Probably the guest room. I set Caleb's bag down and plug in his tablet to charge.

Caleb dumps out its contents of cars, trucks, and Legos.

"Hey, buddy, do you want to rest a little before your appointment? I want you to drink your water, too." I know he's going to have bloodwork done, which he's actually used to by now, but I want him to be well hydrated.

I get him settled into the guest bed with his tablet and I head down to what is essentially a dream kitchen. The huge island in the middle with wicker pendant lights is my favorite. I run my fingers over the butcher block and itch to pull out supplies and bake something delicious in here. I open the pantry. Not much food in there, just a few basic items. I look around at his white dishes and mugs and wonder if he picked any of this out or if he had help.

I pour two glasses of water and carry them to Logan's office, handing him one.

"Thanks, babe. Did you get settled?"

"I did. Caleb's resting a little. We still have about an hour before his appointment." I take in his wall-to-wall bookshelves, filled with books. There's a whole shelf of Beth's books.

"Wow, this is a lot of books," I say.

"I had my New York apartment packed up and brought here. I'm selling my other places, actually. Everything will be here and in New Hampshire. Speaking of, I want you to have this." He pulls a card out of his wallet and slides it across the desk. It's a Visa card with my new name on it.

Allison Nolan.

My heart stirs just seeing the name. *I am his wife.* This will probably never get old.

I pull my hand back. "I don't—"

"Allie, I'm going to need your help sometimes with ordering things. This is our household account, okay?"

"I'm going to use my own money for Caleb..."

"Whatever you feel comfortable with."

"I guess." I reluctantly slide the card into my pocket, not planning to ever use it. I calculate how many pans of cinnamon rolls I'd need to sell to pay the mortgage on this place. A lot.

Logan lets out a deep sigh and leans back in his chair. He yawns.

"Do you need a nap, too?" I ask.

"With you? Sure," he says with a slight wicked grin.

I laugh and playfully swat his arm. "How's work? You look a little stressed."

"It's just busy right now, but it's fine. I have a few meetings later on today and tomorrow before we head back. Speaking of, I won't be here for dinner tonight. Will you and Caleb be okay? I can order in for you guys, or I also have some groceries being delivered."

"We'll be fine," I say. "I brought my laptop and I'm going to start working on my business plan for the bakery. I really want to do this, Logan."

"You already know I think it's a great idea, and I will help in any way. You know that." He crosses his muscular biceps behind his head. He's so freaking fine.

"I can think of a few ways you can help me," I murmur under my breath.

"Oh, yeah?" His eyes darken and his mouth turns up a little. "Well, we are technically on our honeymoon. We just have to make sure Caleb is asleep. The master bedroom door locks." He winks.

"That shower upstairs? Holy shit, Logan. Have you seen that shower?" I say, excitedly.

"I'm aware. I've showered in there."

"Well, that shower is just *screaming* for us to have shower sex in it. Don't you agree?"

His mouth turns up on one side, his eyes not leaving mine. "Yes, it is."

The doorbell rings and rudely interrupts us, but he still doesn't stop fucking me with his eyes across the desk.

"Should I... get the groceries?" I ask, looking out toward the door.

Logan swings his legs down off the desk and shakes his head, mumbling something about the shower as he heads to the front porch. He grabs the bags and carries them back toward the kitchen.

I follow him and put away everything with him, our fingers brushing each other a few times and sending a zing through my body. Damn, I want him so bad. He shuts the fridge and spins around, grabbing me and scooping me up before putting me on the counter. He kisses me deeply as he pulls me against him.

"Momma," Caleb says from upstairs.

"Yeah, baby," I say, scooting down from the counter.

"Can I have a snack?" he says, wiping his eyes.

"Let's get you lunch before we go to the doctor, okay?"

Logan smiles at us.

"What?" I ask.

"Nothing, I just love having you both here. Feels more like a home."

Logan takes a shower, unfortunately by himself, and gets dressed while I get Caleb fed and ready for his appointment. I walk in as he's buttoning up his pants and his dress shirt hangs open. He leans down to put his socks on and looks up at me, his eyes darkening again.

"Tonight we have shower sex," he murmurs as he slowly buttons his dress shirt one by one, not breaking eye contact with me.

I stare at him. "Oh, yeah?"

"Yeah," he says matter-of-factly. "This bed? It's new. I think it needs to be broken in, too."

"Sounds good to me. When will you be home?"

"I have meetings and then a work dinner that should be over around eight or nine. I'll come straight home after that."

Holy shit. I'm in trouble.

He slides into his jacket. "I ordered a car to take you to Caleb's appointment. Charles will wait for you while you're in the hospital and bring you back, okay?"

"I can just drive Beth's car," I protest.

"Yeah, but this is quicker. It'll be rush hour and you can just focus on Caleb. I also ordered you guys dinner and it'll be here at six. I want you to use that card to order Caleb some things to make his room more comfortable for him, toys and stuff."

He wants to make this a home for us and for us to be here, in his space. My heart swells, but still, I have to keep boundaries.

"Thank you for offering, but he has plenty of toys. I do appreciate the dinner and ride, though."

Logan closes the space between us and kisses my forehead. "Let me take care of you guys."

I know I should be infuriated. I am used to taking care of us on my own, but I have to admit it does feel good to have a partner to share life with, to not have to do all of the mundane daily tasks by myself anymore. I can't remember the last time I felt lonely since Logan's been in my life. Now that he's here, I can't imagine him not being a part of our lives.

Finally, he looks at me and says, "Let me be a husband and dad."

I can't argue with him. We are married. Ordering us a ride and dinner is what a normal husband and dad would do. But I won't be using his card for anything unnecessary.

He slides his wallet and phone into the pocket of his dark navy suit. He's so hot it hurts my eyes to look.

"What?" he asks, his eyes moving over me appreciatively.

"Nothing, you're just so damn hot. I was just thinking of some ways to cool you down later."

He walks over and leans over the bed, pulling me up to him and kissing me deeply, leaving me wanting to unbutton those buttons one by one.

He pulls back. "I gotta go. To be continued…"

I immediately love the Boston transplant center and their whole team, and I already feel like this might be an even better fit than San Diego. I'm pleased. They said everything is looking great for Caleb. That he's doing well and we'll need to come back in about a month for another follow-up.

Charles drops us off and I let us in with the key Logan gave me. I get Caleb set up in the living room and put on a show on Disney Plus as we wait for dinner to arrive. When the doorbell rings, I'm surprised to find it's not our dinner delivery but a man in a suit.

Logan's father.

My stomach feels sick standing here with him. His fake smile doesn't reach his eyes, ones that are the same blue green as Logan's, only his are dark and irritated. I want to slam the door and lock it, but I'm frozen in apprehension.

"Logan's not here. Was he expecting you?"

"No, he isn't, I'm afraid. I'm here to talk to you, if I could just have a minute of your time?"

I don't want to let him in, but I do. My first mistake. He scans the house, as if he's never been here before, which doesn't surprise me.

"Quaint," he remarks, looking unimpressed.

Quaint. This is not quaint. This house is amazing. Where the hell does this guy live if this place is considered quant?

"What can I do for you, Mr. Nolan?" I ask firmly, folding my arms in front of me.

"Well, I think we're past formalities, don't you, Allison? You're Mrs. Nolan now, and I think we can both just go with first names, don't you?" He forces a fake smile.

Just then, he realizes Caleb is in the corner on a couch. Luckily, we're across the room in the foyer and Caleb doesn't seem to hear us or be paying attention. Our trip to the hospital wore him out and he's on the verge of falling asleep.

"So this is the child you're in a custody dispute over? The one you needed to trick my son into a fake marriage for?" I must have looked surprised because he says, "Yeah, I know all about that, Allison."

I don't bother to correct him on my name, because my friends and family call me Allie, and this man is neither as far as I'm concerned.

How does he know this? Why is he here talking about my child? I feel like I am going to throw up, but I pull it together and put my best poker face on even though I'm crumbling on the inside.

"What do you want?" I ask him sharply, cutting to the chase. He's brought my kid into this now and I'm done with his shit.

"Direct, I see. I can appreciate that," he says. "I'll be direct myself. I want you to get an annulment and end this now."

"And why would you even care?"

"Because if you don't, I'm going to terminate my son's thirty-five-million-dollar trust fund and his shares in our family's company. He has everything to lose. He's throwing away his future, and you are the cause of that. I want you out," he says bitterly, trying to intimidate me with a glare.

"Don't you want him to be happy? Is money all that matters to you?"

"How much will it take to make you go away?" he asks. "What's your number?"

"I don't have a number. Because, unlike you, I don't need money to be happy. I have my family. And you clearly have no idea what that must feel like, because you don't seem to have real relationships with anyone in your family."

I must have struck a nerve because his jaw that matches Logan's twitches. I recognize it because Logan does the same thing when he's feeling vulnerable.

"Everyone has a number."

"Why are you like this?" I ask, not backing down. "Why do

you treat him like crap?"

"He's a Nolan. He has family obligations," he says, his gaze flickering to Caleb and back to me.

"We're his family now."

"Playing house is over. Go back to your little family inn. Leave my son alone. End this, or you will cause him to lose everything."

"I don't appreciate being threatened."

"No? I don't appreciate you near my son. So, either you end this, or I will make sure your ex wins custody."

"I think you should go now." I show no emotion as I open the front door. I just stare past him, waiting for him to leave.

"Think about what you're doing to your son," he says. "Don't be selfish."

I shut the door behind him and turn the lock. I lean against the door and take a deep breath to gain my composure as I blink back my tears. I knew this was too good to be true. People like Logan don't happen to people like me.

I don't know if he's bluffing or not, but a powerful and spiteful man like that could destroy us. He could destroy anyone. I have had to fight like hell to show Logan that he is worthy of being someone's husband and father because this man wrecked that for him.

What if he loses everything for me and Caleb? How can I do that to him?

I can't.

CHAPTER 22

Logan

What are you going
to do about it?

I finally let myself in at 9:15 p.m. and don't say anything in case Allie's trying to get Caleb down for bed. I take off my jacket and lay it on the back of the chair on the kitchen island. I head up the stairs and notice it's dark. I turn on the bedroom light, starting to get worried. I head back downstairs and check my office, finding a note on my desk.

Logan,

I am so sorry. It's not going to work. There's too much at stake here for both of us. Family is everything to me, and if we're together, we both lose everything. I'm going home. I'm so sorry. Please don't hate me. You are too good for us and we don't deserve you. I know you'll find someone for you that can give you more than what I can.

Love,

Allie

I can't even breathe I'm so upset. What the hell does this even mean? It's late and she left? Are they safe? I pull my phone out of my pocket and call her; it goes straight to voicemail. I leave a message, "Allie, it's me. Call me back. I need to know that you're both okay."

I call Beth and wait for her to pick up. Hers also goes to voicemail, so I text her.

Me: Call me back ASAP. Emergency.

I pace across my living room. What happened in the past few hours that would make her take off like this?

I go upstairs and start packing. I'm going back to New Hampshire. She's not giving up on us like this.

Beth calls me back. "Is she there?" I ask without even saying hello.

"No, but she's coming. What happened, Logan?"

"I don't know. It was fine. She was going to her appointment with Caleb and we made plans to hang out when I got home from work tonight. Then when I got home, they were gone. What did she say?"

"She told Evan she was heading home tonight and would be in around eleven. Evan said she sounded okay to drive, but she said she was upset about something and would talk to us about it when she got here."

"Something happened." I pace the living room. "I'm coming now. I have to fix this."

"Why don't you wait a day? Let's see what happens. Maybe she needs to get her bearings. Let us talk to her and then you can decide tomorrow."

"I don't like this, Beth."

"I know. Maybe you both just need a break. A lot has happened very quickly."

"Yeah, we're *married.* She shouldn't just take off like this. Did something happen with Chris?"

"Not that I'm aware of, but I'm assuming she'll tell us when she gets here."

"Yeah, well it would be nice if she'd have told me. Her *husband.*"

"I'm sorry. We'll find out what's going on."

"Okay, I'll call you in the morning," I say reluctantly. "Thank you."

"Get some sleep. It'll be okay. Evan and I will talk to her."

"Night," I mumble while hanging up the phone. I stick my phone on the charger and pack my bag.

I take a shower to wash off the stress of the evening, but it takes me back to how Allie was flirting with me just a few hours ago about being in the shower and now she's gone.

What the hell happened?

I wake up to no messages from Allie and one from Evan.

Evan: They made it safe. Call me when you get up.

"Are they okay?" I ask when he answers.

"Yeah, they're okay. But we have some things to talk about. Have you talked to Preston?"

"No. Why? What happened?" I head downstairs and start the coffee. I slept like shit. I couldn't stop thinking about what I did to make her leave like that.

"Well, apparently Chris and his family aren't as wealthy as we thought. Mostly, they're all talk. But Preston has a private investigator on them and their finances. Apparently, a very large donation was given to them to fight their child custody battle. Any idea about that?" he asks.

All of a sudden, I feel sucker-punched. My fucking father. He's gone too far.

"Are you kidding me?" I yell.

"Yeah, that was pretty much my reaction, too," Evan says. "She didn't even know that part until she got here last night.

She was just pissed off about his visit."

"Visit?"

"Apparently your dad came to your house last night and told her that if she stays married to you that he would cut you off completely and that she will be the cause of you losing everything. She felt awful and said she didn't want to be the cause of you losing your inheritance, so she packed up and came home."

What the actual fuck? My father was here?

"You've got to be kidding me."

"Take a deep breath, they're okay," Evan says reassuringly. "They're sleeping. Allie just looks... sad, to be honest. I think she really loves you, Logan."

"I love her, too," I say without hesitating. "I love them both. They mean everything to me now. I couldn't sleep last night without them here."

Evan takes a deep breath. "Okay, one thing at a time. Let's give her a few days. I have a feeling this is going to work out, but she's got a lot on her plate and you both rushed into this really fast. A lot is at stake here for both of you."

"You're probably right."

"There's more, Logan," Evan says quietly.

"What?" I ask, defeated, but what could be worse? My father is funding the person trying to destroy us. What could possibly be worse?

"Preston said they have a fifty-fifty shot of getting Caleb.

Your father is willing to testify in court against Allie, saying that your marriage is fake."

My head is spinning, wondering how he could possibly know that. I know Kat and Maggie wouldn't have told him, so Sarah must be grasping at straws from our encounter with her. I feel so defeated.

"I just wanted to help her."

"I know. Your dad is a real piece of shit, Logan. He's really doing my family dirty right now." Evan sounds pissed off and I don't blame him.

"Trust me, I know. He's done this to me my entire life. He's tried to sabotage me anytime I am not falling in line with whatever he wants me to do."

"Allie said if she doesn't divorce you, you'll lose your thirty-five-million-dollar trust fund. That's a lot, Logan."

"That doesn't matter to me," I say, shaking my head. "I haven't taken any money from my dad since college. I don't care about that money. I support myself just fine."

"I figured. I'm just telling you what your father said to Allie," Evan says. "She feels terrible."

"He's not my family. Allie, Caleb, and you all are my family now," I say adamantly. "Family doesn't treat people like this."

"What are you going to do about it?" Evan asks.

"I'll give her until tomorrow, but I'm coming back the day after. I have to try, Evan. I have to fight for them."

We hang up and I go for a five-mile run around Boston. It's cold and I'm not even sure I feel it. I feel empty. I feel like I'm losing everything.

Later in the morning, I head to my home office to take some meetings and get caught up on everything going on at work. Afterwards, I notice that Allie did my laundry and put it away. My heart drops. I might get this promotion and this big job, but what good is any of it if I'm alone and have no family? I had a taste of what I could have, and now I want it more than ever. Who does my dad think he is that he can just take this all away from me?

But for now, I have calls to make. I have to fight for my new family.

Allie

I need to fight
for my son.

I haven't been sleeping much since we left Logan's apartment. It's weird without him, and I'm worried about what's going to happen. With us, with our family, with the custody case. With everything. Luckily, Caleb doesn't seem to understand what's going on.

I look at the clock on the stove, seeing that it's already two a.m. I knead out cinnamon roll dough as I have done hundreds of times before and set it to rise.

I look up to find Beth standing over me in my brother's old

worn black bathrobe that's way too big for her.

"What are you doing up, Allie? It's the middle of the night."

"I can't sleep, and I wanted to get my baking done before Sasha gets here at five to start cooking for the day. I don't want to get in her way." I roll out more dough and punch it down. It feels good to take my frustrations out on something productive.

"Let me help," Beth says, walking over and switching her robe for an apron. She stops by the coffee machine and starts a fresh pot.

The back door creaks open. It's Mellie, ducking in and shutting the door quietly. "I saw the lights on and wanted to make sure everything was okay," she says.

"Everything's fine," I lie, trying to keep it together as I swipe a tear away and begin taking my anger out on the dough.

Mellie comes and sits at the counter in front of me while Beth slides mugs of coffee toward us. She cups her own mug in her hands and plops down on the chair next to Mellie.

"Talk to us."

I take a deep breath and look away, opting to tell the truth. "I love him. I tried not to, but I do. And I feel like he's too good for us. We don't deserve him. I mean, look at me! I'm *not* a catch. What would a man like Logan want with *me*? I just lost my job, my car is a million years old, I am a single mom, and now I might lose my kid. Everything just feels out of control."

Beth looks at me and her face softens. "Allie, you are *such* a catch. And Logan is a really good guy. He loves you, too."

"How do you know that?" I ask, wiping my face.

"Because he told Evan. And he feels really bad about what happened with his father. He misses you and wants to come back for you."

"We could lose Caleb if I go back to him. I can't lose Caleb, Beth. If I have to choose between Logan or Caleb, I have to choose my son."

Caleb is my world and I'm all he has. I hate his dad for ruining this for us. We could have made a family together. We could have been so happy.

"What are you going to do with all of that?" Mellie says, sipping her coffee, eyeing the dozens of cinnamon rolls I've already stress-baked.

"I'm going to open a bakery. I need your help, ladies. I'm going to support my son. That's all I can do right now. One foot in front of the other. I have orders for thirty-eight pans of cinnamon rolls this week from the inn's Facebook page. So, I'm going to bake and stay busy."

"I can help you set up all of your social media," Beth says, taking a napkin and a pen and starting to make a list. "I can also set up business accounts for you and an L.L.C. for the bakery," she adds.

"What's the name?" Mellie looks up at me.

"Baked Inn Love," I say without hesitating. It just rolls off my tongue. I pause and look at them. "What do you think?"

They both nod excitedly, as if they love it.

Beth says, "I'm also setting up a portal so people can order online. And a way to order custom cakes."

"That sounds amazing. Thank you!" I start to feel a little better and add another pan to rise.

"When are you going to bake all of these?" Mellie asks, looking around, concerned.

"I set up a schedule to bake every morning from two to six a.m. and then catch a little nap before Caleb gets up. Then I'll bake after he goes to bed for a while at night. The inn is licensed as a commercial kitchen, so this is perfect. I can do this until I can save up to have my own place."

Beth and Mellie get their laptops and start tapping away to help me as I bake. By the time Sasha comes in to start breakfast at five, I have the kitchen clean and one last cinnamon roll pan baking.

Sasha looks surprised at first, but her expression quickly warms. "Why don't you head back to the cottage for a nap and I'll finish the last pan?"

I agree to let her help, because that's what I'm doing these days. When I get back to the cottage, I fall into a deep sleep and wake briefly to my mom telling me she has Caleb and to get some more rest. I drift off again. I'm emotionally and physically exhausted.

I wake up to two strong arms circled around me and I know he's here, I know he came back for us.

I freeze for a moment, reveling in his scent, before reality hits me and I shimmy away. I watch him sleep in a hoodie and jeans, and damnit, he's even beautiful when he sleeps. He hasn't shaved and he looks disheveled and… sad.

"Logan," I whisper. His eyes blink open. It all but guts me to see his face like this. "What are you doing here?"

"I missed you guys."

"We can't do this, Logan," I whisper and start to cry.

"Why?" he murmurs back, looking miserable.

"Because I'll lose Caleb. You'll lose everything, too, Logan. It's just too much." I wipe tears from my eyes and sit up, trying to keep it together.

"Why am I not enough for you?" he says quietly.

"Of course you're enough, but there's just too much at stake," I say. "This isn't going to work."

"Look at me, Allie. Tell me that while you're looking at me. I don't believe you," he says, upset. "I love you both. And I want to be here for you both. You're my family."

"Go back to Boston, Logan," I say as I get up and go into the bathroom. I shut and lock the door. I slide to the floor and sob. Why the hell does my brain tell me it makes sense to send him away while my heart tells me it's all wrong? I can't let everything around me get destroyed because I selfishly choose him.

I wait until I hear the front door shut. I come out and he's gone. And so is a piece of my heart because he took it with him. It's his anyway, he might as well. I don't deserve him.

I go back to bed and don't wake up until after three when my brother stands in my doorway, his arms folded over his chest.

"Why are you staring at me?" is all I can muster.

"You know who's a dumbass?" he asks, a pinched look on his face.

"Ugh, Evan, I can't do this. I don't have the energy." I pull a pillow over my red, puffy eyes.

"You just did what I did to Beth a while back. And I almost lost her, Allie. I almost *lost her*," he says angrily.

Now I feel even worse. I had something great, and I broke it. Logan fit here with us, with our family, and I let his dad get in my head. Instead of fighting him, I ran, and now I don't know how to fix it. I'm not even sure that I could if I tried. His dad has an insane amount of money and the power to destroy us.

"Now, I definitely didn't like that little pretty boy the first time I met him. But that city slicker has grown on me, and Beth certainly loves him. So, you messed up, Allie. You need to fix this."

Tears fill my eyes. I can't look at him, can't think of Logan. *Put it in a box. Push the hurt away. Don't think about it.* I try to repeat this mantra, but it's not working anymore. The box has exploded and hurt is everywhere.

"I can't…"

"He didn't deserve that. He came for you. And you just sent him away. What the hell, Allie?" he whispers. "You should have seen him when he left. You destroyed him."

I don't have an answer. I just stare out the window from the bed and cry. If he stayed, he would have been destroyed even more. It's not an easy decision, it's not even what I want, but I had to make the call for both of us.

"Think about what you're doing, Allie," Evan says as he slowly closes the door and heads out.

I can't think. That's just it. I don't have that luxury. I need to fight for my son.

I text Mellie and ask her to bring Caleb to the cottage so that we can spend the evening together. I make dinner for us, and afterward, we curl up on my bed, snuggling while we read a few books. Before I know it, it's time for him to get ready for bed, and I'm sad thinking that our time together could be cut in half soon. I give him a bath and tuck him into his bed.

"I love you, buddy," I whisper.

"I love you too, momma," Caleb says.

I shut his door on my way out, heading to the kitchen to make my baking to-do list for tonight, as well as jot down a few ideas for the bakery. I leave Caleb in bed and my mom listening for him when I head over to get to work.

I look like hell and badly need a shower, but I figure I'll get half of my orders done and then go shower and sleep and come back and do the other half. It's probably a lie, though. I'll bake all night like a machine. Because when I close my eyes, I see him. And I can't handle the sadness that comes when I do...

I walk into the kitchen and preheat the oven. An envelope with my name on it lays on the counter. I open it to find $360 from cinnamon roll orders.

I feel a swift wind of relief come over me that this is *working*. I'm going to bake to support my son. I'm going to build something for us. Something no one can take away.

I tuck the envelope into my back pocket, put my apron on, and get to work.

Evan comes in from stacking firewood and just stares at me for a minute before shaking his head and helping himself to a muffin. He sits at the counter and watches me bake, not saying anything.

"What?" I finally exclaim, throwing up my hands.

"The band is playing a gig this weekend. We need you to sing backup for a few songs. Paid gig."

"Okay," I breathe. At least he's not here to ream me about Logan again.

"Okay," he repeats calmly.

"I can use all the money I can get right now. The court is going to be looking at all my bank statements, so I need to show a steady flow of income." I measure more ingredients into the big commercial mixer.

"Okay, well it's Saturday. It's in Boston. Mom can keep Caleb, I already checked."

I keep mixing and nod. "And Allie," he says, looking over at me.

"What?"

"Love you," he says quietly and walks out. My heart fills before immediately breaking again. I want Logan to be the one telling me that right now; it's too bad I messed everything up.

CHAPTER 24

Logan

I'm not done
fighting.

I got the promotion. I figured I would, but there's never a way to know for sure. It came with a nice raise, and I can work remotely while traveling thirty percent of the time. Perfect if you have a family, but now I have no family. What good is any of this without them? I worked for over ten years and told myself that this job, with its perks and its schedule and its flexibility, was all that I needed. Now that couldn't be further from the truth, because if I don't have my family, I don't have anything.

The court hearing is still happening tomorrow, and I'm testifying. I've been staying in touch with Preston, so he's aware, and he says he's got a plan. My father may be funding Chris and his family, but I have faith in Preston. And in Allie, in all that she's done for Caleb over the years. We just have to hope the Court sees it, too.

I'm waiting until this hearing is over, but I'm not done fighting for us. I'm no quitter.

I'm back in a conference room, waiting to testify. We want the opposing counsel to think they have a handle on this, but they don't. Margie, Evan, Beth, and Allie head in fifteen minutes before the hearing starts; I enter the courtroom after them and sit alone in the back.

Chris's attorney is wearing an ill-fitted suit and looks inexperienced. I watch him paint a picture about Allie and her parenting that's extremely difficult to listen to because it's all lies. My knuckles flex on the bench in front of me.

"How do you plan on supporting Caleb?" the attorney asks.

Allie looks professional in a dress and cardigan. "I own my own bakery and bake for my family's inn."

"Why do you feel he belongs with you?"

"Caleb has never even met Mr. Carson, or any member

of his family for that matter. My family is all Caleb has ever known. We have supported him for his entire life, and we all love him very much," Allie answers calmly.

"And you don't think Caleb's father should get to love him?"

"Your Honor..." Preston starts.

"That's enough," the judge chides Chris's lawyer.Finally, Preston gets his turn. Now shit gets real. I've seen this guy dismantle entire companies, mergers, and multi-million-dollar deals. If you come for him and his client, he will destroy you. He knows the law inside and out.

Preston stands and places a lineup of photos of little boys around Caleb's age in front of the Carsons, asking them to identify Caleb.

Their lawyer rejects this, of course, but the judge tells Preston to continue.

"Your Honor, some of these photos are the very same pictures Ms. Harper has sent to the Carsons over the years. Photos they rejected and sent back to her. They have made no effort to try to get to know Caleb, nor do they even know what he looks like."

Their lawyer asks for proof. Preston holds up a letter with "Return to Sender" written on it that was sent back to Allie.

"Is this your handwriting, Mr. Carson?" he asks, holding it up to him before spinning it around for the rest of the courtroom to see.

"Yes, but I didn't know what she wanted," he says defensively. "We thought she was trying to get money from us," he says defensively, sniping a look at Allie.

The judge looks at Preston. "How many letters did your client send to the Carsons?"

"Eight. And they are all right here, Your Honor."

The judge looks at the Carsons. "Did this young lady ask you for financial support?"

"Not directly, no, Your Honor," their lawyer says.

"What did you ask for?" he asks Allie directly.

"At first, I simply asked for them to get to know Caleb. Later, I asked them to get tested for a kidney transplant that Caleb needed. They carry a hereditary kidney disease gene that was passed onto Caleb. I needed their help. My son would have died without the kidney my brother gave him."

"Why would you not support your son?" he asks Chris.

Chris's lawyer whispers something to him and he puts his head down. The lawyer answers, "Mr. Carson is hoping to take care of him now and make up for it, Your Honor."

"Proceed with your presentation," he says to Preston.

"Your honor, I have a photo collage of four different kids. I want to see if the Carsons can pick out which one is Caleb."

Preston walks over and shows the lineup to Chris and his parents. His parents don't respond and Chris stares at it for a moment before pointing to one of the kids.

"That's not your son. That is a stock photo. Your son is

here, here, and here. You don't even know who your own son is. And he doesn't know you. And yet you showed up at his home, trying to take him from the family he does know, on two separate occasions. Your Honor, I have one last witness to call."

"Very well."

"Your Honor, I call the stepfather to Caleb Harper, Logan Nolan."

Allie quickly turns and looks at me with tears in her eyes. I make my way to the front and sit next to the judge, facing Allie, my nerves tense. I dial in deep and compose myself, then don my best poker face, the one I use during tough negotiations to close big deals. I lean in and mouth the words, "Hi, honey," making it just obvious enough for Chris and his parents and the judge to hear.

Allie looks shocked at first, then she quickly recovers and smiles. She glances over at Preston for reassurance.

"Your honor, this is Logan, he's Allie's husband, stepfather to Caleb. He and Allie have made their home in Freedom Valley and have plans to open a family-owned bakery together." Preston directs his attention to me. "Logan, can you describe Chris's demeanor when he was at the inn looking for Caleb?"

I clear my throat. "Yes, he was sneaking around and trying to talk to Caleb and another child of one of the inn's employees. I tried to introduce myself to him, because I didn't realize who he was at the time. At first, I thought he was a guest."

The judge peers at Chris, whose eyes are downcast. He looks angry.

"Are you and your wife able to provide for Caleb?"

I look at Preston and he nods. I lean forward to speak into the microphone. "Yes, Your Honor. We are a team, dedicated to working incredibly hard to provide for our family."

"I'd like to enter a financial document to the Court, representing all of Allie and Logan's assets." He hands a paper to the judge who reviews it. His eyebrows raise slightly, then he sets the document down.

The judge clears his throat and turns his attention to Chris. "With all of this information and in light of it being the holidays, I find it extremely tragic that you are just now seeking out your son. Not only did you not provide support for him financially, but you also ignored a mother's pleas for help during a life-or-death situation for your own son. I find your actions deplorable."

Chris looks vacant. His wife, on the other hand, looks upset.

"Your Honor, I'd like to just submit one more piece of evidence for the court," Preston says. "May I approach the bench?"

The judge nods and motions for him to come forward.

Chris's attorney joins him and Preston hands the judge a

stack of papers.

"Your Honor, I have several documents right here showing that Mr. and Mrs. Carson submitted documents to adopt and were denied for various reasons. They listed that they struggle with infertility and wanted a child of their own. It appears the Defendant then must have remembered he already had a son. Instead of doing the right thing by providing support and asking for reasonable visitation to get to know his son, he shows up and demands the boy he has previously rejected for the boy's entire life. This is a mere act of convenience and bullying on the Carson family's part, to pull a boy away from his mother and support system who has advocated for him and helped him when he struggled with serious health situations."

Preston paces and stops in front of Chris. "Did you or did you not ignore this child for over four years and offer no support?"

"Yes," Chris bites out, bitterly. "But at least my marriage is *real*."

"Nothing more, Your Honor," Preston says.

I'm dismissed from the witness stand, and Preston and I both confidently stride over and sit down next to Allie, completely ignoring that last statement from Chris. I protectively put my arm around Allie and she leans into me, shaking.

"Well, I'm actually at a loss for words," the judge says to

the Carsons. "At this time, I want you to go back to California and think about what you've all done and how you've treated this little boy and his mother. I'll reconvene in six months. If you have made it a point to get yourselves and your reasons right, I'll consider partial custody. Custody for the non-custodial parent is denied at this time. The child, Caleb Harper, will stay in the full custody of his parents, Allison and Logan Nolan. This court is adjourned." The judge stands and exits toward his chambers.

I hold Allie. I realize that just looking at Chris is upsetting to her. This has all been so hard for her. I'm so glad I'm here with her, even if she doesn't want me to be.

We put our coats on and I hold her hand as we walk across the hall to where Preston is standing with Evan, Beth, and Margie. I watch Chris and his parents come out and look at us all with disgust and anger. I keep my gaze level and steady and stare at them, daring them to talk to her. I'm ready to tear them apart. They thankfully choose not to and keep walking. When they're about fifteen feet away, Chris's wife turns around and mouths, "I'm so sorry." Then she ducks her head down and follows them out.

Well, at least one of the Carsons has a soul. If that woman was smart, she'd run far away from that family.

Allie looks at me sadly. "You came."

"Of course I did. I love you, Allie."

Preston taps his pen against his notebook and makes

a note on his legal pad about Chris's wife. "Weird," he murmurs.

Allie tears up and whispers, "Can I talk to you?" After so long not having her with me, I've missed her so much.

"Sure," I tell her, and we walk over to the stairs.

She takes a deep breath and looks away. "Thank you for doing that. I'm so sorry, Logan. I'm so sorry I pushed you away. We don't deserve you."

"Allie, why can't you look at me?" I ask her.

"Because I know I hurt you and there's nothing I can do to take that back. I'm so sorry."

"Why do you think you don't deserve me?" I keep my eyes locked on her even though she still won't look at me.

"You aren't real," she whispers.

"I am real. Remember?" I reassure her.

"I don't know if *we* can be," she says, tears running down her face.

I pull her close and hold her as she sobs into my chest, breaking me down even more. I can't live without her, but I also can't keep fighting for someone who doesn't want me to fight for her. She has to choose. I can't force this.

Finally, I pull her back and say, "Allie, I promise you that if you do choose us, I'll love you forever. But I can't keep doing this." I choke up as I say it.

She blinks and looks at me, scared. "What about your dad?"

"I took care of my dad. He'll no longer be bothering us."

"What did you do, Logan? Tell me." She looks worried.

"Don't worry about it. I handled it, and he will no longer be in any of our lives. Trust me on this."

"How can I trust you when you won't tell me?"

Because if I tell her, she will definitely not be happy, and it won't help things. I want her to want me for me.

"I'm going back to Boston. You know where to find me," I murmur into her ear. I kiss her salty cheek and do the hardest thing I've done so far: Walk away.

On my way out, I stop and hug Beth, clap Evan's back, and head out. I leave a piece of my heart right there, crying at the courthouse. The same courthouse I married her in.

Over the next few days, I throw myself into work, burying myself in meetings. The more time I stay busy, the less time I have to think about Allie and Caleb. My phone dings and I look to see a text from Beth.

Beth: Hey, call me when you get a chance please.

"What's up?" I sit back in my chair, ready for a lecture.

"What are you doing Saturday night?" she asks in a breathless one-word sentence.

"Nothing, why?" I ask, shaking my head and rolling my

eyes. "I'm not coming to New Hampshire."

"Evan and his band are playing at The Tap House in Boston and I need someone to go with me."

"Yeah. Is there a sneaky agenda here to connect me and Allie? Because I told you where we stand. I'm not playing games with her. She needs to figure out what she wants," I say.

"Have you been sleeping? You sound exhausted," Beth replies. Is she panting? Why is she panting?

"Nope, I've been working. And why do you sound out of breath?" I ask, now glancing out at the window where snow is falling.

"I'm just carrying laundry upstairs."

"Is that your exercise for the day?" I tease.

"Maybe," she laughs. "I'm helping Mellie get some rooms ready. We're booked up, thanks to your *People* magazine article. Also, now I have to hide more," she teases.

"I'm glad that worked out."

"Speaking of working. I finished the first half of my new book today. Want to see it?" she says proudly.

"Absolutely," I say, grinning half-heartedly. "Send it over."

"Okay, I will after we get off here."

"I'm looking forward to reading it."

"Okay, so can you meet me at The Tap House at seven on Saturday night? We can catch up while Evan plays. I heard they have good food there, too."

"Yep, sounds fine."

"Thanks, Logan."

I don't want to ask but I can't help myself. "How's she doing?" I regret asking as soon as the words come out. "You know what, forget I asked. I don't want to know," I tell her. "I'll see you at seven on Saturday." I disconnect and take a deep breath.

Yeah, it's going to take a while to get over her. If I ever can.

~

CHAPTER 25

Allie

Wasn't meant to be.

"Buddy, you're staying with Grandma tonight while I go with Uncle Evan to sing with his band. Okay?" I scoop him up for a hug and kiss his head.

"When is Logan coming back? I miss him," he asks, his big green eyes piercing me with their sincerity.

"I know, buddy, I miss him, too," I tell him, skirting his question. I hold him close. I wish I hadn't screwed that up, but some things just can't be fixed.

I pack my only good dress in a bag to change into at the venue. Maybe we'll make some good tips tonight. God knows

I could use the money. Evan said he'd pay me $400 for this gig, but I also really want to help him out. Not to mention I really could use the distraction right now. I'm operating under the guise that the busier I am, the less sad I am.

Beth grins at me as we head outside and put our bags in the back of the truck, along with my guitar in there. Evan told me that I'll be singing a few cover songs that we could go over on the drive to Boston. Honestly, I don't even care what we perform. I just want the money and to come home. I need to work on my bakery business. I have a lot of things to figure out, and working with a broken heart is just so freaking heavy.

I sleep the whole drive to Boston. When I jolt awake, I ask, "Are we almost there?" and wipe the drool from my chin. Lovely.

"Almost. We're going straight to the club and then we'll go to our… hotel afterward," Evan says while giving Beth a look I can't understand.

I briefly wonder what they're up to, but decide I'm too tired to care.

"So what's our set list?" I ask as I yawn then take a sip from my water bottle.

"It's in the back, in my bag there," he says, turning his turn signal on and sliding into the parking lot of The Tap Room.

I lean down and flip up the flap of his messenger bag and

pull out a piece of paper.

"Really, Evan? 'I Won't Give Up'? Is this a joke? Am I being punked right now?" I shake my head. The rest of the list looks fine, but that one hits too close to home right now.

Beth and Evan exchange another look and he turns to me. "It'll be okay. You kill that song and you know it. We practiced that one."

"Whatever." I slide back in my seat, defeated.

I feel like shit. Like when you have something nice and then it's destroyed and taken from you in the blink of an eye. And the worst part? I did it to myself. I destroyed us. Sometimes it feels easier to destroy something before it gets a chance to destroy you. I am not good enough for him. And there's still so many things I don't understand.

I lift my guitar case and bag out of the truck bed and carry them inside to warm up and get ready. Luckily, since I'm the only female in the band, I get my own room to get ready in and that is perfectly fine with me. I just want to be alone anyway.

I set down my bag, close the door, and hit the lock. I sit on the worn couch and put my face in my hands. How did I get here? If you rewind my life to watch it back over the years, it all started here. Evan and I played here before he went out to California to the Marines. Before I followed him out there. Before I fell for the wrong boy and got pregnant. Before I was a single mom who was barely making it.

Before, before, before. We are here and now, though, and that's the reality. That's who I am. I don't fit in with his brilliant world. I can't ask him to give up his identity for us.

Ugh, pity party over.

I rummage through my bag and slide out my curling iron. I plug it in and set out my hair products before pulling out the purple lace dress Logan got for me. A last-minute costume change I now regret as the memories flood back to me. I can almost feel his hand in mine as he walked me to dinner that night. Busking in Vegas. Picnics in Moab. Playing games around his sister's table and laughing. All of our road trip memories come flooding back. Jesus, I'm a mess. I miss him.

I wipe my eyes and take a deep breath. The show must go on.

I put on my makeup and curl my hair in long beach waves down my back. I put my dress on and slide into a pair of black sparkly pumps I will probably regret by the end of the evening. I'm going to tell Evan I'm not playing that stupid song. He can pick any other song, but that one's not happening.

I decide to do some warm-ups and sing a few songs from our set. Most of them I'm singing backup for, and there are a few Adele covers of my own to do. This is a pretty good gig for us, so I don't want to disappoint Evan and his band. It's a great opportunity and easy money.

Someone knocks on my door and I walk over, opening it

to find Beth is standing there in dark jeans, a black satin tank top, and a purple cashmere cardigan with long zip-up, high-heeled boots. She looks me up and down. "You look gorgeous, Allie. This is the dress you wore in Chicago?"

My eyes fill with tears with that question and I look away. I take a deep breath. Beth nods and steps in and shuts the door.

"He misses you, too," she says quietly.

"It sure doesn't seem like it," I say, looking down.

"He thinks he won't be enough for you, Allie," she says quietly. "It was a lot for him to put himself out there for you. He made some big choices here recently."

"He said that?" I ask quietly.

"Yeah," she says.

"He hasn't called or texted me."

"Have you called or texted him?" she says.

"No."

"You can't have it both ways, Allie. You can't risk love without taking risks. It doesn't work that way. Do you think it was easy with Evan? Our pride could have gotten in the way of what we have now."

There's another knock at the door. Beth opens it to a server holding a tray of snacks and cocktails.

"Thank you," I say, setting the tray down and handing Beth a drink as I take one for myself.

She looks surprised for a brief second before she shakes

her head and says, "No, thanks."

"Beth, are you pregnant?" I ask, tilting my head.

She takes a deep breath and smiles. "Yes, but I haven't told your brother yet, so don't say anything. You have to promise, okay? I want to tell him at Christmas in a few weeks."

I wrap my arms around her and give her a big hug. "This is great news. When are you due?"

"Late summer," she says. "I'm so glad you figured it out, because keeping this inside has been killing me. I'm going nuts. I haven't told Cara or Log…" she quickly stops and course-corrects. "Or anyone."

"Evan's going to be delighted, and so is Mom. I'm so happy for you, Beth."

"Me, too."

"Wow. My brother is going to be a dad." I smile at her. "You two are going to make the best parents, you know that?"

"I hope so," she says. "He's probably going to be shocked when I tell him. This wasn't planned."

"The best surprises aren't. How are you going to tell him?"

"I haven't decided yet. But maybe you can help me come up with something fun."

"Absolutely." I hug her.

"So, what are you going to do about Logan?" she asks, taking a sip of her water.

"I can't have him give up everything for me. That's huge, Beth. Who am I to do that to someone?"

"Even if he did give in to his dad, he'd never be free. Logan can't live like that. He's not wired that way. You have to give him a chance. You both deserve to be happy, and I think deep down, you two know you belong together."

I look away. "It's just a lot, you know? I'm scared."

"I get it. You're both scared. But you know what? Do it scared."

Another knock sounds at the door and I say, "Come in."

Evan comes in wearing a black button-down shirt, sleeves rolled up, and dark jeans. "There's my woman." He smiles and gives Beth a kiss that makes me blush.

"Geez. Get a room, you two," I say, shaking my head.

Evan gives me the once-over then says, "You look great. Are you ready to go on in twenty? We have soundcheck right now."

I stand, brushing crumbs off my dress. "Yes, let me put on more lipstick."

Beth looks at her phone. "I have to go anyway and secure my table. You've got this. Knock 'em dead. Which you will in *that* dress."

When Evan and I head out, he asks me, "Are you nervous?"

"I wasn't until you said that just now, but now I feel a little like throwing up," I say, looking at him uneasily.

"If you can busk on the streets of Vegas, you can sing here," he says, grinning at me as he picks up his guitar and adjusts the strap over his shoulder.

There aren't a lot of empty seats, which makes me even more nervous. We begin to play a few songs and the mood and energy is great in the tavern, but despite this being a fun event, my heart feels so heavy and sad. I fell in love with performing again when I met Logan and felt good about singing and playing when he was around, but now nothing feels good. Everything feels like a chore. I have just been burying myself in my baking.

It's hard to see the audience with the lights in my eyes so I focus on performing and getting lost in the music. It feels good to play and sing again with Evan and I try to focus on that.

"Okay, and now for a special dedication," Evan says into the microphone. "Beth, you are my love, and I want you to know that this song is for you..."

He begins to play "Marry Me" by Train. Surprise and happy applause ripple through the crowd as Evan walks out into the audience singing, the spotlight focused on him. He heads to Beth's table and gets down on one knee. He pulls out a velvet box and sings to her while he opens it. Now the spotlight is on her table and she's not alone. Holy shit... Logan's there, with his arm around her. A touch of sadness shows in his eyes as he watches them. Then his eyes shift to mine.

Beth says yes, causing the crowd to erupt into cheers, and Evan walks back, grinning at me. I hug him and kiss his cheek. I'm so happy for them.

Evan takes a break to go have a moment with Beth, and it's my turn to do a solo now. I blink back tears. I focus on getting ready for my next song. Once it's done, I'm making a beeline for my dressing room. The band doesn't need me for the last set.

I begin, looking out and realizing Logan is frozen watching me. Just like that, something in me breaks apart, and I know that I want him back. This isn't right. Us not being together isn't right.

So, I decide to sing this song to him, and I give it—and him—my all. Maybe he'll give me a second chance. I hope he feels me singing this to him, telling him that I'm scared, but I won't give up. Not on us. Not again.

I get lost in the song and sing it in his direction, my eyes locked on his table even though I can't see him over the house lights.

Memories of us in the past few weeks pour through me, a connection to him that I feel in my bones. I messed up. I need to fix this. I need to be brave and risk it, because he's worth it, I'm worth it, and we *do* deserve this.

I finish the song and look over, but he's gone. Beth sits there and claps for me, tears streaming down her face.

Well, there it was. If there was ever a moment for us to reconnect, that was it. And now he's gone, so it obviously wasn't meant to be.

CHAPTER 26

Logan

Fight for her.

It's just a song… That's what I keep telling myself. When her velvety voice begins to sing, I feel paralyzed. I only realize where I am when Beth puts her hand on my arm. I look over at her and blink, shaking myself back into reality.

She isn't singing that to me. No way.

"Are you okay?" Beth says, turning in her chair.

I shake my head, unable to speak. I take a long pull on my beer.

Allie sings and looks over at me, and I'm not sure what this means. Does she want me back? Is she willing to work for this? Is this just a song? What the fuck is going on here? Emotions pour through me, and I panic.

I lean over and whisper to Beth, "What does this mean?"

She looks at me deeply and replies, "Fight for her. Fight for you."

I feel like I'm going to have a panic attack and I shove my chair back and stand. "I gotta get some air," I mumble as I hurry toward the exit.

I shoot out into the cold, brisk New England air and breathe deep as I lean against the brick side of the bar. I have to get out of here.

What does that even mean? Fight for her? I did my part, didn't I? Why hasn't she called or texted me? If she had, I would have been there immediately. I miss her and Caleb so much.

I know I need to make this right. I shrug into my coat and shove my hands deep into my pockets and walk home. I have a lot to think about.

Beth comes out the door, pulling her coat over her and rubbing her hands together. "There you are." She looks at me and says, "Come here," and pulls me into a hug.

"What is going on?"

"I'm sick of the back and forth. I gave up everything for her. Why won't she come back? Why the mixed signals?"

Beth's face softens. "Maybe that was her waving her white flag, singing that song to you."

"I can't keep doing this."

"What do you mean you gave up everything?"

"I don't want to tell you."

"Tell me."

"You have to promise not to tell her or Evan."

"Okay." Now she looks worried. "What happened?"

"In order to get my dad off my back and out of Allie's custody battles, I offered a trade."

"What did you do? Oh my God, you're scaring me."

"I traded my trust fund for my freedom."

Beth stares at me, her eyes wide. "And she doesn't know?"

"No. And it has to stay that way."

CHAPTER 27

Allie

Hey, Ace.

I slide the last pan of orange cranberry scones into the oven and load the last of the dishes into the dishwasher. I'm exhausted. Baking around Sasha's schedule is exhausting.

I wish I could rent a space somewhere; we're definitely getting there, but we aren't quite there yet. Orders are flying in, and I couldn't have done it without Mellie and Beth. I am so thankful to them.

I wipe down the counters, store the cooled baked goods, and lay out one last cooling rack for the last batch. I'm going to literally roll into my bed and hopefully get a good solid four to six hours of sleep before Caleb wakes me up.

Feeling rested finally, I wake up to the sun coming in off of the cold winter windowpanes. I look over at my phone and jump when I see it's already after one in the afternoon. Geez! I slept for nine hours! I haven't slept that long in one stretch for years.

I throw on the leggings I had abandoned on the floor and climb into a hoodie. I run my fingers through my hair and toss it up with a clip. I walk out of my bedroom and jerk back when I catch my reflection in the hall mirror. Damn. I look awful. When was the last time I washed my hair? Ugh, I need to get it together.

I head outside to the main inn and sneak in the back door, hoping not to run into too many people or guests.

I make my way to the coffee pot and Sasha hands me a mug with coffee and cream, just the way I like it.

I smile meekly at her. "Thank you."

"You're welcome. Your orders were all picked up," she says, sliding an envelope of cash across the counter toward me.

"You're the best," I say, tucking it into the front pocket of my hoodie.

"Where are Caleb and my mom?" I ask, looking around.

The inn feels strangely quiet.

Sasha shrugs, then takes a sip of her steaming mug of coffee. "Doing errands. Last-minute Christmas stuff, I guess. Did you get some good sleep?"

"Yeah, I guess I needed that," I say, taking a large gulp of coffee.

"You've been working so hard, you have to remember to take care of yourself, momma. You can't build an empire if you burn yourself out. Trust me, I know."

"Yeah, you're right. I just feel like I need to get a handle on everything, you know? I really want Baked Inn Love to be a success. I don't want to let all of you down. I appreciate your help so much."

"I know, baby, I know," she says, pulling me in for a side hug. "You could never let us down. We're all so proud of you. Caleb is a lucky boy to have you as a mom. You know who else would be lucky to have you..." she says, trailing off, looking out over the backyard.

I hear what she's saying, I just don't feel like I can agree. I feel like I'm drowning lately and can't seem to get my head above water.

"I gotta go, Sash. I'm going to shower and get ready so I look like a human," I say, dodging the question. I need to think about things and make a plan. I can't keep going on like this.

"Hey, come back by five-thirty, okay? We're doing a fun

Christmas picture thing tonight. Beth's idea. I don't really know much, but I know she already has an outfit for Caleb, and she says yours is hanging on the back of your mom's closet door."

"Pictures?" I ask suspiciously.

"Beth said a family picture or something, I don't know. Maybe marketing for the inn?" She walks over to the stove to stir one of her pots. She then pulls a lunch bag out of the fridge and hands it to me.

"Here's a sandwich. Go eat and get ready at your mom's, then meet us here at five-thirty."

"Okay, thanks, Sash," I say. I head out the back door, pulling my hoodie tighter as I make my way back to my mom's cottage to get ready.

I'm starving, so I waste no time tearing through the bacon, avocado, and ham sandwich she made for me. I notice she made the sandwich out of the sourdough loaves I left on the counter for her. I feel like maybe the bakery is the one thing I have going for me that isn't a mess right now. It gives me a slice of hope.

I scroll through my phone as I eat. My finger hovers over Logan's name. I want to call him, but I know it's over. I tried to sing to him in the bar and I ended up looking like a fool. He's done with me. It's time I accept that, so I delete his contact information. I can't be hurt again.

Just then, Evan comes in, a manilla envelope in his hand.

He looks grim.

"Al, this came in the mail for you," he says, running his fingers through his hair and setting the envelope down on the table. I start to feel sick.

Divorce papers.

I don't want to open the envelope; I don't want to know what's inside. Tears immediately begin filling my eyes. Jesus, this is real. He really is done with me.

"Okay, thanks," I say, trying to swallow the lump in my throat and sliding the envelope to the side. Evan sits and looks at me for a while. He doesn't say anything.

"What?" I ask, looking over at him.

"Nothing, just worried about you," he says, his green eyes meeting mine. "We all are."

"Well, you don't have to be. I've been through worse. I'll be just fine on my own. Always have been."

Evan looks at me pensively for a minute then nods and stands. "Okay."

"Thank you for everything you've done and have been doing for us. I feel like everything is still chaos, and I'm just trying to find a new normal for us."

"A lot has happened, but you and Caleb are going to be just fine. I'm glad you're here."

"Thanks." I sniff back a tear. "I see everything you've done at the inn here for our family, and I'm so proud of you. You've done some really great things."

"I couldn't have done it without Beth. She's been a huge help."

"Maybe someday I'll find my person."

"Maybe you already have."

"That's over now. I can't fix that."

He takes a deep breath and looks at the ceiling like he's frustrated with me. I mean, I am frustrated with me. Join the club, buddy. My life is a complete shitshow right now.

"Be ready for pictures at five-thirty. Beth has the boys."

"Fine," I mumble as he leaves and shuts the door firmly behind him.

I look at the envelope again. All I hear replaying in my head is Logan telling Beth he isn't enough for us, and it breaks my heart every time. How could he even think that? He's amazing and we were so lucky to have him, if only for the short period of time that we did. I really hate his family for making him think otherwise.

I take the papers and angrily tear them in half.

I get ready, then pad into my mom's room in my robe to look for whatever outfit Beth left for me. I spot a garment bag and open it to find a beautiful long ivory dress with a boatneck collar and fitted empire waist with a beaded lace shawl. Interesting choice for a dress for family pictures, I think, but whatever. Beth and Evan come up with strange ideas for marketing.

I put on the dress and touch up my lipstick, then slide on

my boots and my wool dress coat. I tuck my phone in my pocket and head outside.

When I get to the back of the inn, I hear a sharp whistle. I look over to find Evan standing next to an old-fashioned carriage wearing dress slacks and a button-up hunter green shirt, along with his dress coat.

"Well, well, well. Don't you clean up nice, big brother," I say. I walk over to him and kiss his cheek.

"You don't look so bad yourself. Let's head out," he says, putting out his hand to help me climb into the carriage.

"Where is everyone else?" I ask, looking around the driveway and noticing most of the cars are gone.

"They're getting ready, too. Beth wants this carriage for part of the pictures, so we'll head over in this." He pulls a thick wool blanket up around our legs.

"Where are we going?" I ask, looking around and taking a deep breath. "It's so beautiful out tonight," I say, looking off into the distance.

"Back of the property," he says as he pulls out his phone and takes a selfie of us.

"This is over the top, even for you and Beth. How fun," I tease.

"Oh, you haven't seen anything yet," he says cryptically. I feel a mix of excitement and nervousness, still unsure what we're doing.

I notice lights up ahead and that we've crossed onto the

Donegal property.

There's a tent with vintage lights strung from the top. And candles, hundreds of candles in lanterns, lined for about two hundred feet leading up to the tent.

"Look," Evan says, pointing to vintage white signs with old-fashioned black lettering.

My hand flies to my mouth.

"Okay, we're walking from here," Evan says.

"Evan, what is this?"

"Come on, Allie. Come see." Evan puts his arm around me.

We walk up to the first hanging lantern and a sign that says, 'I LOVE YOU, ACE.' I open the envelope in the little basket and find a guitar pick from Las Vegas with a picture of dice on it. I smile and tuck it into my pocket. There's also a printed picture of us from when we went hiking in the Red Rock Canyon. We took so many selfies on this trip. I cover my mouth with my hands. Oh my God. Seeing him in the picture and holding the pick makes me miss him so much. I love him, too.

Evan holds my hand and we walk to the next sign which says, 'YOU ARE MY PERSON.' I walk over and open the second basket, my hands shaking nervously as tears stream down my face. Inside is a picture of Logan and me together in Moab.

"There's more."

"This had to have taken days. He couldn't have done this

alone," I say, taking in all the tall oak trees, their trunks wrapped in white lights, with more strands strung over posts, lighting the dirt road.

I walk to the third lantern and read the next sign, reading, 'WILL YOU BE MY FOREVER?' I open the basket to find our receipt from our last dinner in California. On the back of the receipt, it reads, "I knew on the first date you were special, so I saved this in my wallet. Our first date. Only you didn't know it was a date."

I wipe my eyes and swallow. There's also a picture of us right before we FaceTimed with Beth, standing together on the beach with the ocean at our backs.

I head to the fourth lantern and read the sign that says, 'YOU AND CALEB ARE THE MOST IMPORTANT PEOPLE IN MY LIFE.' I wipe my eyes and open the basket to find a note that says, "Look over to your right." When I do, there's Caleb in a tiny suit standing with Chip and Bossy, their tails wagging, who are also dressed in adorable outfits. Caleb holds roses in his hands and waves at me. Tucked inside is a picture I've never seen before of Caleb and Logan both in suits, Logan kneeling down next to Caleb, both smiling big at the camera.

I look over and see Caleb waving, walking toward me. He hands me the flowers.

"Hi, Mommy!" he says excitedly.

"Hi, baby," I say, a sob escaping my throat. I hug him and

look up as Beth motions him back.

"Let's keep going." Evan pulls me toward the next sign.

'I WANT TO SPEND FOREVER WITH YOU. HERE. YOUR DREAMS ARE MY DREAMS, ACE.' I open the basket and pull out a bill of sale for the Donegal property. It's in our names. Logan and Allison Nolan, property owners. There's a picture of the front of the Donegal property. Taped on top of the paper is Logan and me in Montreal, standing together smiling.

Scrawled across the top of the Donegal picture is "The Nolans."

"Oh my..."

I turn to find a tent covered in white lights. Logan stands in the center in his navy-blue suit with a crisp white shirt and a red tie. He has a red rose pinned to his jacket. With his hands in his pockets, he looks at me nervously. "Hey, Ace."

Behind him, the words 'WILL YOU MARRY ME? AGAIN' are spelled out in a light-up sign. He stands in the center of the tent, a heart-shaped pattern of red rose petals surrounding him.

I wipe my eyes and stand in front of him. I'm shaking. He gets down on one knee in front of me.

"I want to spend forever with you, Allie. I love you. Will you marry me and be my forever?" He chokes back a sob as he reaches for my hands and holds them in his.

My eyes lock on his and I nod. "Yes, Logan. I love you so

much," I say as I wrap my arms around him and hug him tight, pulling him up.

He slides a beautiful oval-shaped diamond ring onto my finger.

Applause ripples around us and I realize we aren't alone. My entire family and Kat and Maggie are here, all clapping. Pete, Sasha, Mellie, and Kase are all here, too. The whole family, together.

We kiss, and I hear pops. Fireworks are going off behind us not too far in the distance.

I cling to him, not wanting to let go. "You bought the Donegal property?" I whisper to him.

"Yes, for us. We can plan a home, bakery, hobby farm, gardens, farm-to-table restaurant. Whatever you want, Ace. We're going to build it from the ground up. Together."

"But what about your family?"

"Allie, I gave it up. I walked away. They can have the trust fund. I'm not living in bondage to that anymore. It's not what I want, it's not what I need. I need you."

I choke back tears. "What? That's a lot to give up. Why did you do it?"

"Because I love you. I love Caleb. I love all of us together, and I can't wait for the life we're going to make here."

I kiss him again. "I get to kiss you forever."

"Yes, you do," he murmurs into my ear, pulling me in tighter.

"I love it so much," I say, hugging him back, looking around the beautiful tent. "All of it. I can't believe you did all of this."

"You're my Ace. You mean everything to me. We're going to create an amazing life together," he says, looking into my eyes.

"We're going to be so happy here," I tell him.

Caleb runs up and hugs our legs and we hug him back. "Hey, buddy, you did so good. High five," Logan says, reaching his hand out to Caleb.

My mom hugs us both. "I'm so happy for you two," she says, stepping back and wiping her eyes. "I know your dad would be, too."

I notice a makeshift pallet stage, where Evan and the band have set up to play. Evan strums the first notes of "This I Promise You" and begins to sing.

Logan wraps his arms around me as we dance with my mom and Caleb next to us.

"I'm going to make you happy," Logan whispers in my ear.

"You already do," I say.

Later that night, we make it back to Mom's and I help Caleb brush his teeth and get to bed. I kiss him and tuck him in before sleepily walking down the hall and pausing in the kitchen doorway. Logan stands in my mom's kitchen with the divorce papers laying out on the table.

"Um, babe. Why are our insurance papers torn in half for the new property?"

"I thought those were divorce papers," I manage to get out before covering my mouth with a laugh.

In seconds, he's across the room and pulls me into a deep kiss and embrace. "I love you, Ace. Forever."

"I love you too, Logan."

Logan

Forever.

We made it. No pressure, no fake commitments. Just the real deal. Broken people can be put back together again with love. Because love wins. I got the girl; she got the guy. We're a family, and I'm so grateful.

It's Christmas day, and I look around the big, crowded dining room table covered in bowls and platters of delicious food, Christmas candles, and greenery. I smile at Allie, whose face is glowing in the candlelight. "I love you," I mouth to her.

Her eyes twinkle as she smiles and mouths, "Forever."

Evan interrupts. "Okay, everyone, let's do a toast." He taps his wine glass.

"It's been an insane year for all of us and we all came through even better than we thought we would. I'm so thankful for each and every one of you. Let's toast to a holiday season with family. Old and new. Cheers."

There's a round of soft cheers as I look around at this family who has accepted me, taken me in, and taught me what a real family looks like. A lot can change when you open your heart.

"Hey, Beth, when is *your* wedding?" Allie asks.

"Well," she says. "I was thinking we might have a quick wedding. Before the baby comes."

Evan's eyes get huge and he chokes on his wine. "Baby?!" He jumps out of his chair and pulls Beth in, kissing her.

She looks at him with tears in her eyes. "Yes, baby."

A round of cheers and applause break out at the table and my heart warms as Evan pulls her close again. My big brother is living his dream; he gets to be a dad.

Kat and Maggie sit to our right, and they look so happy. Maybe to know they're also part of this wonderful family. Sometimes family is what you make of it, and we're making something pretty amazing here.

Pete claps Evan on the back and my mom wipes her eyes.

"I get a new grandbaby," she says.

"I'm getting champagne," Sasha says as she heads to the

kitchen.

I look over and see Preston and Mellie speaking and smiling, their heads together. Mellie laughs, and I realize I haven't heard her laugh like that before. She looks truly happy. Preston is a great guy, and it thrills me to think he might just be what makes her laugh and be happy again.

It's going to be a good year at the inn.

FREEDOM VALLEY SERIES

Falling Inn Love

Baked Inn Love

All Inn Thyme

All Inn Books

Forever Inn Love

Inn the End

NON-FICTION

Writers Inspiring Writers

Erin Branscom has read everything she can get her hands on for as long as she can remember. To this day, her favorite place is still the library. In 2021, after a decade of writing novels just for fun, she finally decided to finish a book series and has found writing novels to be her greatest escape. Erin is a passionate author's advocate and loves sharing other authors on Tiktok and Instagram. She lives in Oklahoma and loves traveling and spending time with her husband, four kids, and best friend Molly, a Boston Terrier mix.

ACKNOWLEDGEMENTS

Dusty, Kameron, Ethan, Audrey, and Charlotte, thank you for being the best family I could ever ask for. Thank you for always supporting me on my crazy adventures. I love you all so much!

Mom, thanks for reading my books and encouraging me. Also, thanks for letting me be born. You're the best mom.

Dad and Michael in heaven, I miss you both so much. Every day. It's not fair. I wish you were here. I hope I've made you proud.

Julie and Elizabeth, thanks for being great sisters. We've been through so much in the past few years. Our family is still standing strong.

Auntie Susan and Auntie Paula, you are the best aunt's anyone could ever ask for. I love you both so much.

Molly, you are my best friend in the entire world. Thanks for listening to me talk about all this book stuff and for always keeping me warm in my chair. You deserve all the bones and snuggles.

Erica, you're my favorite human. Period.

Brianna, thanks for all that you do! Couldn't have done it without you!

Kristi, your taco dates and brainstorming sessions mean the world to me. I'm so thankful for you and your friendship. Also, your success is so inspiring. You work harder than anyone I know!

Willow, thanks for all of the sprints! You're so motivating and inspiring to me!

Enni (Yummy Book Covers), thank you for bringing Freedom Valley to life. I love all these covers so much! Thank you for all that you do! Your books are amazing! You always inspire me.

To everyone reading this… Thank you for taking a chance on me and my Freedom Valley world.

Coming up next in the Freedom Valley Series:
All Inn Thyme

Read the first chapter...

~

CHAPTER 1

Allie

I had no idea what he was fixing, but mine was broken.

When I first got married five years ago, I pictured a dream life with a beautiful cozy home, a family sharing loud dinners, belly laughs during game nights, and fun vacations to the beach or the mountains.

That's not even close to the hell that I got.

Now, my son and I are truly *living* in a cozy loft of a garden shed behind a family-owned inn in New Hampshire. Our entire living space could probably fit into the kitchen of our old home, but at least we're safe now. My son and I have been through so much, but we've made it out.

Deep breaths. Deep breaths.

We're safe in Freedom Valley. We're not in Mississippi anymore.

Breathe, Mellie. Breathe. In and out.

I turn to scan my garden as I focus on my breaths. I clench my fist and run my knuckles over my chest, trying to ease the tightness.

A sense of warmth comes over me like a wave as I take in the rows of dirt, seeds planted under the dark soil by my very own hands, and growth beginning to sprout. The sun heats my back as I take in the colors—pops of dark and light greens and brown dirt, wet from the rain. The rich garden aroma brings me back to where I truly am, and not what makes me anxious. This is my safe space. The place where I can think and finally dream again.

I make my way back to the inn and look down at my clothes streaked in dirt. I need to shower before dinner, and I still have some laundry to catch up on. I need to get my linen carts stocked for tomorrow so I can hit the ground running and free up more time to garden.

I step into the shed and find Beth, who's become one of my best friends this past year. She's been through her own hell, and she knows some of my story, but not a lot. When her fiancé Evan, the owner of the inn, brought my son and me here to the Golden Gable, he agreed to keep it between him and me, and so far, we've done that. Beth helps out wherever needed, and to my confusion, she actually likes doing the laundry, so that works out for both of us.

"We're almost ready to eat. Sasha's made an Italian-themed feast for dinner: stuffed shells, homemade garlic bread from Allie, a huge garden salad, and tiramisu for dessert." She rubs her small baby belly bump with one hand and continues to fold towels. "It smells so amazing in that kitchen. I can't get enough garlic with this pregnancy."

My stomach growls as if in agreement. "I'm starved. I haven't eaten since breakfast."

Beth's face scrunches up in worry. "You need to make sure you're taking care of yourself. You're working too hard."

I know she's right, but the garden isn't work to me, it's my therapy. "How have you been feeling?" I ask, changing the subject.

"I'm finally past all the morning sickness, and now I just feel tired sometimes but I'm mostly doing great. I can't believe we're really having a baby. Evan is over the moon. He barely lets me lift a finger."

I chuckle at Evan's overprotectiveness. "I bet. He's so good with Kase, I know he's going to be such a good dad."

Beth looks around. "Speaking of, where's Kase?"

"He just left with Logan and Allie to play with Caleb."

"Why don't you go take a quick shower and I'll finish up." She looks around, her face taking on a look of dismay.

"What?" I laugh as she scans the chaos of the space.

"I wasn't going to say anything, but honestly, the garden shed is feeling more like an actual garden shed these days." She laughs as she stacks a pile of towels onto the cart neatly.

She's not wrong. Every surface available is covered in starter plants under grow lights as I get ready for our spring planting. I have papers taped to the walls with colorful hand-drawn diagrams of where everything will be planted in the new gardens I set up at the back of the property. Over the past year, I have been able to explore my passion for gardening, and I feel like I've finally found my purpose. When I'm not cleaning rooms at the inn or taking care of Kase, I'm reading gardening books, watching videos on YouTube, and researching new things to grow. It's become a big part of my healing. When I'm with the plants, I have peace.

The garden shed, as everyone calls it, is actually a cool "barndominium"—a small barn with two levels. The stairs on the side lead to a small studio apartment I've made cozy with thrifted finds, DIY crafts, and a revolving selection of books I check out from the library—plus more plants. All things that make me feel cozy and happy.

I do feel a bit guilty, though, for taking over the laundry space with my plants, and I tell Beth, "I know. I'm sorry. As soon as I can get my greenhouse together, all of this will go out back there."

"Oh, I don't mind it. It's kind of cool, Mellie. I love

seeing you so happy with all your plants. You've really, um, blossomed." She says the last part with an exaggerated wink.

"You and your dad jokes." I laugh, shaking my head.

"Yeah, and you love me." She pulls me into a side hug.

"That I do," I say as I hug her back.

"Okay now, don't make me get all sappy. Go take your shower. These hormones are all over the place and I cry at everything these days."

"Thank you," I call as I quickly jog up the stairs.

We had a lot of guest turnover today and I worked hard to get all the rooms fresh and ready before putting in a good hour outside. I'm exhausted and sweaty. I think I can smell myself at this point. I wish I could crawl under the covers and go straight to bed, but that's not a possibility.

Beth doesn't know that every single surface up here is covered in plants as well. I quickly move the ones from my shower, perched on the overhead window, basking in natural light.

Once I'm showered and clean, I grab a t-shirt and my better pair of jeans from a basket on the floor. I don't even own enough clothes to put away. I wash and re-wear everything practically daily, and mostly I wear older clothes to clean and garden in. Who cares about clothes when you can buy more seeds and plants?

I gave up on caring how I look a while ago. I just want to be comfortable and have my hands in the dirt. My eyes roam over my plants as I quickly dry my hair and pull it back. I can't wait to see them thriving outside as they grow into fresh veggies for us to eat.

Spring is here and it feels so good outside as I head over to the main house, thankful for some good food and family time. No, I'm not related to these people, but they have all gone out of their way to make me and Kase feel like we're part of their family, blood or not. I ease in the backdoor, looking around. The sounds of chatter and the smells of garlic and Italian food greet me, my mouth instantly watering.

"There you are," Margie says in a motherly tone. Evan and Allie's mom beams as she comes over and pulls me close. "We waited for you," she says as she guides me into the kitchen and hands me a glass of wine.

Warmth spreads through my chest over that simple, small gesture. They waited for me. I feel wanted here. Needed. These people are my family now, and I love them so very much. I am constantly reminding myself to never take this for granted—even the small things. I swallow a sip of wine, hoping to keep my emotions tucked away.

"Thank you," I murmur with a smile. "Where's Kase?"

"He's in the other room playing with the puppies and Ty's dog," Margie tells me.

"Ty?" I ask, startled as she wanders off, not hearing me.

As in *hot Ty*? Hot mechanic Ty I've seen around but never been brave enough to speak to? Suddenly, I'm wishing

I'd spent a little more time on my hair and maybe some mascara. Oh my God. Ty is *here*?

I head into the next room and freeze when I see a huge grey Pitbull staring at me with its tongue hanging out one side of its mouth, drool dripping onto my son who lies under it, giggling.

"Hi, Momma." Kase giggles. "Look at Nova. I love her." He wraps his feet around her, wrestling with her, and the dog leans into him and closes her eyes in utter bliss, clearly just as happy with him. Kase is always finding time to play with the dogs, he loves them so much.

"I see her," I say, hesitantly reaching over and scratching her ears. She's big, very stocky, and could easily be intimidating. Chip and Bossy, the black and white mutts that Evan rescued, are wrestling in the corner and tugging on a toy back and forth. About six months ago, Evan was out running when he found them abandoned in a trash bag. How anyone could ever do that is beyond me.

We had to leave our mini dachshund, Sassy, behind when we left Mississippi, and I miss her every day. Sometimes, in my mind's eye, I can see her propped up on the back of the couch, staring out the window, waiting for us to come home. She's probably so sad and doesn't understand that I didn't have a choice.

Pitbulls sometimes get a bad rep, but judging by this dog's demeanor, she's more of a goofball than a threat. She leans in and closes her eyes again, seeming to enjoy the scratches from me.

"Good girl," I coo softly.

Our guests don't typically bring their pets to stay at the inn, but Evan doesn't discourage it. He loves animals and can't say no to anyone who asks. A while back, someone brought a cute ferret that liked to collect and hide things. He only stayed a short time, but he sure made life interesting when we found piles of random possessions it had hidden for weeks around the inn after he left.

Watching my son adjust over the past year has been such a relief. He smiles more, he doesn't jump at loud sounds as much, and he's a lot more relaxed. We both are. I wonder, though, how much he remembers about our old life, about Sassy, even about his former name. He's never said anything, and I never bring it up.

Brianna and Jase became Mellie and Kase. I got Mellie from the show *Scandal,* one of my favorites back in the day, and Kase sounded like Jase. I wanted to give him a name that was easy to remember so he wouldn't slip up and tell anyone his real name. So far, it's working out.

We've had no issues so far, thankfully. When I'm around guests or in town, I typically wear a hat and keep my head down, just to be safe. No one has ever seemed to recognize us, and the longer we're here, the more at ease I feel. Everyone here at the inn has just accepted us as is, without questioning our backstory or forcing us to open up about our past. We created a basic story, and that's what we go with if we are asked. It's a relief to not be constantly fielding questions, to just be Mellie and Kase. The past is in the past.

"I see you met Nova," a deep, friendly voice drawls from behind me.

I startle and quickly lower my eyes, instinctively going into chameleon mode when I recognize that voice. I've seen Ty around town often, and I'm well aware of who he is, but he probably has no clue who I am given that we've only actually spoken one time. To say he's good looking is putting it mildly. He's like the ultimate manly-man cinnamon roll.

I've had a crush on him since the first time I laid eyes on him. It was last summer when we were both new here in town. I saw him fixing something at Sam's Auto Body when I walked by with Kase. He probably didn't even see me, but I couldn't have missed him, especially with his baseball hat on backward. I had no idea what he was fixing, but whatever it was, mine was broken. His intense blue eyes mirrored his dark blue coveralls and the way he leaned over the engine with his biceps flexed still make my heart go into overdrive when I think about it.

After that, I'd see him around town sporadically—at the local pizza place, the hardware store. And each time, I'd crush just a little bit harder. Then, I found out that it had been Beth's car he was fixing at the shop, and when he dropped it off at the inn last fall, I had been the only one there. I still remember taking the keys from him, the way my hand felt like it was on fire when I brushed his hand. Sure, he was friendly to me, but he didn't say much more than a handful of pleasantries. And I said nothing. I just continuously nodded like a yuppie and all but tripped over my own two feet.

Smooth, Mellie.

I still cringe at how awkward I was that day. God only knows what Ty must have thought of me.

I think every woman in Freedom Valley has at least a small crush on Ty, if the talk around town is to be believed. I mean, how could they not? His dark blond, neatly trimmed beard, his piercing blue eyes, and charisma that could charm anyone. He's got the blue-collar mechanic hotness going for him, but he also cleans up nice and looks smoking hot when I've seen him around in jeans and a flannel.

I'm a housekeeper at an inn, a single mom just trying to survive. He's way out of my league, anyway.

But to say my life is complicated is an understatement, and I have no time for getting involved with a man, no matter how hot. So, I'll just admire from afar and keep it moving.

"We haven't formally met," I say softly, coming back to the present, still stroking Nova's silky velvet head as she leans into my thigh. My gaze is still on the dog. I'm trying not to look at him because I'm afraid I'll spontaneously combust or forget my own name if I do.

"I'm Ty. And you're Mellie, right?" He squats down to pet Nova, who's now lying on her back, her feet in the air, accepting all the scratches and belly rubs with glee.

She reminds me of Sassy, who also loved belly rubs. Pain stabs me for a second, and I try to shake it off just like I do every time I remember something from before. Something that we had to leave behind. Most of it I can live without, but some things I do miss. Like my dog. I'd give anything to go back and get her. To some people they may say, it's just a dog, but to me, that dog is my family.

"Yes, and this is my son, Kase." I wave. *Ugh, why am I waving?* Keep it together, Mellie. *Keep it together.* I smooth my hoodie and stand. He's so handsome, it literally hurts my eyes to look at him, so I go back to petting the dog.

"It's nice to officially meet you both," he says with a tiny hint of a southern drawl that you might miss if you didn't listen for it. I actively try to hide my own drawl, so I'm aware of it when I hear it. Surrounded by all the New England accents, it's not hard to stand out if I'm not careful.

He speaks softly and slowly, almost as if he's trying to hold it back. *Interesting.* I suppose it takes one to know one. I wonder if he can detect the accent that I'm trying hard to hide. Honestly, I have tried so hard to blend in and suppress it, and I think I've done a pretty good job of it.

What are *you* hiding, I wonder to myself as I sneak a glance to look him over.

Ty showed up in Freedom Valley around the same time that I did, and I don't know much about him. Come to think of it, I don't think anyone does. He reminds me a little bit of myself, like he's also sort of a chameleon.

I hate that I'm like this now. That I have to try and get reads on everyone to figure out if they're a potential threat or not. It's probably something I'll be doing for the rest of my life.

"Nice to finally meet you, as well," I say as I try not to stare, but he's making it hard. He continues to pet his dog, running his big hands over her head and ears.

And if all of this isn't bad enough, he also smells so good. Like pine, laundry soap, and something else I can't figure out. Maybe leather and motor oil. I catch myself staring at him, getting lost in his deep blue eyes, and quickly blink and look away. When I finally turn back, he's smiling, and he does not look away. *Nope.* He's smiling at me like he likes what he sees, and I'm starting to lose my senses. *Again.*

"You work here?" he asks, and something tells me he probably knows this already. Maybe he's just being friendly and I'm reading more into it.

I clear my throat. "I'm the inn housekeeper. What about you?"

He runs his hand over his beard and says, "I work nights

over at Larkin as a mechanic, and I sometimes help Sam Sr. in his auto shop here in town."

"I remember you dropping Beth's car off a while back." I gaze at his trimmed beard and catch myself wanting to reach out and touch it. I wonder how old he is. He looks young with no grey in his beard or hair and he has light wrinkles on the sides of his eyes when he smiles, so I'd guess early thirties. *Hot. Older man hot.*

Stop it. Ugh, I need to get out more. I've turned into the lonely lady creep here at the inn.

"Dinner!" Evan calls from the kitchen, interrupting us. Thankful, I stand and say, "Well, it's nice to meet you both." I give Nova one final scratch on her ears.

"You, as well. I hope to get to know you more." His gaze is warm on mine. The way he looks at me makes me nervous, but in a good way. Like he's interested in me, and that feels. . . strangely warm and fuzzy. If Evan invited him here, he must like him. Evan is former military, so nothing gets by him, which makes him outstanding at reading people and knowing who is good and who is not.

My stomach dips nervously and it's not because I'm afraid, which is my usual go-to. It's because I think we just had a moment right now. He had to have felt it too with the way he was looking at me.

"Let's go, buddy," I say softly to Kase, taking his little hand in mine.

"Nova, stay," Ty says as Nova's little nub of a tail wags so fast her whole body sways back and forth before she lies down and puts her head on her paws, keenly watching us.

"Wow. She'll just stay there, just like that?" I'm impressed at how calm and well-behaved she is.

"Yep. She won't go anywhere once I put her in place." He casually stands and tucks his hands into his front pockets, his blue eyes still focused on me. He's commanding, he's sexy, and he's making this room feel like a furnace all of a sudden. Jee-zuz.

Kase lets go of my hand and races to meet his friend Caleb in the dining room doorway, leaving me to walk down the hall next to Ty. I try to sneak another peek, noticing again how tall he is as he confidently walks in stride beside me. Not to mention that he seems at home here at the inn. I wonder why he's here for dinner, but knowing Evan, he probably ran into him in town and invited him, unofficial town mayor that he is.

As I step into the dining room, Allie hands me a plate and motions for me to get in line for the buffet. "Hey, girl! Can Kase sleep over with us tonight?" she asks. "Caleb got a new game he's dying to play with him. Some Pokémon thing. Then tomorrow, Logan wanted to take them both out to play Pokémon Go."

"Sure. Sounds fun. That'll give me some time to get some more garden work in."

I'm supposed to have help getting my greenhouse put together, but the crew hasn't showed up—for three weeks in a row. They're probably not even coming. I just need to figure it out myself.

"You look lost in thought." Allie looks over at me.

"Sorry, just trying to figure out some things with my greenhouse plans."

"Ooohh, like what?"

Allie's brother Evan is who I would consider my best friend in Freedom Valley, but Allie and Beth have become my close friends, too. There's no mistaking her and Evan for siblings, they look so much alike, with dark hair and the brightest emerald green eyes. Allie's encouraged me with my gardening dreams, and sometimes she gets so excited for me that I forget that they're my dreams and not hers. I'm lucky to have a friend who has become like a sister to me. Our sons became inseparable from the moment they met, acting like best friends almost immediately.

"I've been trying to get my greenhouse together so I can do more seed startings. I just got more seeds in, and I'm excited to get them going. I was counting on the greenhouse space. I need to get everything growing now so that I have plenty to sell at the farmers' market all summer and fall."

I work on my garden plans when I'm not doing my housekeeping duties, so my time is very limited. Not having the greenhouse finished has set me back, but I don't want to tell her that. It's my problem, not theirs. Allie, Evan, and everyone else at the inn have their own stuff going on.

The farmers' market started as a result of me wanting to give back to the community here in Freedom Valley and bring positive attention to the inn. This past year was a rough time for the inn, and Evan almost lost it due to the bank threatening to foreclose. But we brought back the fall festival tradition and made enough money to turn the inn around and save it. Without Beth's help with all of that, I don't know if we'd still be here right now. We're trying to integrate the inn into the community as much as we can. There's a spot on the back of the property where we host the fall festival that I dreamed of using for a farmers' market. I thought it would be a good way to bring in more vendors, customers, and the community. It's been coming together, and I can't wait to host the first one as soon as everything is ready.

"I can't wait to see your farmers' market come together. Oh, and before I forget, I baked you a loaf of sourdough with roasted garlic and rosemary from your garden herbs. It's still warm." She motions to her purse sitting on a chair in the corner of the room, a foil wrapped package next to it.

"Thank you." My mouth waters at the thought of her bread. "I'll never turn down your sourdough. It's the best."

Allie's baking is on another level. I've never tasted such delicious breads and pastries, and her passion for baking is like mine for gardening. Watching her do what she loves every day has inspired me and given me permission to pursue what I love. Allie's success isn't surprising, though, because she is one of the most persistent people I know. She began her bakery business out of the kitchen here at the inn and has now been able to open a new location here in town called Baked Inn Love—another extension and nod to the Golden Gable Inn that's been in her family for generations. She's planning on moving the business there within the next few weeks.

We move up in the line and I make plates for both Kase and me. By the time I get Kase set up next to Caleb at the kids' table, there's only one seat left at the big table: next to Ty.

Great.

I'm nervous as I move toward him, but a small part of me is excited. I want to have grown-up conversations and make friends. *Friends*, I tell myself. It's okay to have friends. Nothing more.

I remind myself that he's just a guest here, having dinner like the rest of us. I slide in next to him with a small, hesitant smile, and he smiles back but continues talking to Logan. Even so, his body shifts to the side to include me in his conversation at the table and I feel a little bit giddy that he wants me to sit there. I catch him look over every so often and smile when he catches my eye. I can't even help it. Ugh.

I'm ridiculous. What is this, high school?

Logan leans forward to get my attention through the buzz of noise at the table. "I picked up some of that deer netting you were asking about that we can put around the garden area. I left it in the barn for whenever you need it."

"Thanks, that's going to help so much. There's always a ton of deer back there and I can't have them eating up all my vegetables."

"It's a hundred-foot roll, so that should do it. It's heavy, so when you're ready, Pete or I can help you get it set up." He forks a bite of his pasta and leans back in his chair as he shoves it into his mouth. "This is so good."

"Yeah, it really is good," I say, looking over to Sasha and smiling. "Thanks for dinner, Sash."

Sasha beams at us from across the table. "My pleasure, love. When are you going to be bringing me my bountiful produce to cook with?"

"Hopefully here in a few weeks you'll have more produce than you'll know what to do with. Forget the grocery store. I'll have you covered with organic fresh-grown goods right from my own two hands."

I accidentally graze Ty's hand with mine as we both reach for a piece of garlic bread. My hand zings where it touched his and my heart flutters with unexpected excitement. Ty seems unfazed by the contact and casually asks, "So, how did you get into gardening?"

Now my heart races with panic. The truth is right on the tip of my tongue, but not something I feel comfortable sharing. I swallow and finally pull it together enough to reply with not the whole truth but at least part of it.

"I started playing around with the herb garden last year and I really enjoyed it. So, this year I decided to take a part of the back property that already had a few garden plots cleared and turn them into full gardens. I'm growing vegetables for the inn and starting my own locally-grown farmers' market. You know, something to bring the Freedom Valley community together."

He nods. "That's really cool. My momma gardened a lot, I used to love helping her."

"Your momma sounds like a good southern woman," I hedge, hoping I'm right in my accent assessment.

He pauses, then gives me the side eye and says with a chuckle, "Who says she's southern?"

"Isn't she?" I ask, playing it cool. "Pretty sure I'm detecting a hint of southern accent." Now I give him the side eye with a smile.

"I guess it takes one to know one," he says with a sly grin.

My heart is pounding in my chest with panic washing over me. *Shit. Shit. Shit.*

I quickly recover and say, "Why do you say that?"

"Darlin', you sound about as southern as I do." He relaxes when he says this, and his southern drawl is now full-on, like he's not even trying to hold it back.

His eyes lock on mine, and we stare at each other for a minute, like this is a duel. Finally, he says softly, "Alabama."

And I whisper, "Mississippi."

"Howdy, neighbor," he says, breaking out of our stare down and taking another bite of his food like it's no big deal, his eyes still flicking back to me in a way that makes me feel comforted instead of fearful. Nothing about Ty screams scary or alarming. Something about how he carries himself is just. . . calming and peaceful. He's like a big teddy bear. I bet he gives really good hugs.

It may not be a big deal for him, but I can't believe I just freely admitted that to him. I have no idea why I even did that, and I feel my ears begin to burn with regret and worry.

"I don't talk about home too much. This is home now," I start rambling, trying to steer him back to Freedom Valley.

"Same," he says. "I like it here." He focuses on me when he says that, and he doesn't look away for quite a while. When he finally does, he flashes me that panties-dropping grin again.

As bowls of warm and buttery sourdough, rosemary, garlic bread are passed around, I grab another piece and take a bite. I close my eyes and try not to moan, it's so good.

I glance at Allie, who's watching me with a smirk on her face. She's enjoying watching me squirm next to Ty and I know she's going to tease me about it later with Beth. I feel my face get hot and I focus on my bread. "Great bread, Allie. How's the bakery coming along?"

"Good. I'll be glad when it finally moves out of my kitchen and officially into the new building in town."

"I got you covered with fresh herbs," I offer.

"I'm counting on that. Fresh is always the best. My sourdough loaves with fresh herbs always go fast."

"Because they're so good, Ace," Logan says as he leans over and kisses her on the cheek.

She smiles warmly. "Thanks, babe."

We enjoy our meal and conversation. Every so often, loud laughter breaks out, and before we know it, we find ourselves still chatting long past when everyone has finished eating—plates pushed back, utensils abandoned, some making room for seconds, nobody feeling lonely or hungry.

Whenever I leave one of these big family dinners at the inn, my heart is happy and my cup is full. It's like my soul has been recharged.

As Ty gets up to get more food, Logan beams, "Hey, look who's here!" He's looking beyond me, toward the doorway. "Preston, my man. There's still plenty of food left. Grab a plate."

"Sorry I'm late. Traffic coming up from Boston was a nightmare." Preston waves at everyone as he heads to the stack of plates at the buffet table.

"Glad you made it," Evan says, standing to shake his hand.

"How long you here for?"

"About a week. Do you have space available?"

"No problem at all." Evan claps him on the back. "Get yourself some dinner and let's catch up. Beer?"

"Sure," Preston replies.

Preston and I have always had a strong friendship, but I think he may like me in a different way than I like him. "Hey, Mel. Save me a spot, will you?" he asks, gesturing to Ty's empty seat.

I watch Ty slide back into his seat, setting his plate full of seconds on the table. He turns to me, a satisfied smile on his face knowing there isn't a spot for Preston now. I give Preston an apologetic smile with a shrug before refocusing on Ty next to me.

He did that on purpose, I'm sure of it. What in the world?

Keep reading: books2read.com/FVS3

www.ingramcontent.com/pod-product-compliance
Lightning Source LLC
Chambersburg PA
CBHW070608300726
48975CB00006B/1751